LEGACY AWAKENED

PRIME PROPHECY SERIES
BOOK 4

TAMAR SLOAN

Copyright © 2018 by Tamar Sloan

All rights reserved.

No part of this book may be reproduced in any form or by any electronic or mechanical means, including information storage and retrieval systems, without written permission from the author, except for the use of brief quotations in a book review.

*To the readers who fell in love with the Prime Prophecy series (you guys planted the seed that saw this book grow) -
Michel, Tonya, Jackie, and so many more.
Oh, and to Sean...*

1
AVA

"He's close." My mother hoists the bulky vet pack further up her shoulder, a frown in her voice.

Almost two decades of culling has meant the wolves are shy, their natural inclination to avoid humans so dialed up that it's rare to see a wolf in the wild. The reality is the ones who learned this lesson, and learned it fast, are the ones who survived.

Which is why it's all the more surprising that Achak isn't far from the Glade.

Dad narrows his eyes, his Were nostrils flaring. "Yep, I can smell him."

I've sensed Achak, the alpha male of this wolf pack, too. Our connection meant that our thread started pulsing the minute we climbed out of the car.

Our thread, the shimmery, gossamer fibers that no one else sees, is one of the strongest I have with any animal. I was there when he was born—he was one of the first litters in the captive breeding program desperately working to save these wonderful creatures. I helped coax milk down his baby wolf throat when his mother died. His sister has become an ambassador for their plight, a placid, tame beauty that humans can touch and pet and discover exactly how unthreatening wolves are. Despite this, Achak left for the woods the minute the gates of his crate opened, the need to be away from the same species who caused his endangered status too strong.

That hasn't stopped me from visiting him regularly.

At first, it was because I was fascinated but also worried. The threads we all have, the ones that are living proof of how connected we all are, are becoming weaker and weaker between humans and wolves. And I knew that wasn't good. But then I discovered how our threads strengthen with time and contact. Maybe it's the Fae in me, drawn to our natural world. Maybe it's the dash of Were, sensing a kindred spirit. I doubt it's my human genes, for they're the very ones trying to exterminate these beauties. Either way, roaming these forests, Achak and his pack loping at my side, has created some of the most special memories in my seventeen years.

Achak looks like he's pacing amongst the trees. Mom frowns. "Symptoms?"

"Hoarse bark, a bit drooly." I remember the pacing that he couldn't seem to stop when I was here yesterday. "He just seemed...off."

Dad angles his head, eyes staying narrowed. "A wolf cold?"

I glance at Mom. Although I have the Fae connection to animals, I've never had the drive to be a vet. I know the procedures and surgeries are for the ultimate good of the animal, but I can't bring myself to hurt them. Which means I have no idea if there's such thing as canine flu.

"Maybe." But Mom doesn't sound convinced. "We'll take some blood if we have to. His annual health check was due soon anyway."

Without warning, Achak slips forward from between the trees and stands there. Tall and broad, shades of grey and depths of red, he is magnificent.

Not as magnificent as my wolf...

I quickly glance at Dad, glad the hitch in my chest doesn't translate to a blush. No one knows about my wolf because no one shares my dreams. I've thought of telling Mom or Dad or my cousin Joshua many times, but something has always stopped me.

Maybe because they'll try to tell me he's not real.

Dad glances back, his blue eyes curious. Pushing away thoughts of shimmery, beautiful animals that I know aren't imaginary, I turn back to the trees. "I told you he was acting strange."

Dad's gaze is already focused back on Achak. "They don't normally come this close to the Glade."

Achak pauses at the edge of the trees, watching us. The growl that powers over the clearing has us all stilling. I've never heard him growl while looking in my direction.

He starts pacing again, several loping steps to the right, before tracking back, zigzagging at the edge of the trees. From here I can see the line of white froth circling his panting mouth.

It was a two-hour hike to find him yesterday. Now, it's like he's waiting for us.

My body tightens, not understanding why the back-off signals are being thrown our way. Is it because Dad's here? I glance at Mom, knowing she's probably thinking the same thing.

"Noah, maybe you should back off a bit?"

"Not happening, Eden." Dad's voice has a thick vein of inflexibility running through it.

Oh yeah, Dad's protective streak.

Instead, I step forward. Mom will be working her Fae magic, and Achak knows me. He'd never hurt me.

I keep my voice calm and level. "I didn't think you were feeling well, Achak. I came to check up on you."

The edgy energy driving him one way then the other doesn't stop. His trajectory stays the same, although he seems to speed up and slow with no discernible rhythm.

"Let us help you."

My response is another growl. Not just any growl, but a rumbling, threatening growl. I don't understand. Why would he tell me to stay away?

I take another step forward, now worried. Achak must be really sick.

"Ava..."

Dad's tone is low, my name heavy with warning. I reach backward, holding up my palm. "He won't hurt me, Dad."

I can hear Mom rustling in the vet pack. Good, hopefully she has an idea of what's wrong with him. All I need to do is calm him, then we can make him better.

Getting closer, I see the sheen of fever in Achak's eyes. Normally a golden glow that reminds me of dawn, his eyes are wide, flaming, and feral.

He looks really, really mad.

"Did someone hurt you, Achak?"

Oh god, please don't let the poachers be back. Hunters still come around, looking for trophy kills. They know that even if the quota of wolf culls for the month has been reached, no one is going to check. The majority of humanity is too frightened after they discovered what these usually gentle creatures are capable of.

Achak stops, and I use the pause to come a few steps closer. His glowing, golden eyes watch me as he pants. Up close, I see the drooling has become worse. His tongue lolls, the saliva that doesn't catch around his mouth dripping to the ground. Worry tightens my chest. He's gotten worse faster than I expected. If I'd known, I would have brought him in yesterday.

"Ava." It's Mom's soothing tones that reach out to me. "I don't think you should go any closer."

I want to ask if she's figured out what's wrong, but I don't turn away from Achak. I tap into our connection, finding the place where every living being meets. Here I show him the truth of who I am and who he is. Different in so many ways, but the same in so many more.

Mom and her brother, Orin, another of the Fae Elders, have taught me everything I know. What's more, I'm the only one who sees the visible proof of our interconnection. Achak and I have a bond nothing can break.

Achak stops and I hope it's a good sign. In a flash, he spins around and disappears into the trees.

"I'm going to get the tranquilizer gun from the truck. Just in case."

I turn to tell Dad that would never be necessary, but he's gone before I can open my mouth. Darned Were speed. Another Were gene I don't seem to have been blessed with.

Mom comes forward, wrapping an arm around my shoulder. "You know he likes to be safe."

I roll my eyes. "Yes, I do." I glance up at my mother, her mahogany hair tied back, the green eyes I inherited smiling, but framed by worry. "What do you think's wrong with Achak?"

She looks to the place Achak was a second ago. "I'm not sure..."

I pull back a little. The connections are strongest with those we care about. The link between myself and my parents is a powerful one—reinforced by time and unconditional love. "But you have an idea?"

"The symptoms fit...but it doesn't make sense. Too fast and too uncommon."

"Less vet talk, more making sense, Mom."

Mom walks back to her bag, pulling out a solid little tome of a book. She flips through, the frown that has never really left since we arrived, deepening.

I look up towards the trees, holding still. Joshua tells me I do this when I sense a disturbance in the force. Achak is moving. I can't see him, but our connection is changing. Thinning one moment, thickening the next. It's like some sort of metaphysical tug-of-war is going on.

For the first time, I take a step back. Unease is rising up my spine, starting to feel a little like fear.

"It's almost like it's..." Mom's voice sounds like she's worried she might be right. "Ra—"

The shimmery, gossamer thread that disappears into the trees, the one that ties Achak to me, pulses, grows, and then thins until it's barely there. I blink, except there's no time to process what that means.

Achak spears from the trees, but I barely recognize him.

"Run, Ava!" It's my mother's voice, shouted in alarm and high with fear.

For a second, I hesitate. Achak was the wolf who first taught me how wolves hug. Who refused to let anyone else touch him from the moment he was released.

Achak is the wolf who's barreling straight for me, nothing but rage in his eyes. Froth frames his exposed teeth and flicks back onto his red-grey coat as he propels forward.

I turn and run. I try to match my feet to my thundering heart, needing to rival the pace. I latch onto my mother's frantic eyes as she powers forward, running toward her in a desperate, uncoordinated sprint.

Even as I know that it will only buy me time. Achak is an alpha male. The strongest and fastest of his pack. Sometimes we'd pretend to race, me running my heart out, him loping and leaping like he was teasing me.

He'll reach me within moments. And my scared brain has no

idea what will happen when he does.

The boulder that knocks me over feels like a mountain. I have no choice but to honor the laws of physics as gravity slams me to the ground. The grass feels like cement, unable to absorb the speed I'd desperately built, or stop the forward momentum I'd hoped would save me. I tumble, rabid growls and snatches of sky flashing past me as I roll over and over.

"Ava!" This time my mother's voice is a desperate scream. All the sound tells me is that she's too far away to help me.

I stop with an oomph, not because I've hit something, but because a weight lands on me. I roll onto my back, hoping to get away, but Achak pins me to the ground. The first snap at my face peppers me with canine spittle. I throw my hands up, fingers sinking into thick fur. I feel the amped-up heat radiating from what could only be described as a rabid beast.

"Achak! Stop!"

Achak's eyes glow with hatred, his body vibrates with explosive energy. There's no reason in those eyes. No desire other than violence.

There's nothing left of the wolf I helped raise.

He snaps at the arms that restrain him and I feel his claws dig into my shoulders. The next wild bite grazes my arm, and I release my hold as pain ruptures along with my skin. A thin graze oozes crimson blood down my forearm. Maybe this will be the wake-up call to snap Achak out of this furious rage.

"Please." This time I whisper the words, my throat too tight with fear to squeeze out anything else. Achak would feel my terror through our connection. Please, let him feel it.

Please, make him stop.

His mouth, open and snarling, powers down. My blood is a pale pink smear across his gleaming teeth. Frantically, I wrap my fingers around his neck, hands digging into his throat. Despite the pain, despite the hopelessness, I lock my arms and push.

Snap! Teeth gnash past my nose. *Snap!* His jaws slam together, angry that they haven't connected with anything. *Snap. Snarl. Snap.*

Fevered breath spills down on me, nothing but growls of rage fill my ears. My heart feels like it's trying to squeeze as many beats as it can into its last moments of life. Dad went to the car and Mom isn't going to get here in time. Plus, there's nothing she could do against the strength bearing down on me. It would be safer if she doesn't reach me before...

My arms tremble with the strain, muscles knowing they can't hold this back. There's a pop, and another and another. All that dominates my vision are wide, feverish eyes and deadly, sharp teeth.

My hands feel the growl that throbs in Achak's throat, my ears register the intent. My heart denies it as my arms collapse.

My mind realizes I've run out of time to discover all the answers I've been seeking for seventeen years. I'll never find them now.

Achak blinks, seems to lose his hold on the fury that was powering him, and collapses onto me. Frantically, the will to live a living, breathing being, I struggle and push.

It's a limp body that I push off, and I'm surprised I have the strength to move it. Achak flops to the side, eyes shut, tongue lolling from his foamy mouth.

Great mother, no. I clamber to my knees, trembling hands reaching out to his still form. Achak doesn't move. He's gone from furious energy to deathly still.

He can't be...

It's then that I see the three darts, red tufts jutting up amongst the mottled hair, their needles embedded in the wolf's hide. I look up to see Dad throw aside the tranquilizer gun before running to my side.

I roll over and empty my stomach onto the emerald grass.

2

AVA

We never thought we'd build by the Glade. For generations, it had been a sacred place that could only be accessed by the privileged—essentially those who knew of its importance, Fae and Were.

But the legacy I was born into changed all that.

The Glade was exposed by bulldozers. Humans were attacked by what they thought were wolves.

From as early as I can remember I tried to tap into the threads, help the land restore so the Glade could disappear back into obscurity. But hiding the Glade was never what we needed to do. Humans had bigger things to worry about—their fear of wolves—and they attacked right back. Wolf numbers shrank.

In the end, the most logical place to build the captive breeding center was the location where humanity, Fae, and Were intersected.

Those determined to make sure wolves don't become vulnerable to extinction built on my parents' land. Here they could research the remaining wolves, see which ones held the greatest complement of genetic diversity, capture them, and then help nature take its course.

Achak was born here. Spent his early months here. He may not exist if it wasn't for the captive breeding program.

But it still hurts to see him back, caged and unconscious.

Mom pushes away from the microscope she was leaning over. "He's rabid."

Rabies? "Are you sure?"

"Pretty sure."

"So, there's a chance he's not?" I don't need to say out loud that there's no cure for rabies.

"Well, there's no definitive test for rabies, unless we do it posthumously."

Joshua frowns, his dark brows low. He crosses his arms as he leans against the cupboards lining the wall. "Thankfully, we're not there yet."

I cross my arms too. Although I don't want to be a vet, I've grown up around them. I know what Mom just said. "You can only know for sure after he's dead."

"There are some pieces of the puzzle that don't fit. There's no sign of a bite wound that would've been the infection site. And even the furious form of rabies doesn't usually progress that fast." Mom glances at the microscope again. "But I checked his saliva, spinal fluid, and did a skin biopsy. They all showed signs of the virus."

Furious form. That's exactly what Achak was. Furious beyond reason.

Mom reaches the shelves above her and pulls down a small bottle. She scans the tiny lettering on the label, her usually serene face grave.

My arms untangle and I step forward. My heart lodges in my throat. "You can't—" I stop although there's nothing but silence in the lab. There's no way I can finish that sentence.

Mom looks up, her whole face drawn. "We don't need to euthanize him at this stage."

Now my heart plummets painfully. At this stage...

"I'm going to vaccinate him."

Josh rubs his chin. "And what does that do?"

"He was already vaccinated, but this gives him a booster if he was exposed." She scans the shelves again, then grabs a second vial further down. "And I'll add some immuno globulin."

Josh walks over, studying the little bottle. "To help him fight whatever it is?"

Mom nods. "It'll provide immediate antibodies until he can respond to the vaccine and produce antibodies of its own. It's a long shot and not something I've done before, but worth a try."

Josh nods too, looking thoughtful, and my hopeful heart decides that must be a good thing.

Mom draws the white liquid into a syringe. Heading to the metal cage that holds Achak, still unconscious thanks to the multiple sedatives Dad pumped into him, she kneels. Through the bars she gently grasps his leg and stretching as far as she can, injects the vaccine into his shoulder. Stretching even further, she administers the second dose in his hind leg.

I glance at Joshua and his lips thin. He, too, noticed that Mom didn't go in. The Queen of the Fae, the leader of beings so deeply connected with animals that they can influence them, doesn't trust to go in the cage with Achak.

Straightening, she steps back. We stand there, staring at the gentle movement of his chest. His stillness is such a contrast to the violence that drove him just an hour ago. The cut on my arm, now sterilized and bandaged, still stings.

Joshua is the first to move. "Now what?"

Mom sighs. "We see how he is when he wakes up. If things are looking better, we quarantine for ten days. We monitor for restlessness, saliva production...aggression."

I tilt my chin up. "And when there's nothing?"

The door opens and Dad comes in. He takes in Mom's

expression, probably reads the hope in mine, and comes to slip an arm around my shoulder. I feel like a child who's being braced for bad news.

Mom disposes of the syringe in the biohazard container. "If there's no other sign of illness," her tone says exactly how likely she thinks that is, "we decide whether he can return to the wild."

Because Achak attacked me. Even if there was a miracle and he woke up his old self, he still attacked someone. We can't afford to have a wolf out there confirming the human bias that already exists.

The window of this small building looks out onto an enclosure. It's a big one, as enclosures go, with eight-foot fencing. Inside are the wolves who work as ambassadors. They were the ones drawn to humans, the ones who are put on a lead and taken to schools and fairs. They show humans that wolves don't have to be a threat.

Is that where Achak will have to live? Contained and corralled?

That's not a life he'd want. Achak's name means 'spirit' in Native American. We chose it because there was no denying he's the essence of everything that is wolf. Wild, independent, and full of vitality. There's no way he can live in that overgrown cage.

Mom gets another syringe from the metal drawers. "And you need a shot too, Ava."

"Can I do it?"

We all turn to Joshua. He rubs the back of his head, sheepish as he tousles the dark hair he inherited from his father. "I've been practicing on oranges if that counts for something."

Joshua is my best friend. His passion for medicine started when we were children. When I wasn't at the Glade or the reserve with the wolves, we were at my house, using Mom's scarves as bandages for imaginary emergencies.

I shrug. "I trust you." But throw him a glare for good

measure. "Plus, if you miss or make it super painful I'll tell the twins you probably fed them those oranges."

Joshua pales. His parents, Dad's twin and his wife, had not one set of twins, but two. Breanna and Belinda, Layla and Luna, are the reason Joshua first looked into medicine. When we were six he wanted to know whether you can sew lips shut with dissolvable stitches just to get some peace and quiet.

But then he grins. "It was only saline. I told them it was a new strain of sweet and salty oranges."

I shake my head. "You know we don't mess with Mother Nature, it's bad juju."

Mom looks between the two of us. She holds up the syringe, her eyebrows hiked in question. She's checking to see if I want to reconsider.

But I do trust Joshua. And if he's going to stick someone with a needle for the first time, it might as well be someone who isn't likely to deck him. "Go for it."

Josh takes the syringe and I look away before he moves closer. I don't want to see the tip pierce my skin, nor do I want to see Joshua's face as he does it. He'll either be terrified, which won't help my nervousness, or excited, which isn't normal if you ask me.

There's a sting, enough for my jaw to tense, and I wait for the real pain to start.

"All done." Josh sounds as surprised as I feel.

I look down at my shoulder as he presses a cotton ball onto it. "I barely felt a thing."

Josh waggles the fingers of his other hand. "Doctor's hands," he grins. "Let me know if you ever feel any twinges in your appendix or something."

I push off the table, holding down the cotton myself. The thought of surgery on anyone, including myself, makes me queasy. "I'll keep you in mind."

There's a rustle from the cage behind me, and the subtle sound arrests all movement in the room. Achak is waking up.

The step forward is instinctual for me, and I guess Dad's arm shooting out to stop me is too. He shakes his head before returning to watch the wolf stirring in the cage.

I'm about to brush off Dad's arm and move forward when Achak opens his golden eyes. Flashes of the last time they were close pierce my mind like a machine gun. Furious speed. Deadly teeth too close. Violence without restraint.

Shame fills me as I stay where I am.

I've never felt more human or Fae than right now. My frozen fear is a glaring reminder of how little Were there is in me.

Achak slowly pushes himself up. I'm not surprised he's uncomfortable remaining prone. He looks arthritic as his front legs straighten, the back legs taking seconds to mirror them and bring up his haunches. His nostrils work, registering where he is. He would recognize the smells from when he was a pup.

He's about to realize he's in a cage.

Images of this wolf, violent and furious all over again, slamming himself against the bars, snarling, snapping, salivating, almost have me closing my eyes. If that happens, it will be his death sentence.

Achak glances around, seeing the humans all still, all waiting. His lips twitch up, there's a flash of teeth. A noise is strangled in his throat.

"Stay back," my mother warns. It seems the same pictures are being painted in her mind.

It's the briefest lick of his nose, the pink tongue flicking over his black snout, that has me moving forward.

I've seen that little tick many times before. Just before he left his cage, an army of unfamiliar trees waiting for him. When he first met his Alpha mate, Kiowa. When he sees another human.

It's all this proud wolf will do to show that he's nervous. Probably scared.

Dad tries to grab me, but I push his hand away. They need to see he's not dangerous.

I kneel at the cage, extending my hand slowly, but without hesitation. Dad is standing right behind me, coiled and waiting to use his Were reflexes.

"Ava..." It's Mom this time, her voice quiet but urgent.

"He's okay. You're going to have to trust me."

Achak's yellow eyes, black pupils at their center, dark circles surrounding them, reach out to me. So familiar. So full of confusion. Our connection glows and thickens, a thread that can never be broken. My hand sinks into his fur, past the greys and into the deep reds. He's no longer hot. He's no longer angry.

I can feel the collective sigh in the room.

I relax, crossing my legs and resting my forehead on the bars. "You feeling better, Achak?"

Achak's tongue laps my fingers. He pushes himself closer, forehead coming to rest on mine. The bars between us feel alien and unwanted.

"You still need to be careful, Ava." Dad's voice is low, calm, but heavy with warning.

But he doesn't see what I see. Our thread is back to the shining, gossamer strand that's alive with love.

Achak's head droops as his eyes close. I stroke his head. "Have a sleep, friend. Tomorrow you'll be better."

Like he's exhausted, rather than having spent almost an hour asleep, Achak's body folds down. His regular breathing fills the room within moments.

I stand up and turn toward my parents and Joshua. "The vaccine and the other thingy must've worked."

Mom shakes her head. "There's no such thing as a therapeutic vaccine for rabies, Ava."

"I have no idea what that is, but you just saw that, he wasn't aggressive or sick at all."

Josh's eyes light up with recognition. "They're trying to develop those for cancer."

Dad rubs his chin with his finger. "A vaccine for cancer?"

"Not quite." Josh's eyes are bright with interest. This is the guy who pours over medical texts just for fun. "A therapeutic vaccine is given after the disease has started. It triggers an immune reaction that attacks the active virus."

"And like I said, there's no such thing for rabies." Mom crosses her arms. "And I'm not convinced that's what it was. Rabies doesn't work that quick."

Dad hasn't lost his frown. "So, what are we dealing with, love?"

Mom moves to him, like the undeniable thread that connects them is a line reeling her in. He opens his arms and she tucks herself in. "I'm not sure."

I look at Josh, who gives the smallest of shrugs. He's not sure what happens next either.

I swallow down the hope building in my chest. "If Achak is better, then it can't have been rabies."

Which is a relief. There's no cure for rabies. Apart from death.

Josh comes to stand beside me. "And that's got to be a good thing."

Dad has his I'm-not-convinced face on. "He was going to kill you, Ava."

There's no point saying I could have reached him. It's not my ability to connect with animals that has me standing here now. It seems I'm only part Fae after all. I rub my upper arms like I'm cold, then stop. Weres don't feel the cold. In fact, I'm even less Fae than I am Were, and I don't do that part of me so well.

I look back at the wolf asleep in the cage. There's no sign

that he was so sick he attacked the one who helped raise him. No frothing mouth, no agitated energy.

None of this makes sense.

"Let's get home, get a good night's rest." Dad is already fishing the car keys out of his pocket.

Sleep. The place of dreams and possibilities. The place where my wolf is.

Mom comes over to wrap an arm around my shoulder. She squeezes and I pull up a tiny smile. She tucks a stray blonde hair behind my ear. "Let's let him rest, see where things are in the morning."

I sigh. "Okay."

We head to the door, and it's Dad who looks back one last time. I know exactly what he's thinking, and it has nothing to do with how close we are. Everyone who will hear this story is going to think the same thing.

Even if Achak completely recovers, what had him acting like that in the first place?

3
AVA

As my head sinks into the marshmallow that's my pillow, I smile. Not because anything is resolved. Definitely not, because the serious expression on my parents' faces never changed, even when Uncle Mitch and Aunt Tara brought all the twins over.

And certainly despite the fact that I'm lying on a cold, tiled floor with just a blanket around me.

This isn't the first time I'll sleep at the lab, nor the first time I've spent beside Achak. I just couldn't leave him alone tonight.

If I'd actually changed at sixteen like I was supposed to, I could have shifted and been here in minutes. But I haven't, so I rode my bike like some lame human, as I have so many times before. The lab, the wolves and their plight, have always drawn me. There's plenty of times I've snuck out to visit pups or sick wolves. Mom actually bought this pillow just to stay at the lab for nights like these.

The smile is because when I'm asleep, I'm actually free of threads and responsibility and expectations. And yet I'm more connected than I've ever felt.

I'm with him.

Between the big day and late-night bicycle ride, I'm asleep quickly. Maybe it's because I welcome the dreams. It doesn't really matter, because I'm with my white wolf almost instantly.

He's with them, like he usually is.

He turns when I arrive, sensing me. His copper eyes catch me and draw me in like no other connection can. I don't see the threads in my dreams, but I don't have to.

My soul is connected to this wolf.

I walk forward, not feeling the cold in this snowy landscape, and touch my forehead to his. I wish I could smell here, but I can't. I feel my lungs inflate anyway and my whole chest fills with enough emotion to make up for the loss.

He comes around so we're standing side by side. His size dwarfs me as I sink into his thick fur. So many nights have been spent like this—standing, touching, just being. But I can already tell tonight isn't going to be one of those nights.

The wolf pack several yards away is restless. The alpha, big, but not as big as my wolf, is pacing. The others, five of them including the alpha's mate, have taken his cue. They move around each other, zigzagging in and out, weaving an invisible mat of unease.

My wolf moves forward a few steps and looks back at me. He arches a canine brow. Excitement coils through my muscles—I know that challenge and the answer is a resounding yes.

He circles the pack and I follow him. Looks like we're heading west this time. Once he's on the other side he throws back his head. I close my eyes as the howl fills the night sky. Deep and profound, it carries the power that I feel deep in this animal. Full of authority and passion, it tells the wolves that they aren't alone.

I revel in the feeling that I'm not either.

The pack joins in, voices marrying with his, telling him

they're ready to follow. With that, my wolf starts to move, plotting out a trajectory across the snow.

I love when we run just as much as when we do nothing but stand. It must be the dream world, because despite my limbo existence between Fae, Were and human, I can keep up with him. No matter how fast his powerful legs propel him, I'm by his side. His copper gaze catches mine, alight like a comet and my heart feels the same. A sunrise is blooming in my chest. I step to the side, brushing him, and he does the same, bringing us closer. His face, all wild lines and soft fur, dominates my vision before he steps out again. With a burst of speed, he shoots ahead.

So that's how we're playing it, huh?

The snow doesn't slow me, seeming to compact and become a springboard for every step. Air injects into my lungs as I gain speed. In seconds I've caught up. This time when I step in our contact has more impact. With a playful push, I use our joint speed to give me the advantage and power past him.

It doesn't last long, although I knew it wouldn't. It probably doesn't help that I want to be caught.

He shoots past me and swerves in front. I twist right and we fan out, only to angle in again. Neither of us wants to be apart for long. We start up this rhythm of in and out, our tracks weaving a double helix in the snow behind us.

I'm not sure how long we do this dance of excitement and exhilaration, but we eventually slow. The wolves behind us are panting heavily when we reach a rocky outcropping. My wolf slows and I come to stand beside him as the others spread out. They begin scenting their new area and I wonder if they've been here before.

I feel a nudge and turn to find my wolf close. I don't know why, but I never seem to be able to reach up and touch him. In this space, I'm the surreal mix of sensations but no body. I long to feel the velvet of his muzzle, to trace those copper eyes, to know every inch of him. Instead our heads come forward to rest, two halves of a whole fitting into each other.

He sits and I feel his body wrap around me as I sink in. This is how we usually end, whether we've run or just reveled in the stillness and silence we weave. A sense of completeness floods my senses. It's a wonderful merging of a future I can't see and an emotion that is undeniable. I've only ever felt like this with my wolf.

With him, I'm everything I'm meant to be.

Bam! The slamming of a door jars me awake.

"Thank goodness. There you are, Ava."

I struggle to sit up, not wanting to leave the realm of sleep. What's going on?

There's a flick of a switch and light fills the room. I shield my eyes with my arm. "Mom?"

Mom seems to stop in the doorway, taking me in lying on the floor, and Achak who is now wide awake in the cage beside me. She doesn't move. In fact, she seems to sag.

I stand up and shuffle back, for some reason feeling the need to protect Achak. "Mom, I told you he wasn't dangerous anymore."

My words seem to diminish her even more. Her stooped shoulders speak of bad news. They have me stepping backward until the bars jam between my shoulder blades. Achak licks at my fingers and I let the sensation calm me.

I pull in a soothing breath. "Yesterday was some weird glitch, you can see he's back to normal now."

"This isn't about Achak. I need you to come to the main lab."

Achak whines. He's picked up on the tension Mom's words keep dialing up. I turn around and bend down. "I'll be back, beautiful boy. This won't take long."

I follow Mom down the hall, noticing how tense her shoulders are. The windows along the way tell me it's barely morning. Our steady steps feel like an ominous, slow drumroll.

It's the other end of the building that houses the real deal. Metal and white, microscopes that make the one Mom was using yesterday look like a child's toy, frosted fridges and glass shelves the main decor. This is where Dawn, my mother's friend and the oldest and most respected of the Fae elders, worked her magic.

The most surprising sight is finding my father there. His arms are braced along one of the benches, his head hanging down. He shoots up when we walk through the door, wiping his hands down his face. As a local police officer, I've seen him look like this before—after particularly harrowing night shifts.

But never in the lab.

And never directed at me.

"What's going on?" I make a conscious effort not to cross my arms.

Mom and Dad glance at each other before Mom reaches out to grasp my arm. "Kiowa was shot last night."

"No!" Shock slams through my stomach. Not Achak's mate! I shake my head in denial. "We haven't seen poachers in over a year."

"It wasn't poachers. It was one of the staff at the center."

What? They know how precious every last wolf is. Every loss is another life, another unique individual we'll never see again. Mom's face, so serious, so sad, has my whole chest tightening. "Why?"

"She tried to attack another of the pack."

My hands clench by my sides. "That's not a shooting offense. The wolf probably tried to upset the hierarchy."

But Mom is already shaking her head. "And then tried to attack them."

I gasp. This is too similar to what happened with Achak yesterday.

I look at Dad, who's never been the silent partner type. He's always known the right thing to say when things are tough. But his lips are a tight line. It tells me there's more to be said.

Oh no. "You've tested her, haven't you?"

Mom nods. She says what's already written in her frown. "It was rabies."

I'm gone in a breath, racing back down the hall, barreling into the room holding Achak. He stands in alarm, then relaxes when he sees me. I open the cage and throw myself inside before shutting the gate. My arms are clamped around him by the time my parents have followed me.

Several tears have already fallen onto his fur when Mom comes to kneel on the other side of the bars, Dad standing behind her.

I look up at them. "If it was rabies, I wouldn't be able to do this."

"I know."

"When we deliberately sever a thread, it bleeds."

Only three people know I see the threads. Mom, Dad, and Josh. And although they seem to understand how overwhelming seeing the intricate web that we are all part of can be, they've never seen what happens when an animal is killed. Their ties to those around them, to Mother Earth and life itself, snap. The stump left behind eventually shrinks and disappears, but not before it weeps and hemorrhages like a cut vein.

"Oh, honey. I know that too."

My head sinks into Achak's fur, losing myself in his familiar canine scent as he curls protectively around me. I wish I had something else to say...but I don't.

"It's still too early to tell, but I think you're right."

I look up. "What?"

Mom reaches out to grasp one of the metal bars. "It looks like he may be cured."

I suck in a breath. We all saw how sick he was. Achak jostles me with his head, like he does when he's ready to play. I scruff his neck, knowing I'm going to have to disappoint him, but glad of the proof of what Mom is suggesting.

Dad kneels beside Mom. "Maybe we can talk about this sitting on a chair or something? You may be okay with lounging around on tiled floors, but this old body likes its comfort."

I roll my eyes. Dad is one of the youngest fathers I know, even by Were standards. "Like a lab stool or something?"

Dad straightens, making a show of doing it like he's eighty. "Right now, I'll take it."

Shaking my head, impressed that my dad almost has me smiling, I stand. With a quick hug, I promise Achak I'll be back soon. Being in a cage for this long isn't going to be easy for him.

In the next room, I'm not sure how to feel anymore. The past twenty-four hours have been a yo-yo of emotions. I cross my arms, wishing I felt prepared for this. Why does it feel like we're standing at a precipice?

"So you think Achak had rabies?"

Mom nods, letting me process this. "The frothing, the tests, the aggression—it all fits."

"And you think the vaccine worked on Achak after he developed rabies?"

Mom glances at Dad before settling her gaze back on me. "As far as we know, there's no therapeutic vaccine for rabies, but it's the only explanation that makes sense. It must've been the blend of vaccine and globulin."

Dad's rubbing his chin in that way of his. "That was some pretty intense aggression."

"This was no run-of-the-mill strain. Faster, more virulent," Mom says.

The flashes of what I saw, and how it felt when my beloved friend attacked me, are still fresh in my mind. "More furious."

Mom nods. "Far more furious."

Dad narrows his eyes. "So, you're saying the vaccine worked on it after infection, because this strain is different somehow?"

Mom shrugs. "It's a hypothesis."

Hope flares fast and bright. "Which means Achak is cured."

But Mom's face doesn't match the light that's sparked in my chest. "Only if the theory is correct. And if it is, we have a much bigger problem on our hands."

Dad's hand drops to his side. "A fast-acting, highly aggressive form of rabies amongst wolves."

Mom looks out the window to the forest beyond. "The few wolves we have left."

4

HUNTER

24 MONTHS BEFORE

"You're not heading out tonight." My sister uses her Were speed to slot herself between me and the door, like her small form would stop me going through it. She flicks her chestnut fringe back from her forehead. Ever since we were kids that's signaled 'I mean business.'

I keep pulling on my boot. "Bad weather never stopped us."

I wince at my choice of wording. There isn't an us going out. Tonight, and every night, will be just me.

Riley crosses her arms, dark brows frowning. "You know it's not the weather. You'll probably strip down to a t-shirt the minute you're out of human sight."

For a short period of time, for only a few weeks after changing at the age of sixteen, I did love doing that.

I grab the other boot, letting my actions speak rather than trying to find my voice.

Riley's arms tighten. "KJ rang. He wants you to stop by."

Jamming it on, I don't look up. "I'll do that tomorrow."

Riley's arms flop to her side, the sadness we all live with rising to the surface. "I hate it when you go out alone."

The ache in my chest intensifies, but I ignore it. "It won't be the first." I make sure I'm looking straight at her. "And it sure as heck won't be the last."

Purely because I'm the only one left to do it.

Grief, it's the aching mix of pain and anger and another emotion I refuse to acknowledge, sledgehammers my chest. One day that feeling will diminish. One day...

"Maybe I can come?"

That has me smiling, especially when the clatter of a dish in the sink reaches us from the kitchen. "And miss Bachelor in Paradise?"

Actually, Riley hates The Bachelor. She used to rant to Mom that any woman who had more depth than her foundation wouldn't dream of watching it. But that clattering plate tells us Mom is listening. She always does, as we go through some variation of this discussion every night.

Riley's shoulders drop another notch. The Bachelor was always Mom's escapism from an isolated, sub-arctic island. But Bachelor in Paradise, filmed on a tropical island, is the only hint of warmth she seems to find right now.

"You could stay home?" The hope in Riley's face is about as authentic as a fluorescent light. She already knows what the answer to that will be.

"Then it would all have been for nothing, Riley."

Silence falls over the house. I've said the words that acknowledge exactly how cemented my destiny became two months ago, only a few days after my sixteenth birthday. Only a few days after I shifted for the first time and finally became a Were.

"Be safe, Hunter." Riley's voice is a whisper, but she knows I can hear it. It's the hitch that I choose to ignore.

"Always my first priority."

There's a snort and a muttered 'bullcrap' as I pull on my coat. I shut the door behind me, welcoming the sting of wind on my face, my mantra my only companion as I head for the road.

I won't let Dad have died for nothing.

The Ski-Doo bumps over the snow, the rumble of the engine sounding more and more alien the further I drive out. I leave it as soon as I'm out on the tundra, striding into the desolate wild. Evelyn Island only has one inhabited area, weathered houses that line the southern edge, looking over the water. Originally, the Inuit people were the ones tough enough to brave this snow-drenched land. But Evelyn Island, the largest in the archipelago dotted between Canada and Greenland, developed into something different when white people saw its potential.

It's a good thing the Rendell pack was already here, because as the township grew, the space shared by humans and wolves began to grow too.

For the most part, the intersections were rare. The odd wolf tearing open someone's rubbish or dragging away some roadkill.

Until some power crazy Were back on the mainland left behind a legacy.

Kurt Channon. His name is as well-known as the Phelans. He wanted Weres to stop hiding, to show their power. To dominate humans. So, he set in motion a domino effect that he never lived to see. He had his followers attack humans. He butchered animals at a sanctuary. He left behind video footage showing a massive wolf tearing apart a bear.

And so, the culling began. Population control they called it. For everyone's safety.

Tell that to the poachers who had their sights on the white wolf standing on the top of Resolute Mountain. Tell that to the guy who pulled the trigger. Tell that to the family left behind because as that wolf tumbled over the other side, he shifted back to his human form.

Bitterness floods my mouth, and I resist the urge to swallow. If I'm not careful, it will start corroding me from the inside out.

As I head inland, the landscape becomes wilder and more rugged. The isolation here has always called me. I suspect it's the lack of eyes that also attracts the poachers. Arctic wolves have never attacked anyone but their pelts are the color of snow, and in a world where the killing of wolves is encouraged, that's a pretty cool trophy to spread over your shiny timber floor.

But we haven't lost one since we started the patrols. There's so few of them left that we can't afford to.

I shove back my hood and undo my jacket as I look around. My Were sight scans the twilight, wondering if they're still here. They've been hanging out in this neck of the tundra for a few days. It makes me nervous as it's closer to the town than I would have liked. It might be time to move them on.

I shift to wolf form before I let myself think about it too much. In the space of a heart-beat I've multiplied in size, everything exploding outwards and it feels like I'm made of fireworks. The thrilling change into something that should be impossible is discouraged nowadays, but I know I'm unlikely to see them if I don't. I've learned that the sight of any human spooks them. They don't hang around long enough to find out if it's friend or foe.

I scent them almost straight away, loving the extra layers of information I can extract with my wolf senses. They haven't gone far at all. I head north, paws powering over the ground. At this time of the year, the beginning of summer, the vista is a mismatch of harsh rock and white snow. The cold stings my eyes as I push to go faster. It would be exhilarating if it wasn't so important that I find them.

I spot them in the distance, white moving on white. The average human is unlikely to see them from here, which is a relief because it seems they haven't moved far at all. I throw my head back and howl, letting them know I'm coming. I see one head hike up the tallest. Zephyr, the alpha, has spotted me. He arches his head back and throws out his own greeting. With the green light given, I break into a lope.

As I come closer, I do the headcount. It doesn't take me long, there's only six of them. All largely related now that so few are left. Except I can only count five. I pick up the pace, registering that Sakari isn't amongst them. As the alpha mate, she's always close by.

Checking again, I only come up with five.

Please no. We were so sure we'd halted the steady decline of these amazing animals. That's what Dad put his life on the line for.

And lost.

As I near, the wolves start to pace, contracting around Zephyr. Although they're used to seeing me, they still look to their leader to gauge how they should respond.

Zephyr, white except for the mane of grey that surrounds his broad head, watches me. I slow, never coming too close. We have an understanding, Zephyr and I. He is the alpha, the one who belongs to this pack.

My role is protector. The one tasked to keep safe what little of the world they have left.

He barks once and turns, running a few yards before stopping. I follow, tense at what I'm going to find.

Only a few feet away from Zephyr I discover why these animals, usually nomadic around their massive territories, haven't moved. Sakari, the alpha mate, is curled up in a rocky outcropping. What little soil there is has been padded down to create a shallow depression. The squat rocks around her offer limited protection from the elements. It's about as good a den as you can create out on the tundra.

I glance at Zephyr, wide-eyed. Wolves don't build their dens until the birth is near. Looks like he's going to be a dad very soon.

I can't help but sit, my back legs giving out. I nod at Zephyr and I swear he grins, white bushy tail high, probably feeling quite proud of himself.

Well played, you sly dog.

I head back, finding a vantage point on the largely flat ground. I need to be close enough to see the makeshift den, but far enough to give these wolves their space. Sitting, I take it all in. For the first time since we lost Dad, since the role of Alpha was placed on shoulders too young, a new emotion flickers.

Hope is about to be born in that little alcove.

Hope that I am going to have to protect.

Challenge. Accepted.

As the night becomes absolute, I feel my body yearning for sleep. The battle I have with the Sandman is a nightly one. I've discovered if I half-doze, it lulls him into a sense of security. I'm convinced Sandman believes that when my defenses are down, he'll be able to strike.

But he hasn't won yet.

Ultimately, his pull is strong, but my determination is stronger.

I must have one foot in slumber land a few moments later because a wolf appears. One that has my spine straightening because this isn't one of the snow colored animals that camouflage in this mostly white world. This one is beautiful. A golden, glowing being that I know has to be a dream.

Dammit. Sandman won.

I struggle to wake myself, but I can't seem to find a way out. It's like I'm being held by something that doesn't exist.

She stares at me across the rocky tundra. I've never seen a wolf, or a Were, that color. She's layers of gold, from burning ember through to sun-on-fire. Her gaze doesn't leave mine, like a connection was just forged. Forged and set in ancient stone.

She moves forward, not in the least bit nervous. Maybe there's nothing to be afraid of in this dream state. I blink, no longer caring how she materialized or from where. In a world that is cold and desolate in more ways than one, I'm drawn to her.

A few feet away she stops. I try once again to wake myself, only to find there's no foe to fight. Although this is a dream, nothing seems to be holding me here. I admit it's a battle I didn't want to win as I move forward too.

Her eyes are an amazing shade of green, her face fine and graceful. She looks like she's full of curiosity and I'm totally captivated. We hold there for long seconds, studying each other, and I'm lost in the moment.

Until she moves. She walks past me, behind me, before coming up beside me. There's a chance I'm hallucinating.

Standing beside me, slightly smaller, so much more impressive, she looks around. Seems she's visiting my dream world. I look over at the wolf pack, they're all asleep, curled and furled around their alpha pair.

I look back at her. I want to share this magical place with her. No one gets to see the wolves like I do. And if this is my dream, I'm going to make it a memorable one.

I take a few steps forward, and she's there with me. A few more and it's like an invisible rope has attached us because she's still by my side. Fine by me. Right now it feels like I've found my mate.

We cover the space between where I was resting and the

wolves. Seeing as this isn't real, I take us closer than I've ever been. Sakari opens her eyes, takes us in, and closes them again. She's never minded me being around. The others are just as unconcerned.

Zephyr looks up, a low rumble vibrating past his throat. At least the dream is realistic. Our relationship has been based on a mutual agreement. You help me look after them…but don't mess with the system. Seeing as I'm bigger and faster, I can pose a threat to his status as alpha. He stands, obviously not comfortable lying prone with us so close.

Good on him. A protector is always ready.

The golden wolf doesn't seem fazed. She leans into me like we've done this all before, as if we haven't just met, and I marvel that I can feel her weight and warmth. The sensation has awareness zinging along every nerve ending. The touch is far more electric than should be possible in a dream.

She straightens all of a sudden, head tilting like she heard something. I glance around, surprised I hadn't heard it. But there's no noise to register. The tundra is silent.

I turn back to find her gone. I jump to the side, loss a sharp pain in my chest. Zephyr growls beside me, but I ignore him. This is my dream, and this is not how I want it to end. She only just got here, for Pete's sake.

Another growl and Zephyr steps forward. I ignore him again —it's not like he can hurt me here. Can't he see she's gone? I step around again, walking in a circle. Weird things can happen in dreams, maybe she's playing teleport hide-and-seek or something.

When Zephyr leaps forward, it's not the whistle of wind past my ear that has me freezing. It's not the snap of teeth so close to my face that has me jumping back.

It's the undeniable drop of drool that has landed on my muzzle that has my jaw go slack with shock. It sits there and I almost go cross-eyed as I stare at it. I can feel its slight weight, the pinprick of warm that is rapidly going cold. What ultimately has my breath evaporating is that it doesn't go away.

Holy crap. It's not possible.

I've been awake the whole time.

5

HUNTER

24 MONTHS BEFORE

"Whoa. You don't actually look like crap today."

I pass KJ the cup of coffee I brought him. "And I call you my best friend." Then look a little more closely. "Seems like the tables have turned..."

KJ is sitting where he usually does—at his desk with multiple screens surrounding him, in his usual getup: black cargo pants, grey sweatshirt, and the always-there grey beanie. Except today there's a slump to his shoulders, like his body is too heavy to carry.

Normally, that's my look thanks to my evening jaunts, but today I feel invigorated. It's probably because of Sakari and the den, or maybe it's because my mind hasn't slowed down since she appeared...

KJ grabs the coffee, rubbing his face with his other hand. His fingers spear under the wool on his head to scratch his hair. A beanie in this neck of the arctic circle isn't unusual. A beanie on a Were in this neck of the arctic circle? Now that's not something you see, like, never.

Then again, if there's one thing KJ doesn't want to be, it's a Were.

I reach out to grab it, but KJ ducks like this is a dance we've done before. He pushes my hand away, a grin nudging at his lips. "We don't touch this remember?" He waves his coffee around the general area of his head. "This, cousin, is sacred space."

We're not cousins in the strict sense of the term, KJ is the nephew of my grandmother. We've never bothered to figure out what exactly that makes us because it doesn't really matter. When he moved in a few houses down several years ago it didn't take us long to become the best of friends.

I roll my eyes as I flop onto the bed. "Whatever you're trying to hatch under there, I think it's cooked."

KJ's baby grin dies. "A solution?"

My coffee cup stops its journey to my mouth. "Has something happened?"

He turns around to face his screens and wiggles the mouse. The screen on the left comes to life, and a frozen face fills the screen.

I sit up, shifting to the edge of the bed. "Not that prick again."

With a glance over his shoulder that says 'yep, that prick again,' KJ clicks the little white triangle at the bottom. Alistair Davenport begins to move, and I realize I'm watching the replay of a news report.

"It is only a matter of time before another one happens." He slams his fist into his palm. "Wolf attacks are on the rise." I clench my hand. Wolf attacks have remained at what they always have—less attacks than hippos for Pete's sake—they've just been on the news a thousand percent more. "Their threat grows daily. Women and children are the most vulnerable to attack." My teeth grind into each other. Technically, that's true.

Any predator goes for the most vulnerable. "And it's our role to protect them."

I sigh. "Next, he pulls on the heartstrings."

Alistair rearranges his features from evangelical to that of a martyr. "My father, a gentle man, is a silent victim of these menacing animals. A lover of nature, he was witness to the violence they are capable of. He has barely survived the heart attack it caused. Weakened, the trauma of those images have stayed with him so indelibly that he can no longer leave the house. He lives in fear of what they are capable of."

I want to throw my coffee at the screen. The truth is, Alistair feeds that fear.

KJ is frowning just as ferociously as I am. "And now the promise."

"I vow to you, our world will be safe. We will be free to walk the woods and not have to look over our shoulder. We will not feel vulnerable or weak or scared. Culling is how we ensure this."

The screen changes to bring us a young reporter with her serious face on. "That was Alistair Davenport, son of Harold Davenport. Harold was the groundskeeper of a wildlife sanctuary before taking an early retirement. He now lives with his son, Alistair, a passionate campaigner for wolf population control."

I snort. What an emotionally sanitized term to call it. Indiscriminate killing would be more accurate. Legal slaughter of innocent animals would hit the nail on the head. I have to put my coffee down before I crush the cardboard cup. The levels of unfairness in this whole mess always piss me off.

KJ clicks the mouse and the image minimizes, but he doesn't turn around straight away. From the moment he arrived to live with his Aunt Lou about seven years ago, the plight of the wolves has been his personal mission. Discovering that we're second cousins only cemented our relationship.

It means I know how hard it hits him every time Alistair Davenport stirs up trouble. It also means the vigilance on the patrols will have to be taken up a notch.

It also means I may see her again...

Thinking of the golden wolf reminds me of what I shared with her. I open my mouth, the good news I've brought bursting to be told, but KJ hasn't finished.

"Oh, and she emailed again."

My mouth shuts and my lips thin. That woman is tenacious, I'll give her that.

I grab the coffee again, taking a sip before I respond. "Same old, same old?"

KJ wheels to the right and lights up another screen. "Yep." He clicks open his email. "And nope."

Dawn's letters are always lengthy. She's obviously as passionate about saving the wolves and ending this all as KJ and I are. She just has a different view as to how to go about it.

"Give me the short version," I mutter.

KJ pushes his beanie up a bit as he leans in. "Ah, all the usual stats about the captive breeding program. The genograms are pretty interesting. The level of sophistication they go into to get the genetic profiles of the wolves is cool."

I relax a little, zoning out just a tad—all the genetic, scientific stuff is KJ's kettle of joy, not mine. I'm not sure why these emails get me wound up. Dad's answer was always the same, and mine won't be any different. There's no way our arctic wolves are going to be part of some glorified lab project.

I guess they would be easier to ignore if Dawn wasn't a Fae Elder.

"Their first litter's been born."

In an overgrown cage.

"She even sent a photo."

KJ scans down and a picture rolls up the screen. I've just decided that I'd rather not know, when something about it captures me. I'm at KJ's side in a second.

"Who's that?"

The photo shows a grey-haired, lean woman with a blonde teen beside her. KJ points to the older woman. "Well, that's Dawn."

"Ah, I figured that."

KJ leans back, all of a sudden interested in my reaction. "And the one holding the cub?"

I nod, eyes glued to the screen. The blonde girl isn't looking at the camera, she's far too engrossed in the young wolf she's cradling. It's a grey pup, with a deep red undercoat, and it's staring up at her with just as much fascination. They're both far more interested in each other than the camera. There's something about her...

"That's Ava Phelan."

I quickly squash whatever emotion was germinating. That must be why she feels familiar. Everyone knows who Ava Phelan is. The child of the Prime Prophecy. The only one we know who carries Were, Fae, and human blood. Dad told me there were high hopes when she was born. What could this nexus of beings mean?

But as the true inheritance of the legacy became apparent, so did the fact that she, and the Phelans, had about as many answers as any of us.

None.

Actually, their solution was to catch wolves and pick and choose who gets to mate.

I shrug. "And why am I not surprised she seems perfectly okay with the program?"

KJ turns back, turning his head as he stares at the photo. "She seems pretty invested in that little one. It's a sweet photo."

I head back to the bed, rolling my eyes. Of course KJ would say that. "Well, photo or no photo, Dawn hasn't shown us anything new. So they've bred a couple more wolves, so what?"

Especially when our wolves are doing that on their own, in the wild.

KJ turns so he's facing me, his eyes assessing me. Great. He's got his thinking cap on. "She said she'd do a complete genetic profile on as many of our wolves as she can."

I narrow my eyes. "So?"

"Our numbers are barely stable." He pauses so I can appreciate exactly how optimistic the word 'stable' is. "Most of the members in each pack are probably related. That's why we brought Zephyr to this pack. The less genetic diversity there is, the more vulnerable the population is."

I wave my coffee across the air between us. I know all this. The more vulnerable they are to catching a sniffle or unexpected change. "You want to capture them and breed them according to some lab results?"

KJ pulls the grey wool on his head down. The bloody thing is like a safety blanket. "I want to feel like we're moving forward for a change." He looks away before glancing back. "And I'll do what it takes to make that happen."

His last words pull a sigh past my lips. "You know I would too."

"Things are starting to get desperate, Hunter."

I know my smile is out of place in this moment, but I can't help it. I make sure my next words explain it. "Sakari has built a den."

KJ shoots up, eyes the biggest I've ever seen them. "No freakin' way!"

"Way freakin' way."

He holds his hands out, one still holding the coffee, like he's trying to capture how monumental this is. "Why the hell didn't you tell me?"

I shrug, my grin as big as his. "Got sidetracked."

KJ puts his coffee down and I know what's coming next so I brace myself. He yanks me up and engulfs me in a bear hug. I barely even wince when he thumps me on the back five or six times.

He pulls back, eyes round with excitement. "Maybe I should come out with you on patrol."

I shake my head. "No need for both of us to be walking zombies. You're better off here, keeping an eye on what's going on around the world."

"Surely you get lonely out there."

I have been… "It's about as much fun as keeping your finger on the digital pulse of this legacy or monitoring our wolf data."

KJ tips his cup in acknowledgment. We chose our path years ago.

He sits back in his seat, that brain of his already whirring with all the implications. "These pups are going to be the first generation of wolves who may actually stand a chance."

"Yep." Evelyn Island holds the last of the arctic wolves. With so few of them left, inbreeding was becoming a problem. But Zephyr and Sakari are from two different packs. They hold everything that arctic wolves can be.

The coffee cup rises, stops, and lowers again. "If we get a female from this litter, we can use her to establish another pack."

Another alpha pair, starting a whole new pack to grow their numbers and their genetic vigor. "Exactly."

KJ slams the coffee cup onto his desk. "We don't need to consider captive breeding."

"We're not that desperate yet." Man, it feels good to say that.

"Send Dawn an email, tell her nature is working its magic all on its own."

"Aye, aye, Alpha!"

I look away so KJ can't see me wince. Alpha was a title I was looking forward to, somewhere in my future. Not at the age of sixteen…

Before the grief can sink its painful claws in, I focus on the positive. Sakari is about to have a litter of pups. Maybe the golden wolf was an omen of some sort. Even if it messes with my sanity, I hope she comes back for more than one reason. Patrols with her by my side could be a real light in the dark times.

I stand up, slapping KJ on the shoulder. I'm going to get home and see how everyone is going. Then maybe I can squeeze a nap in before doing this all again.

KJ is already writing the email to Dawn. I allow myself a smile.

Something pretty drastic would have to happen for me to say yes to that woman.

6

AVA

Achak's first steps outside after solitary confinement are buzzing with anticipation, but cautious. I wait, letting him scent the barely-there breeze, wondering what it's communicating to him. A pack was here a week ago, which means he would be cataloging how many there were, their gender, their age, whether they're something he needs to be wary of.

Nose twitching, he glances back at me. I nod, letting him know it's okay. Those wolves were the latest pack successfully reintroduced into the wild.

As if that was all he needed, Achak bounds out the door and is instantly nose down as he lopes first one way, then the other. I smile as I move out and sit on a log nearby.

Achak is the most alert I've seen him in days. His canine brain is loving being in overdrive as he explores the space around him. He sniffs at rocks and bushes, and I roll my eyes as he cocks his leg and marks his territory. This is where Achak will stay for another couple of weeks as we wait and see whether his clean bill of health stays that way.

Mom still shakes her head every time she looks at him. He was infected with Furious, as we've now named it, but here he is, marking yet another tree. It's like that incident at the Glade never happened.

Except Kiowa, his mate, is dead after attacking the people who raised her. Just like Achak did. And her death meant her brain tissue could be tested, confirming what we hoped wasn't true. And now we're facing the question about whether there are other wolves out there with Furious.

Achak trots back to me and I smile at him. "You're the proof that the therapeutic vaccine worked, my friend."

He watches me for a second. Unlike so many of the other wolves born in captivity, it's rare for Achak to come too close to humans when we're outside. It's like once he's in his natural habitat, his evolutionary brain remembers that we aren't the friends we want wolves to think we are. I've often wondered whether the fact that Achak's mother was baited not long after giving birth to her litter has somehow impacted him. Even though it necessitated being raised by humans, it's like he decided he won't be tamed by our sense of guilt for the loss we've caused.

I respect him for that.

Achak angles his head like he just heard something before loping away. Dawn always said it's respect that forged my bond with him. Achak found someone who saw and loved him for who he really was, and that's all he needed.

Achak comes up against the chain-link fence that surrounds this enclosure. He paces several steps to the right before turning around. I sigh. This captive breeding site is what saved the grey wolf from the threat of extinction. Dawn is understandably proud of what she achieved here and it's why she left to work her wonders further north. The program is an amazing feat of compassion and commitment.

I'm just not so sure Achak would agree.

I stare out to the mountains in the distance, their snowcapped peaks almost matching the pale grey sky. What would my wolf think of this place? Although I've only ever seen him in his magnificent wolf form, I know he's a Were. There's his size, but also the humanity I see in his eyes. Which means he lives in the same world I do—one where wolves could be nothing but YouTube clips in the space of our generation.

I start, but quickly catch myself, when I feel Achak behind me. I hold still, feeling our thread pulse with awareness, and wait. Like he does it all the time, all casual and soft-footed, he comes and sits beside me. I glance at him and I'm pretty sure he grins. I shake my head, my own smile finding life as I nudge him with my shoulder.

"You're a smooth operator, Achak."

His pink tongue slips out and brushes my cheek. The touch is brief and wet, but it lifts my heart in a way I can't describe. Love like this, born of respect and given freely, is what feeds connections. It heals the wounds that we can inflict.

Another sigh falls from my lips as I rest my head on Achak's neck. He leans into me, offering his strength. I turn so my cheek is against his red-grey fur, breathing in the scent of musty canine. We stay like that for long moments, trying to absorb the world around us, the one that is undeniably changing.

I look up at Achak. "We need to make sure it's somewhere we're proud to live in, huh?"

He blinks before his lips pull up again in a grin. I can see where the term wolfish came from. With another quick canine kiss he moves away again. Probably doesn't want to risk any other wolves seeing him have a moment with a human, like the cool kids not being able to be seen with the nerds.

My cell buzzes in my pocket. Crap sticks, I haven't been paying attention to the time. Joshua must be waiting out the front. I get up and dust myself off. The meeting tonight is going to be a big one.

I head for the door, noticing Achak is back at the wall of wire holding him captive. He's watching me leave, that wolf gaze of his unreadable.

"Believe me, my friend, I'd prefer to be here, fence and all."

Walking out to the carpark, I brush the plaque that's embedded into the front wall like I always do. Etched into its surface are the words 'United we Conquer'. The touch is my salute to Dawn and everything her passion has accomplished.

Joshua toots the horn of his truck, and I'm yanked back into the world of expectations and responsibilities. Flipping my hair over my shoulder, I glare at him. "I'm coming, I'm coming."

He grins from behind the windscreen.

I've just stepped onto the gravel when a howl pierces the afternoon air. It's a familiar one, but it has me pausing. This soulful cry has the hairs on the back of my neck springing up. Achak isn't happy that he's been left where he is, that's for sure. But why does it sound like he's worried he's being abandoned?

I shake my head and climb into the car. Josh turns down the music, telling me he probably didn't hear the long, painful cry. I mentally shake off the feeling—if Josh heard it, he'd probably be telling me I'm being melodramatic. My guess is that the meeting we're heading to has me on edge.

In the car, I'm still fastening my seatbelt as Josh accelerates out of the parking lot. I grab the dash as he takes a sharp right onto the road.

"I just figured out why you're so interested in medicine."

He glances at me before looking back at the road. "Huh?"

I assume the usual position for when I'm in the car with Josh. Feet braced on the floor, one hand on the handle above the door, the other gripping the center console. "So you can put yourself back together after you wrap around a light pole."

Another grin is flung my way, a don't-you-realize-I'm-invincible grin, before we squeal around another corner. "Have to get my need for speed fix somehow."

Accelerating down the highway, we pass another chain-link fence. This is for one of the biggest enclosures where wolves can move around in, almost like they're in the wild.

Josh notices me looking. "How's he going?"

"Clean bill of health," I say like a proud mother, but the feeling doesn't last. "Although not keen on being cooped up."

Josh seems to relax a little on hearing that Achak continues to improve. "Better that than the alternative."

Which is true. "I just can't shake the feeling that Achak blames us for being there in the first place."

Josh's lips flatline. "Well, the rabies not so much, but the whole need for captive breeding in the first place? He's kinda got a point..."

His hands tighten on the steering wheel and the car powers forward. Uh oh. I shouldn't have gone there. It was Joshua's grandfather who started the wolf culling and thinking of that always gets him worked up.

Time for a change of topic. "Any ideas what this will mean for the assembly?"

Once a month, a handful of Fae and Were leaders come together to share information on where things are at. Over the past two years, it's been more about desperately trying to come up with a solution to the steady decline we've slowed, but not stopped.

Josh shakes his head. "Mom and Dad said they didn't want to talk about it in front of the twins, which means there's never a time to talk about it."

He's right. With four of them, it seems there's always at least one awake and redecorating a room somewhere in that great big house of theirs.

I cross my arms. "Well, my parents weren't giving too much away, which isn't unusual."

"Maybe there isn't much to tell?"

I use precious seconds to tear my eyes from the road to throw Josh an unimpressed look. "Or?" I prompt.

Josh's lips twitch as he continues to stare out the windscreen. He shrugs. "They're the Prime Alpha pair and they take looking after their only child very seriously."

I wait, even my own safety put aside to see if Josh is going to acknowledge it. "We both know it's more than that."

Josh's teasing glint disappears as his serious face returns. "We don't need to go there, Ava."

Except I can't help but pick at the wound. Its always-there-and-waiting pain means I can never quite ignore it. "They're totally overprotective, Josh, and all because I can't shift. All because I'm a bit of everything," I throw my hands up in exasperation, maybe a little desperation. "Which adds up to a hybrid-mix-of-nothing."

Josh reaches over to squeeze my hand, and I tense purely because now there's only one of his on the wheel. "You're a flower waiting to bloom. Your parents have patience patented."

I turn to look out the window. There's only so many times you can say that line before you start to wonder if you're a fern or a lump of moss—both plants that don't flower.

Josh shrugs. "Besides, there's not much point being able to shift. It's not like we get to do it."

The trees are a blur of alpine green. Maybe my limbo-status is a blessing I should be grateful for. Full moon runs stopped before I was born. Weres are encouraged not to shift. It's just too dangerous. Humans are hyper-vigilant to signs of wolves, and tracks left by Weres have sparked wolf hunts. Members of packs have been lost to rogue poachers looking to shoot a trophy. I've noticed the edginess this confinement sparks in members of my pack, heck, I feel it every time I'm in a car with Josh. I've seen the resentment smoldering in so many Were eyes, each year a little closer to the surface.

I chew my lip, feeling guilty that gratitude doesn't seem to be interested in showing up.

We're at my house quicker than should be possible, and we both glance at each other when we see the number of cars lining the driveway. There are about five times more than the usual handful that make the trip.

Obviously, word has gotten around that something's up.

I was right—this is going to be a significant meeting.

7

AVA

As usually happens when entering a room with a lot of people, I brace myself but still find I'm a little overwhelmed.

The threads spear out, connecting everybody in the room. Each one splits and divides, mapping out the ties we all have to each other. When I've tried to describe what it looks like to my family, I've always struggled. It's like a network of veins, maybe those images you see of brains and their cells. Just as alive, just as complex and three dimensional...but denser, brighter, and seen by no-one else.

Dad is watching me from across the room. I straighten and smile, showing him that it doesn't bother me like it used to. It just takes some time to adjust when I first walk into a crowded room. They tried to have more children, but it seems fate decided I'd be an only child. It means he's always worried this is too much to ask from one girl.

As time has kept moving, I've sometimes wondered the same...

"Ava." I instantly recognize the warm, calm tones and turn.

A tall man, blond hair pulled back into a long braid, his green, tilted eyes smiling, is standing there with his arms open.

"Uncle Orin." I hug him tightly. Although he's technically my half-uncle, our bond is a special one. The son of Dawn and the Fae Elder who also fathered my mother, Orin was the one who taught me the way of the Fae. Long walks in the forest, time spent with not just wolves, but all the animals that came out to visit us, showed me how amazing our connection is. He's the one who helped me understand the threads. He pointed out that they are simply what's always been there.

I'm just lucky enough to see them.

"How's my favorite niece?"

My smile grows. I'm his only niece. "Trying for the favorite uncle title, huh?" Seeing as Dad is a twin, I have two.

Orin's forest colored eyes twinkle. "You've always had an unfair advantage."

I hug him again, because I know what's coming next.

The people in the room move in, preparing to greet me. There's one other Fae elder here, River, and his welcome is warm and genuine. Next, come the Alphas of nearby territories. The Tates and the Lyalls are the most familiar as they're here for most assemblies, the Bardolfs and others who've come from further afield. I smile and pretend I don't notice the courteous nods, my name said with a hint of deference. I'm the child of the Prime Alpha *and* the Queen of the Fae. The one born of the Prime Prophecy.

I'm just not sure when the honor became a weight of responsibility.

I make my way to my parents, waving a greeting at Uncle Mitch and Aunt Tara. It's sad that their brief break from their brood of children has to be a meeting like this. Once I'm by Dad's side, with Mom on his right, he clears his throat.

The silence is swift and absolute. Even if they hadn't called such a big meeting for something so important, when the Prime Alpha speaks, everyone listens.

"Thank you, friends, for attending. We have some important news that needs to be discussed."

Tension winds through my chest as I watch and wait. Achak's fate is going to depend on this meeting.

"We've come across a particularly virulent form of rabies."

Several people suck in their breath.

"And one wolf has had to be euthanized."

A grumble ripples through the crowd. We all know that we're at the stage where every loss is going to have a ripple effect on the overall population.

River frowns. "Why do you say it's more virulent?"

Mom answers this one. "It's faster, with a twenty-four-hour incubation period instead of the usual week. The animals, once infected, are far more aggressive."

Glances are exchanged around the room as the implications settle amongst them.

John Tate is frowning ferociously. "We can't afford to lose more wolves."

River nods. "They're too vulnerable. There aren't enough of them to fight some new disease."

A voice from the back carries across the small crowd. "Human are the ones that made them vulnerable."

"They'd be happy to see them wiped off the face of the earth," comes a quick reply.

Dad straightens. "Not all of them."

Mom raises her hand to curb the malcontent before it gains too much momentum. "We believe we've discovered a therapeutic vaccine. One that can work after a wolf has been infected."

One or two eyebrows raise in the crowd. "How?" says a voice full of skepticism.

"We've successfully treated an animal with Furious."

Aaron Bardolf, a wiry man when it comes to Weres, and a shrewd one, crosses his arms. "How did you discover this?"

I'm not sure if I sense or imagine the strain that forms along Dad's jaw. "Ava was attacked by one of our captive bred wolves."

Aaron glances at me before looking back at Dad. "And she calmed him?"

My stomach clenches and my teeth clamp down. Orin moves a little closer to me.

Dad seems to grow on the spot. "There was no time. The animal was extremely aggressive. I tranquilized him before Ava had a chance."

There's a shifting of bodies in the room, but no one says anything.

I'm the only one standing still. I've hated it more and more as the days crawled past my sixteenth birthday. For two years there's been a collective breath held. All waiting to see what the child of the prophecy is going to mean.

Then started the new looks. The speculation, the worry. The questions in their mind have moved from 'what will she do?' to 'will she even make a difference?'

And I've never had an answer for either.

What no one has realized, is that maybe my mixed heritage has made me a watered-down version of everyone. The sum of the parts is looking like it's added up to a whole lot of nothing.

Mom steps forward. "Humans cannot know of this."

"Damn right."

Mom smiles as the Lyall Alpha slams his fist into his hand.

"But we need to get the vaccine out."

Dad nods. "We need to be able to respond quickly. We're hoping this vaccine is just as effective before a wolf is infected. If we get in quick, we stop this becoming an issue."

Mom grasps Dad's hand, and pride swells my chest at their

show of unity and strength. "We will remain here, monitoring the wolf who's recovered, and vaccinating as many of the wild population as we can."

Aaron steps forward. "We'll head east. Target the packs there."

River is already nodding. "I can head inland, and let other Fae know. We will be able to get close to many of the wild ones."

Dad nods in thanks. "We'll need more than one person to do the west. Those are the territories most densely populated."

Three hands go up as does the sense of determination in the room.

As the diversity within the room births unity, I realize I've come to a crossroads. An opportunity. A scary possibility.

I straighten my shoulders. I was born because my parents had faith in what no-one believed was possible.

Pulling in a breath that I hope feels like courage, I step forward. "I'll head north."

Now that silenced the room.

I don't look anywhere but at my parents. Their over-protectiveness is going to be the biggest hurdle. But even though the idea was only just born, all of a sudden, it's full of life. This is my opportunity to be part of the solution, to show everyone I'm a part of this.

Josh rubs his chin, speaking up for the first time since the assembly started. "Makes sense. Dawn is there, heading the next captive breeding program."

Oh yeah, I hadn't thought of that.

He looks up at Mom and Dad. "And it's the least populated of all the territories."

Gratitude floods my limbs and I want to grab Josh and hug him. He's trying to allay my parents' concerns. Please let it work.

Mom and Dad don't move. They look like my words turned

them into statues. 'No' is stamped all over Dad's stony face. Mom is gripping his hand like it's a lifeline.

And then everyone else is looking at Mom and Dad. Although, now the words are out of my mouth, I realize how it's going to look if Mom and Dad say no to their only child heading off to the arctic tundra. I'll go back to being the mixed-breed child who everyone's starting to give up waiting on.

All of a sudden, a lot is riding on their response.

I know they're balancing their love for their daughter with their love for their people, but please let them see how important this is—for everyone.

Dad pulls in a breath, snapping out of his brief daze. He looks at the Fae Elders and Were Alphas around him. He looks down at Mom, who nods. You don't have to see how tightly woven their connection is to know these two can practically read each other's minds. It means they've made a decision.

Dad's face is solemn as he speaks. "Ava, our daughter, will head to the north."

All the air vaporizes from my lungs. I turn to Josh, trying to curb my wide eyes. Looks like I'm heading to the sub-arctic plains. He arches a brow at me, probably reminding me that I didn't develop the Were immunity to cold.

A jubilant feeling bubbles up in my belly, one that shouldn't belong in this somber space, but it stirs through my blood anyway. It suggests there was another reason I put my hand up to head north. It's a reason that leaves me a little light-headed.

My wolf is the color of snow.

8

AVA

For two years I've wondered.
Every time we connected in the world of dreams, I wondered if I'd ever get to meet my white wolf. We've done so much together. Run miles over so much terrain, explored every season. Wrapped around each other and held still, like maybe we can stay that way for as long as we want. I've felt him breathe, seen his eyes light with a smile.

But we've never spoken. I've never seen his human form.

I've always wondered if maybe I have an amazing imagination that can be mistaken for reality.

When I put my hand up to travel north I realized there's only one way to find out. I don't think I'd ever thought that maybe I could go looking for him. Maybe I should've considered this trip earlier...

But there's no room for regrets, because anticipation has filled me to the brim. I've got to be moving closer to him with every mile north. There's a tightening in my gut, a tension winding higher. I could meet him today!

"Not one tree." Josh is shaking his head as he takes in the framed vista outside the airplane window.

I lean over. "Ah, that's because we're above the tree line. It's too cold and too dry."

"Well, it certainly looks cold."

Even though there's no snow, it's probably the tundra; a patchwork of rock and jagged hills getting progressively more rugged, that give that away.

I nudge him with my shoulder. "Yep. Never a day above ten degrees Celsius."

"I'm not sure you thought this through." Joshua shudders, and I suspect he's realizing the offer to come with me was an impulsive one.

But my decision was made with full awareness of where we're going. After all, I've been here before.

We bank right, and I see a rocky beach, houses dotted along the bay. Even though it's summer, the sky is a pale dove color and the water a mercury blue. Everything is muted, hardened, stark...and I love it. It speaks of peace and patience and most of all, is deeply familiar.

I can feel that my wolf is here.

From the moment our wheels touch the tarmac I feel like my whole body is filled with helium. His thread is one I will recognize instantly.

The airport is a compact, plain building not far away, and I hurry toward it.

"Hey, what's the rush?" Josh lengthens his stride to catch up with me. "Are you cold?"

I slow at the concern in his voice. In my excitement, I didn't noticed the temperature. Now the cool afternoon air nips at my cheeks and settles in my lungs. I wrap the jacket my mother made sure I wear a little tighter around me.

"Stay warm," she'd said, hands holding my shoulders like she didn't want to let go. "And stay safe, Ava."

"Mom. I'm heading to the least populated point I can." I'd rolled my eyes. "And Dawn will be there."

Her tilted green eyes, the ones I inherited, had misted a little. "All true. I just know that for great things to happen, hard lessons have to be learned."

I hadn't bothered to ask what she meant by that, I'm delivering some vaccines...and looking for my wolf. Not starting some epic journey.

Josh tucks his hands into his jeans, his long-sleeved tee catching in the breeze. He winks. "I hope you packed some thermals."

I smile at him. "Your mom is bringing them when she visits with the twins."

Josh's eyes widen and his mouth pops open—a comical expression of horror. I flick my hair as I turn back around and pick up the pace again.

Josh's muttering behind me is barely decipherable. I think I hear something about burning thermals when I'm not looking.

I don't register the inside of the airport. There could be a coven of bloodthirsty vampires for all I know. My gaze is totally focused on scanning and finding the other bodies in the room. There will be a group of people here to welcome the child of the Prime Prophecy; the Alpha and his mate, some extended family, and *he* could be among them.

Except there are only two people standing in the broad room, and they're both female.

The younger one leans toward the older one. "Yep, that's her. Looks just like the photos."

The older woman flaps her hands to shush her before striding forward. "Welcome, Ava. I'm Lauren Rendell. I'm sorry our Alpha couldn't be here to meet you. He had...responsibilities that couldn't be rescheduled."

I don't let disappointment take root. I was being overly optimistic thinking he'd be here. He probably doesn't even know I'm arriving. "Thank you for meeting me. This is my cousin, Joshua Channon."

There's shaking of hands and I take in the two women. Dark haired and dark eyed, the older woman is smiling, but lines of tiredness frame her eyes and mouth. The younger girl looks about our age. Her pixie cut nearly-black hair frames a set of gorgeous amber eyes.

They remind me of him...

"This is my daughter, Riley," Lauren smiles. "We're honored to welcome you to Evelyn Island."

I smile right back. "It's a privilege to be here."

"Now," Lauren puts her hands on her hips. "I'll go track down your luggage. They should have unloaded it by now."

"Oh, I can do—" But Lauren is already striding away, a woman on a mission.

"You're probably used to more of a welcoming committee." Riley's jammed her hands into her back pockets. It's hard to tell if those words are an apology or a challenge.

I open my mouth to say that I've never had a welcoming committee, but Josh steps forward. "I thought the whole town was here to greet us."

What? I spin to look at him—since when was he blatantly rude? He glances at me, a frown scrunching up his dark features, and I realize what just happened. I've traded my protective parents for a protective cousin. Actually, I wouldn't be surprised if Mom and Dad had a word with him, asking him to look out for me.

Riley's hip juts out to the side as her chin tilts up. "Unfortunately, they couldn't make it...they had to get on with their life."

I splutter as a laugh escapes my lips. Riley may have triggered Josh's protective streak, but it looks like I might need to protect him from this girl's sharp tongue. Josh's mouth opens to reply and I'm about to jump in and referee when Lauren returns, pushing a trolley with our bags.

"Got them. Let's head to the car."

Wiping the scowl from his face, Josh insists on pushing the trolley. As we follow Lauren and Riley to the parking lot, I nudge him with my elbow. We can't talk about what just happened, Were hearing is far too sensitive, but I don't need to. We grew up together. He knows I'm going to give him grief about this for many moons to come.

Outside, it feels like the mercury has dropped another couple of degrees, but when I see a tall, broad-shouldered guy climbing from the truck at the front, I almost forget to breathe. I'd walk through a snowstorm if that's who I hope it is.

Beanie covering half his head, the young man walks straight up to me and puts his hand out. "Hey, Ava. Great to meet you."

Hiding the disappointment is hard, but it's not this guy's fault he's not him, so I yank up a smile. "You too."

The guy scratches at the grey wool on his head. "The name's KJ. Welcome to Evelyn Island."

I like him instantly, and it doesn't surprise me that the shimmering thread that links us is stronger and brighter than when I usually first meet someone. Maybe it's because he's a Were, but it doesn't really matter. I know I've found a friend.

Joshua has already unloaded the bags into the back of the truck, so KJ opens the rear door, a broad smile on his good-looking face. "Kept the car warm for you."

Feeling kind of spoilt and hoping this isn't the way I'll be treated the whole time I'm here, I smile back. "You rock."

Lauren climbs in the front as KJ climbs into the driver's seat. That leaves Joshua, Riley, and me to sit in the back. Josh climbs in, obviously deciding he's going to be in the middle. Riley and I take the two window seats.

The interior of the truck is quite spacious but put one Were male in the back and it instantly shrinks. I don't mind being pressed against Josh's side, he's practically like a brother to me, but I realize Riley would have to be experiencing the same on the other side.

I glance over to find them both staring straight ahead and have to suck in my smile. These two are going to be interesting.

Settling back, I take in the scenery moving past. Houses line the bay, parallel to the rocky beach. They stretch back in hodge-podge lines, a delightful mix of red and blue roofs. Surrounding everything is the arid, brown soil. I begin to wonder how many Weres live on Evelyn Island, and whether it's going to be as easy to find my wolf as I'd hoped.

Time to make some conversation. "There's something beautiful about the isolation out here. How many of us are there?"

KJ glances at me through the rear vision mirror. "We're a small but tight bunch."

Lauren turns in her seat. "Our Alpha will take you for a tour when he's back."

The Alpha. He's probably a good person to learn about the members of the pack. "I'm looking forward to meeting him. Will he be away long?"

"I'm hoping he'll be home when we get there."

There's a quiet snort from Riley. "Don't bet on it," she mutters.

Lauren glares at her daughter before turning back to me. "He's been out on patrol." She beams a bright smile. "Protecting the arctic wolf population is our first priority."

Josh is looking out my window. "How often is your husband out on patrol?"

So, Josh noticed that Lauren stated the Alpha lives at their home. It makes sense that the Alpha mate would be here to greet us considering he wasn't able to himself.

Riley turns to Josh, her amber eyes flashing. "Our dad is dead."

My eyes widen. It was an innocent enough question, but Riley just made it look like Josh jammed his foot in his mouth. Crimson creeps up his neck.

KJ takes a moment to throw a glare over his shoulder. "A fair enough assumption, really. Declan was shot by poachers a couple of years back. Hunter, his son, has been Alpha ever since."

Lauren has turned back to the front, staring straight ahead. "A responsibility he shoulders very seriously."

KJ reaches out to squeeze Lauren's hand. "He's not alone. He has a wonderful family to support him."

"I'm so sorry." I glance at both Lauren and Riley. "It sounds like you've made your father and husband proud."

Riley crosses her arms as she looks out the window. "Rendell means 'wolf protector'. Hunter has always done what needs to be done."

Glancing at Josh, I wonder if he recognizes the same protectiveness that Riley's earlier comment sparked in him. She's obviously just as protective of her older brother. But Josh is staring straight ahead, practically pretending Riley isn't there.

Apparently not.

Hunter would have to be a few years older than us to have shouldered the responsibility of Alpha two years ago. He's obviously garnered the respect of those around him. "He sounds like someone I'm looking forward to meeting."

And like someone who would know who my wolf is.

The houses thin the further we drive away from the bay. It doesn't surprise me that the Rendells live on the outskirts. Most Weres do as it provides some measure of privacy.

The Rendell house is a simple, weathered building with a red roof. There are no other cars in the driveway as we pull in, but I try not to take it as a bad sign. It seems that hard evidence doesn't matter anyway, because anticipation bubbles up again. The Alpha is surely going to have the information I need.

I can feel it. We're coming closer together.

Inside, the house is as simple as the outside. The front door opens into a lounge room, with a TV and worn, comfortable sofa. The house is noticeably quiet and I look at the Weres around me. They'll hear or scent if there's anyone in the house.

Riley narrows her eyes. "He'd better be home..." She heads off down the hallway.

Lauren makes a show of smiling, probably already realizing that Riley is going to come back empty handed. "I suppose this gives you guys time to unpack and settle in."

Another wave of disappointment hits me, and I have to wait for it to pass. I know I'm being impatient, but it seems my heart won't listen to reason.

Riley comes back, holding out her arms to show she's empty handed.

Lauren shakes her head. "I told him we'd be back at around this time."

Riley is nibbling on her nail. "I hope he didn't go too far out."

KJ pulls his cell phone out of his pocket. "I'll see if I can get hold of him." Something in his voice says he's not hopeful he'll be successful.

It's then that I remember this family has already lost one Alpha to a poacher. "Is there anything I can do to help?"

That seems to bring a smile to KJ's face. "Nah. Hunter likes to think he's a lone wolf, but family is what recharges him. He'll be back soon enough."

With that cryptic remark, KJ heads out the door.

I look to Josh, who shrugs. Turning to our hosts, he grins. "Unpacking sounds like a great idea."

Lauren relaxes. "Wonderful. I'll get us a warm drink. Riley, can you show these two their rooms?"

Riley goes to grab my suitcase, but I beat her to it. "No need," I smile. "Lead the way."

With a shrug, Riley turns and heads down the hall again. Glancing over my shoulder, I notice exactly where Josh's eyes have strayed. It seems my cousin is intrigued by the sway in this girl's hips. They certainly have a feminine sashay that holds just a hint of attitude.

Following, I curb my smile. These two are definitely going to be interesting.

My room consists of a double bed, a bureau and a wardrobe. A dark blue comforter is spread over the bed. There's something about this room that has me breathing in deeply. I'm feeling closer to him by the minute.

Flopping back on the bed I throw my arms out wide.

I'm here.

Now, it's only a matter of time.

And judging by how I'm feeling, time will only let the anticipation build.

9

HUNTER

24 MONTHS BEFORE

Heading out the following night, my muscles are wound tighter than they usually are. I accelerate the Ski-Doo, letting the wind slap at my face. It's because Sakari is close to giving birth.

It's because you want to know if you'll see her again...

By now I've convinced myself I had some sort of brain-snap, probably brought on by lack of sleep. Or it was some sort of weird sleep-walking incident...probably brought on by lack of sleep. But all the rationalizing doesn't stop my brain from reliving those minutes when she was with me. They were the most amazing moments, moments when I felt alive and vibrant and free.

I shake my head. Alphas don't feel free. They live up to their responsibilities. And for me, that's making sure our arctic wolves are around for longer than this season of The Bachelor.

As I near the area where Sakari has built her den, I cut the engine.

I consider shifting, only to glance over my shoulder. We

thought there'd been no poachers around the last time I was out with Dad...Taking off my jacket, I hang it over the handlebars. Not having to wear all the layers that humans need will have to be as close as I can be to acknowledging I'm Were. Besides, the walk will do me good. Unloading the dead weight from the quad, I head in their direction.

As I drag my gift, I scan the horizon. Behind me, it seems to stretch as wide and flat as an ocean. The horizontal line where harsh earth meets muted sky is unbroken. In front it rises to the craggy, irregular hills and mountains. The furthest and highest peaks hold the snow that will be back before you're ready.

Next, I keep an eye out for where I can set up the camera for KJ. It needs to be close, but not too close. One of the others was knocked over and smashed when Zephyr decided he needed to remind one of the wolves who was Alpha. We can't afford to replace them too often on our limited budget.

As the base of the hill comes into view, I see the wolves go on high alert. Zephyr is instantly at the forefront, ears erect, eyes zeroed in on me. I stop and take a few steps back. Now isn't the time to get them all agitated.

Lifting the head of the roadkill I picked up, an unlucky caribou, I show Zephyr what I've brought. Dropping it, I walk to the left, moving away, but maintaining the distance between myself and the den. Once several yards are between me and the road kill, Zephyr starts to walk down, his head constantly alternating between me and his meal. I put my hands up to show they're empty. Zephyr has lost family to humans just like I have.

Once he's there, it only takes one sniff for him to dive in. Once Sakari gives birth, it will be his and the pack's job to supply her with meat. At least now he won't have to leave her unprotected to do that.

The other wolves follow closely behind and the growls and grumbles as everyone ensures the pecking order is maintained fills the air. In no time their jaws, far more powerful than those of a domesticated dog, have begun tearing open the carcass. I use the opportunity to get closer, eyes darting to the feeding wolves with each step. Judging the distance is tricky. The closer it is, the better we see what these guys are up to. The closer I get, the more I risk pissing these guys off. Too close, and we lose another camera.

Hammering in the stake that will secure it is the most dangerous bit. It's noisy, and right now, this pack is protecting their pregnant alpha mate. But I can't be here twenty-four-seven, so we need this camera. The key is to put as much power behind each hit so the stake goes in with as few strikes as possible. Easier said than done when the soil around here is a token sprinkling from Mother Earth. Just beneath that shallow brown icing is solid rock.

Zephyr looks up a split second after the first *clang*. I pause, waiting to see what he's going to do. He's never attacked me, and normally I wouldn't think it was a possibility. I've spent a lot of time on the fringes of this pack in human form. But his mate is pregnant. And I'm making a lot of noise. Noises—sharp, loud noises—aren't a good thing in Zephyr's world.

He stands beside the carcass, white body tense.

You don't want to come over here, friend.

I slam the hammer down again and the stake buries another inch. I want this over and done with. Zephyr takes a step away from his dinner.

Stay where you are.

If Zephyr decides to get his angry pants on it won't be me that loses the fight. One more hit and I decide that will have to do. These animals don't need their world upset any more than it already is.

Strapping on the camera, I connect all the parts just like KJ showed me, and then angle it toward the outcropping. A quick press of the little green button and I'm walking away, creating distance between me and the den. With each step Zephyr appears to relax and I breathe a little easier. Mission accomplished.

As I walk away I realize I haven't got a look at Sakari. Has she given birth yet? I hope KJ has the link up and running. It won't be long and he could be zooming in and seeing what I can't.

I also realize *she* hasn't appeared…

I sit on the hard earth, feeling disappointment pulling me down as I tell myself I'm being stupid. Sure, if she were to appear again then last time wasn't a figment of my lonely, tired brain. But if she were to appear, then I'd have to figure out what it all means. I have some soulmate who only exits in some weird-ass dimension? I'm crazy either way.

Darkness folds around me as the wolves finish their meal. I watch as Zephyr drags a bloody chunk over to the den. I sure would love to see how Sakari is going…

Glancing around, I confirm I'm alone as I always am. If I shift, I can get closer. I can make sure everything is okay. Poachers are even less likely to come out this late.

Before I can think twice, I shift, breathing in the air that, all of a sudden, holds so much more. I can smell the dry earth, what's left of the carcass, and something else. There's the scent of a different kind of blood—more canine infused, more earthy…

Holy crap, Sakari has given birth!

I'm loping towards the den when she appears, almost like my being a wolf is golden wolf's green light to appear. I stop, and I wish it was surprise that robs me of speed, but it feels a lot more like delight.

This time we walk toward each other, like a thread reeling us in, until we're face to face. Just like before, she's shades of gossamer and glory. I couldn't dream up something so beautiful if I tried. Her wintergreen eyes hold mine, and I haven't known her long enough to be able to read them, but they hold something I'm looking forward to deciphering.

I open my mouth to talk, then remember I'm in wolf form. Looks like we're going to be getting to know each other in this wordless night-world. I step in closer and her eyes light up with delight.

There's nothing I'm looking forward to more.

I angle my head at the rocky outcropping and take a step forward. She's at my side in a breath. Why does it feel like this one will follow me anywhere?

We walk towards the den and my heart starts hammering. Sakari holds the future of arctic wolves in her rocky little hollow. And I get to show my golden wolf.

Zephyr moves forward as we approach, white ears erect, canine eyes sharp in the dark. Disappointment stabs me in the chest for the second time tonight. There's no way this protective alpha is going to let me near his pups. And as annoying as that is, I respect him for it.

Except it doesn't stop my golden wolf. She walks another few steps forward, gentle eyes holding Zephyr's. She waits there, not backing down, but also not crowding him. She's asking him for permission in a, gentle, respectful way.

Whoa. This wolf is something.

Zephyr spends long seconds thinking on it, and I wouldn't expect any less of him. I hold my breath as I wait. Confirmation of what my nose has told me would be nice.

With a last glance between the two of us, and if that wasn't a 'keep your paws to yourself' look, I'd eat my tail, he steps back.

Double whoa! Zephyr just gave us the okay to visit his mate!

We walk forward in the same way you'd enter a church. Soft footed, silent, and reverent.

Sakari is curled in her little depression in the earth. In the cradle formed by her body are three little lives.

I look to golden wolf, as if needing to check that I'm not the only one seeing this. But the wonder and awe I feel blooming through me are dawning across her face. Yep, this is definitely real.

The last one, born not long ago, is still wet, white fur pasted to his body as Sakari licks him. They all curl into their mother, eyes tightly shut, wanting to burrow into the one who'll be their world for the next month or so. One mewls, and Sakari pauses to nudge it with her nose, and I see it's a female. Excitement buzzes through my veins. Rounder, softer miniatures, these guys hold so much future in their little bodies.

Golden wolf leans into me, her warm body pressing against me. I hold my breath as a new sensation rushes through me. Like two puzzle pieces slotting together, I tilt my head down and rest it on hers. I curl around her with the same protectiveness that Sakari has for her pups.

We stand there for countless minutes, watching those little lives become part of this world, bodies pressed together. I can't tell her how monumental this is, but I get to share it with her, and that's more than enough. Together we'll see them open their eyes to a world full of hope, grow into the folds of their snowy fur, and eventually create packs of their own.

We both know when it's time to leave. Zephyr walks over, the proud papa wanting to see his progeny. Knowing he's already given us a great gift, we retreat. Remembering the camera, I steer us in the opposite direction. It takes a little while for the satellite signal to pick up. Hopefully I've managed to avoid detection.

As we head away from the base of the mountain, I revel in the happy energy pumping through my body. I wonder…

Glancing at golden wolf, I go very still. She watches me, eyes narrowing and head tilting. Holding as still as I can, I coil tension through my muscles. She'll never see it coming.

When I spring, I can practically see it playing out before it happens. I'll be too fast, she'll be too surprised, I'll tag her, touch that golden fleece of hers with my nose, before darting away.

I leap, and she holds still. I sail over the distance between us, and she holds still. The outcome seems so certain.

Except it seems she sees me coming as though I'd been a mile away. At the last moment, as I'm supposed to land right beside her, she feints left. I backpedal midair, not wanting to crush her, except she's already gone by the time I land. Rather than gracefully landing on my paws, my pride gets left in the tundra soil as I trip and topple.

I stand, not sure what just happened there. Looking around, golden wolf is a few feet away, once again holding still. But this time there's a great, big smile on her face. It would be adorable and alluring if I hadn't just looked like a five-footed fool.

Who am I kidding? The sight is one of the most beautiful I've ever seen.

Nevertheless, there's the small matter of a score to settle. I lower my head, my own grin almost a reflex, and power forward.

Not bothering to wait this time, she turns and runs. I throw out a bark, a playful, canine you-can-run-but-you-can't-hide and shoot after her.

Running, chasing, wanting to be captured, we spend the black hours discovering that more than three cubs were born tonight.

10

HUNTER

24 MONTHS BEFORE

As I come in with our usual takeaway coffees KJ isn't where he usually is. Instead of sitting at his desk, he's standing in the middle of the room, hands on his hips.

"You're not meant to shift."

Crap. The security camera.

My heart stutters for a second. "What did you see?"

Would golden wolf be captured on camera? Do I want her to be? I'd have confirmation that I haven't dreamed her up...but for some reason, I'm not ready to share. Golden wolf has me feeling things I didn't know were possible.

KJ huffs. "Not much, the signal took a while to connect. And you were smart enough to stay out of range most of the time." He throws me a wry glance. "But enough to see your massive white butt."

Despite the scowl, I grin. "Jealousy suits you."

KJ looks around for something to throw, his grin is obviously unwanted, but there nonetheless. "No way I'd want a butt that white. You're lucky you live in the snow or NASA would think it's another moon." He snatches the pillow and whacks me.

"Hey." I curl around the two coffees I'm still holding. "This stuff is my lifeline."

KJ rolls his eyes. "True. Without it, you're just a cranky toddler whose blanket is in the washer."

"Hey, I only need it on days ending with a 'y'."

KJ grabs one of the cups and takes a seat. He has a sip before speaking again. "I thought you promised your family you wouldn't shift."

I look away, not happy the conversation ended back here. "They needed to hear that." I stare KJ in the eye. "You know I can't get close to them unless I'm wolf."

KJ sighs, knowing I'm speaking the truth. "It's risky, Hunter."

"It's also not optional."

Another sigh and KJ turns back to the screen. "At least the camera means you don't have to be there every night now."

Even though I will be, but I don't say that out loud. No point having to convince him I'm right all over again. A security camera may tell us what's going on, but there's no-one there if anything goes wrong. Not to mention the fact it's not as lonely as it used to be...

I pull in a breath. This news is almost as good as the news I brought yesterday. "They were born last night."

KJ's grin grows to impossible proportions. "I saw. Had to zoom in a bit, but there's three of them."

Right. So no surprise there then. "At least one is a female."

That does the job. KJ lifts his coffee cup and I meet him midair. We toast the future these little fur babies are going to mean.

"You should see them, KJ." I shake my head in wonder. "They look like overgrown balls of cotton."

"Give me two secs and I will."

KJ wiggles the mouse and the center screen comes to life. KJ starts clicking then leans forward. So far, the screen looks like what humans would see out on the tundra at night. Blank blackness.

"Did you make sure there was good reception?"

I roll my eyes. "There weren't any trees around."

"Did you connect the solar panel like I showed you?"

Now I'm frowning. KJ has never asked these questions before. "Yes." I look from the blank screen to him. "Why?"

Click. Click. Click. "I'm not getting a signal."

"Is it the internet connection or something?"

Click. Click. "Nope." *Click.* "It was working fine about midnight last night."

I peer at the screen, like coming in closer will reveal an image we can't see. But it remains blank. "What's it mean?" I ask, even though I already know. This has happened once before.

"Something's up with the camera."

Man, I hope it's not broken again.

I take a big gulp of the coffee, and even though it burns, I know I'm going to need it. I've already got KJ's door open before the keys are out of my pocket. I'm at the entryway before KJ has leaped to his feet to stand in his doorway.

"Wait, I'll come with you."

But I'm already out the door, not bothering with the jacket I don't even need. "The Ski-Doo is quicker without your Were ass on it."

I drive there faster than usual, hating the it-all-seemed-too-good-to-be-true feeling that has lodged in my gut. I don't like to think I've become that much of a pessimist, no matter how much crap life has thrown at me. But it's like a weed, and once it's grown roots, it doesn't go away.

Parking closer than I usually I do, I kick myself when I can't see any wolves where they should be. Even if I did spook them though, I doubt Zephyr would've left his post. Frowning, I figure it might be a good thing. It means I can get close to the camera seeing as I haven't brought a slab of meat for distraction.

I quickly find the camera has been knocked off even though the stake is still in the ground. Great. The wolves must've been playing or arguing nearby. I lift it up to find it's smashed. My hand tightens around it, frustration tangling my muscles. We don't have time to save up for another one. Keeping an eye on these pups is our highest priority right now, so much rests on their furry little shoulders.

As I look up, I realize I'm close to the den, but Zephyr isn't giving me the evil eye. That's unusual in itself. What's more unsettling is the fact I still can't see any of them. They should've come back by now, their need to protect their Alpha mate and her pups a powerful drive. Even for the arctic tundra, it's too quiet. Too still.

Shifting to wolf form isn't a choice.

As I approach the rocky area, heart thundering for me to move faster, I see what I felt. The wolves are gone. But why would they move so soon? I stop to scan around me, fear holding me still. Did the poachers find them?

The thought has me powering forward, caution no longer a priority.

But the den isn't empty.

I shift, falling to my knees, the need to scream trapped in my chest. Three small bodies, motionless except for the wind buffeting their fur, lie tucked in together, forming a perfect circle. I touch them, already knowing they're gone, but needing the confirmation. Their bodies, so small and chalk white, are hard and cold. They may not have been dead for long or they could have died not long after we left them, it's hard to tell with our frigid nights.

Not that it matters. The loss of these three lives is going to be like a sonic boom, the pain amplified over and over as the ramifications expand and escalate. These wolves won't mate again for another year. A year they may not have.

My whole body collapses in on itself, hope crippled and crushed. What do we do now?

Burying the three cubs, not even old enough to be named, is hard, slow work with nothing but the stake from the security camera. I welcome the blisters, the broken nails, the grazes and cuts and blood; they're a physical testament to how damaged my heart feels.

I'm not sure how long it takes, but it's almost dark by the time I'm finished. In a couple of months, snow will cover this area. This grave will be impossible to find. It will be like they were never part of this world.

Like the promise of hope never existed.

I feel like I've let Dad down…my whole family. I know I've let the wolves down.

I know what I have to do. The choice that has to be made. As I drive back home, the decision cements in my mind.

I call Dawn from the steps of my house, wanting the bad news I have to tell my family to come in one sucker punch. The loss of the pups and the need for a captive breeding program aren't words I'm looking forward to delivering.

Dawn answers on the second ring. "Hello?"

"Ah, Dawn. It's Hunter. Hunter Rendell."

"Hello, Hunter." Her papery voice is giving nothing away. "This is a surprise."

"I've rung about the captive breeding program you've been emailing us about."

"Oh yes. Do you have any questions? I've tried to be as thorough as I could with our stats and what would be involved."

"They were very detailed." I swallow. "Thank you."

"Well, we keep a very close eye on our wolves."

I grit my teeth, she isn't making this any easier.

"Excuse me for a moment, Hunter."

Dawn's voice, now muted and further away, carries through my phone. "Yes, I think Achak suits him well. He's a wild one, that's for sure."

"Apologies. We had a litter born last week and you know how important naming them can be."

I close my eyes, unsuccessfully breathing through the pain. It feels like I've been cut loose and I'm drowning in it.

Opening them, I stare straight ahead, speaking through a jaw that feels wired together. "Your captive breeding program. We'd like to begin a similar program here on Evelyn Island."

"Really?" The pleasure in her voice just rubs salt into the wound. "That's wonderful."

"We can't afford to lose them."

"Then you've made the right decision, young man. This is their best chance at survival."

We talk some logistics and dates, but I hang up as soon I as I can. My mouth feels like I've been chewing caustic soda. My pride is shattered along with my dreams.

Sitting down on the front step, I stare at the ground. Right now, this all feels like too much to carry, but sharing the pain isn't an option either—I'm the Alpha. Which basically leaves me in some sort of hellish limbo.

Alone.

A memory from last night blazes in my mind. There are moments I haven't been alone...

I didn't see her today. My guess is night is our time together. I'm tired, bordering on exhaustion. The type that even a coffee

IV drip isn't going to fix. But I know I'll go out tonight, praying that I see her.

My golden wolf is the last thread I have, the one I cling to, that maybe the world isn't as dark as the nights I spend my life in.

I don't want to know what a world would look like where that is taken away from me.

11

AVA

Waking up, I'm disorientated by the silence. There are no blue jays, larks or swallows announcing the morning like they made it happen themselves, there's no movement within the house. Then I remember where I am.

Stretching, I do a catalog of where things are at.

Frostbite? Pneumonia? Not yet, but then again, it's summer here. Nor have I been outside a lot.

Last night was a quiet dinner of mushroom risotto. Judging by the looks Riley had shot her bowl, it wasn't a meal they usually have. I made sure I was appreciative of the lengths Lauren had gone to for me.

Met the Alpha—the elusive Hunter? Nope.

Lauren had stopped apologizing by the time the afternoon came around. I'm pretty sure I heard Riley call him a few choice names under her breath. KJ had looked like he thought it was all quite humorous. He'd pointed out that once the sun had gone down we weren't likely to see Hunter till morning.

Warm, buzzing sense of anticipation still heating my stomach? Yep, alive and well.

That's the feeling that has me springing out of bed and

dressing in a hurry. Jeans and a jumper are my staples. The cream colored knitted scarf Mom made me pack sits on the top of my suitcase, but I decide there's no point looking like too much of a freak...surely it doesn't get that cold here.

In the kitchen, Riley is already at the table eating a bowl of cereal. She jumps up when I enter. "Good morning. What would you like for breakfast? Toast? I'm happy to cook up some eggs?"

"Ah." This treatment is starting to get a bit much. I grab the cereal box sitting before her, reading the brightly colored label. Mocha Munch. Looks like something the twins unsuccessfully try to get Aunt Tara to buy them. "This looks great. Point the way and I'll grab myself a bowl."

Riley heads to cupboards and passes me one. "I could grab you some juice?"

"Riley, I'm not sure what people have said about me, but I'd be far more comfortable if you'd sit down and point me to the spoons."

Riley's brow arches over her amber eyes. "Top drawer next to the sink."

I smile. "Thanks."

Riley takes her place as I grab a spoon. I can feel her watching me. "Mom said you're practically Were royalty."

I have to work not to laugh. I've already figured out Riley is a proud young lady. "As in, like a princess or something?"

"Yeah."

Filling my bowl with the balls of sugar, I wink at her. "Do princesses eat Mocha Munch?"

Riley's smile is big and fast. She grabs a spoonful and brings it to her mouth. "If they know what's good for them."

The laugh escapes, and I have to work on not spitting cocoa-colored milk everywhere. Riley bursts into her own giggles, which just fuel my own. In seconds we're both working on not spluttering cereal all over the table.

Which is just when Josh walks in. Riley instantly curbs her giggles and I use the opportunity to sit back. I'm thinking watching these two is about to become my entertainment in this house.

Josh pauses at the door. "Morning."

I smile brightly at him. "Morning. Mocha Munch?"

Josh eyes the neon box I hold up. Right now, he'd be cataloging the amount of sugar per serving and which preservatives could be considered carcinogenic in this breakfast delight. He glances at Riley, who seems to have been put on pause.

My smile grows. "Look, all-natural colors."

There's a possibility I hear his teeth grind, but Josh still manages a nod. Good to see manners won out for a change.

I grab a bowl and spoon and pass it over. "Luna would kill to have these at your house."

Josh huffs. "She'd use them as ammo against Layla."

Actually, that's true. "Breanna would clean them up."

Josh rolls his eyes. "Right off the floor, too."

"Ah, how many siblings do you have?" The question is from Riley, and I quickly shift my seat back and head to the sink. I feel like a chess player right now, strategizing as I set up my pieces.

"Four younger sisters." There's a clink of a spoon in a bowl. "Two sets of twins, in fact."

"Whoa. What's that like?"

I turn to find Josh's lips twitching. "Like living in an MRI machine."

Riley snort-laughs, then her gaze instantly shoots to her bowl. Josh looks like he's been hit by a bison.

Just then, Lauren enters holding a basket of washing. "Oh wonderful, everyone's up."

We all chorus a good morning. Lauren makes a point of smiling at me in a way that makes me tense. It feels like she's wondering whether she should curtsy.

Riley stacks our empty bowls and takes them to the sink. "Is he back yet?"

Lauren's brow twitches like it would like to frown. Her eyes flick to Josh and me before looking back to her daughter. "Not yet."

They exchange a long glance. Josh looks at me. He noticed it too. It's unusual for the Alpha to be out this long. I tuck away my need to find out about my wolf for the moment. These two women are worried.

Lauren pulls up a blinding, artificial smile. "What would you like to do today?"

I pause. I don't know Lauren and Riley enough to ask if there's anything going on. I can also instinctively tell they wouldn't want an offer of help from someone they think is Were royalty.

Which means all I can do is meet them where they are. "Well, I'd love to see the captive breeding program. Getting these vaccines dropped off is our priority."

Lauren nods. "We figured that would be the best place to call everyone in."

"Call everyone in?"

She nods again. "Our pack will assemble for your announcement. There's work to be done."

My announcement? As in a speech?

"Ah, of course." I take a moment to pull in a breath. "Just let me get my stuff together."

I dart down the hall and into my room. A speech? Why didn't I consider that I'd have to do something like a speech?

I stare at my suitcase, realizing I should have unpacked last night, but my mind was too busy buzzing. What does one wear to an announcement? One where people think you're some kind of Were royalty?

I end up choosing a green top my Mom says brings out my

eyes. With a quick brush of my hair, I open my door to find Josh leaning against the opposite wall. He's making a point of containing his grin.

I want to kick him in the shin. "Shut up."

The grin breaks free. "It'll be fine. You do these kinds of speeches all the time."

I glare at him. I've never done one of these speeches and he knows it. Lauren has assumed I'm some sort of leader back at home, someone Weres look up to.

Man, am I going to burst her bubble.

The drive to the captive breeding compound is longer than I expected, and I say as much in the car.

Riley, this time in the front, looks out the window. "Couldn't have it too close to town."

Josh narrows his eyes. "Because of the townspeople?"

She turns to look at him, and her eyes echo with sadness. "They weren't too happy that it was set up."

Lauren's face is grim as she stares out the windshield. "We've lost too many wolves to poachers. They seem to think they're target practice."

I close my eyes for a brief moment. It always hurts to hear of wolves, or any animal, being deliberately killed. Those people with guns wouldn't see the threads that connect them to the very animals they're shooting. They don't understand what severing them forever means.

Josh leans back in his seat. "I can see why you have patrols."

Of course, the Alpha would prioritize keeping the wolves safe over our arrival. I'm glad he's kept his priorities straight.

When the chain-link fence rises on the horizon a sense of familiarity floods me. Now this is something I know. I take in the format as we draw close. Looks like two large pens, a smaller one close to the building for when wolves are sick, being mated, or need close observation. It's fairly similar to what we have back home, just a smaller scale. Which isn't surprising, considering the same person established them.

I sit a little straighter. I'll be seeing Dawn for the first time since she left two years ago. The woman has been a mentor and teacher to me, someone who shared my passion for the wolves. Her Fae blood meant she understood the connections we have to the animal kingdom, but she was someone who was willing to work tirelessly, to sacrifice, in the name of their survival.

It's a reunion I'm looking forward to.

The building we pull up into is a squat, sturdy, somber-looking thing.

Lauren must notice me taking it in. "It was an old Distant Early Warning Line, a system of radar stations in the Arctic region set up to provide early warning of any invasions."

Riley rolls her eyes at me, telling me exactly what she thinks of that likelihood.

"It was deactivated in the eighties and was abandoned until we took it over two years ago."

I nod. There's certainly some interesting history up here.

Inside, I straight away notice the warmth. Although the building looks like a dreary, concrete bunker, it's obviously well heated. I'm going to enjoy spending time here.

"Ava?"

The tall, lean woman striding down the hall has her arms spread out wide. I rush toward her and our hug is a tight one. I feel our connection warm and glow as we hold each other.

Dawn pulls back. "What a mighty fine young woman you've grown up to be."

Dawn has a few extra lines across her face and her grey hair is tied back in a braid. She looks almost the same as when I saw her two years ago. "You look amazing, Dawn."

Her green eyes twinkle. "The cold air is quite invigorating."

Riley is peeling off her jacket which she hangs on a nearby

hook, a cheeky grin on her face. "Says the woman who's recreated the tropics in here."

Dawn's smile grows even more. "Makes you appreciate the cold even more." She wraps an arm around my shoulders. "Come, look at what we've done here." She leans over, a twinkle in her green eyes. "I named the center Resolve."

I nod, loving the choice of name and excited to be seeing this all, maybe even spending time with some wolves.

Except that is the moment the door opens again.

12

AVA

Along with the cool air, people start to file in. Correction, Weres start to file in. About five of them.

Each one of them scans the room until they find me, and what follows is a mixture of facial expressions. Two smile in the same way Lauren does. Some seem to struggle to keep eye contact. One seems to be fighting back a frown.

Nervousness has my hands wanting to tremble as I'm introduced to them all. Some of these people are expecting something I'm not. Others seem to have an inkling of the imposter I feel like.

But I came here for a reason. And Furious is a threat we can't afford to gain strength.

When a grin that's already becoming familiar makes its way towards me, I smile right back at KJ. Just like with my wolf, there're some connections you know are deeper even though you can't explain why. He indicates for me to follow, and we head to the far wall. Oh dear, where a lectern stands.

"Most people know why you're here."

That doesn't surprise me. The Were grapevine has always been an efficient one.

"Hunter is still MIA, but I say we start without him. Being late is his superpower."

I glance behind KJ, people are chatting amongst themselves, commenting that you can smell summer is almost over. They keep glancing my way, but I could really use a little more time. I turn back to KJ. "So, Hunter is Riley's older brother?"

"Yep."

Except Weres generally have their children close together... Surely not... "How old is he?"

"In human years? Our age. But I'm pretty sure his sense of responsibility was born a few decades ago."

I blink. "He was young when he became Alpha then."

"Just a bit over sixteen. Most other Weres wouldn't have been able to pull it off."

Holy smokes, it can't be! But the pack is all here. Hunter is my age.

I think Hunter is my white wolf!

Except there's no time to dwell on whether that conclusion is correct. The room falls silent and I look up to find all eyes on me. Right. It seems it's time for me to talk.

KJ winks and moves back. I swallow as I step up to the lectern. "Ah, thank you for coming. I...appreciate you taking the time to be here."

Feet shuffle and faces look expectant.

"As most of you know, I'm here because we've come across a virus."

Nods move around the room. "Rabies."

"Yes. But a particularly virulent strain. We've named it Furious."

There are more shuffles as people turn to look uneasily at each other as I go on to explain everything I know about the virus.

It's then that I feel him. Something in the connection that I've only felt while asleep all of a sudden becomes real.

He's here. Maybe in the room. Scanning, I can't find him, even though I don't know what he looks like. The moment I see him, I'll know. I'm sure of it. The heady sense of happiness has me straightening.

"But we have a vaccine, one that works after infection. We're confident it has the capacity to immunize them too."

Dawn is at the back now too, watching me with a smile on her face as I tell them about how the vaccine works.

It feels good to be the one to give them hope.

"We'll be spending the next few days disseminating the vaccine amongst the captive population before extending to the wild wolves."

"And that will cure them?" asks a woman at the front.

"That's what we believe. We've seen it work on one of our own captive wolves."

I notice KJ frown as he looks to the back of the room. With a glance at the crowd, he heads down the passage to my left.

"Have there been any other cases of Furious?" This time it's a man to my right. His weathered skin and dark hair speak of Inuit ancestry.

"Not that we know of, which is why we're confident we've caught it early."

There are some nods and I'm keen for this to be over. Meet my wolf, then deal with Furious. Two goals that are just within my reach.

"Other Weres and Fae are vaccinating other wolf populations. We'll work with Dawn to do the same here."

"Won't take long," the same man grunts. "There ain't many left."

A grumble ripples through the small crowd and I make sure I smile rather than frown. It doesn't surprise me that the dissatisfaction with humans is also here. In fact, Evelyn Island is probably a crucible for all these tensions—a small, isolated population that's amplified what's happening in other parts of the world. But the sense that my wolf is nearby buoys me, reminding me of all the amazing things that exist in this world. I smile. "They'll never lose with you all protecting them."

"Sure as hell better than catching them and holding them in cages."

The last comment is muttered, probably not meant to reach my ears. But I see Josh and Riley stiffen and I know I heard right. I definitely want to wrap this up before any of these sentiments gain too much momentum.

As I answer a few more questions, I can feel the connection weaken, like he's moving away. He mustn't realize I'm here, which means I have to catch him before we miss this opportunity. It's been two years of wondering and hoping.

It's time to bring this to the realm of reality.

Like she's a mind reader, Lauren steps up beside me. "Thank you, Ava. The Rendell pack is willing to help in any way we can."

The crowd starts to move, one or two leaving, some talking to each other, one looking like they're going to head my way. I touch Lauren's arm and tell her I'm going to find the ladies room. She smiles, probably assuming I've had enough of the crowd. She's right, but not for the reasons she assumes.

It's time to meet my wolf.

I head down the hallway KJ just used. It turns right up ahead, and my guess is that this building is a great big square with a hallway that circles it. I can feel myself drawing closer, the connection building.

A voice reaches me. "I'll be back later."

A voice I've never heard before, but a voice I already know. I pause where I am. Why is he walking away?

"You get here late, and now you're leaving early?" I recognize

KJ's voice. "I get that the patrols are important, Hunter, but you've spent almost every night out over the past two years."

Hunter. It's him.

"I don't want to talk about this right now."

I slow again. He sounds angry. Maybe that's why he's still moving. He would have to know I'm here.

"As opposed to all the other times you've wanted to talk about it?"

"KJ, now really isn't the time. I need…a break. Just for a bit."

"Going out alone isn't the answer, Hunter. Take advice from an orphan who knows what they're talking about."

There's a sigh that sounds a little strangled. "I'll explain tomorrow."

"You know what? Don't bother. If you want to kill yourself, don't let someone who cares about you get in the way."

There are footsteps on the concrete, and I figure this must be the time for me to move forward. Maybe meeting Hunter will be the good news he needs.

"KJ, I think we start it."

The footsteps stop. "What?" A moment passes. "You're serious, aren't you?"

There's a pause. "We've run out of options."

Those words have me stopping mid-stride, but I don't have time to wonder what they're talking about. A barely perceptible squeak just sounded when my sneaker stopped in a hurry on the concrete floor.

Silence reigns. They've heard me.

I know I should feel guilty for eavesdropping, but I'll do that later. Right now, I have a soulmate to meet.

Rounding the corner, heart pounding like a drum, I stop the moment I see them.

Great glory, it's him.

It's his copper eyes that first grip me. I've stared into those depths so many times. The familiarity, the sense of rightness, is instantaneous. But then I take in the tousled dark hair, the sharp line of his jaw, those lips...good grief, then the shoulders built of muscle, the lean length, the biceps! I hadn't banked on Hunter, my wolf, being a whole hunk of gorgeous.

I open my mouth to say something. We've spent so much time together, but we've never spoken. Except I'm as silent as I am in my dreams. My only saving grace is that he looks as shell-shocked as I feel.

KJ could have been teleported to another dimension, I'm not terribly sure. All of a sudden, there's only two of us in this building. This continent. This whole, amazing, incredible universe.

"Ava."

Oh god, my name sounds good on his lips.

His face seems to transform. It goes from shock, to raw anger, to hard as the concrete underneath us. "It's true, you're Ava Phelan." In fact, his face seems to be chiseled from stone. "The girl who never changed."

The verbal slap is a painful one. I don't know how my head hasn't snapped to the side. "What?" My first word since we met is a stunned whisper.

"You're not Were." He swallows. "You've never been a wolf, not matter what colour she is."

This time I reel back. The connection is there, golden in a way I've never seen it. His eyes said he felt it too. Except he's just hit me where I'm most vulnerable.

My hand comes to my brow, trying to disentangle what's going on.

"Hey." KJ steps between us. "What's going on?"

I swallow. This moment has taken up so much airtime in my head. In the sweet scenarios we stand there, just like we do in my dreams, our eyes saying it all. In the more realistic ones, I get tongue tied, maybe he does too. There's this awkward silence neither of us knows what to do with...until we both speak at once.

I feel so naive.

So stupid.

And both feelings hurt. Really hurt.

Stepping back, I wish I could stop looking at him. "It seems I've made a mistake."

KJ is looking from Hunter to me and back again. "Dude, I know you don't get out much. But that was just damned rude."

Hunter's response is to clench his jaw even tighter. His whole body looks like a tightly wound coil. "Mistakes." Repeating my last word, he looks away, disconnecting his gaze from mine. "Believe me, they're not a feeling you want to repeat."

KJ gasps, but my lungs don't have any air to do the same. Anguish seems to have filled every crevice of my chest.

Somehow, I thought the dreams meant I had potential. Made me more. Meant I wasn't just a disappointing mix of nothing.

That maybe I had a soulmate.

But the scowling, copper eyed guy before me is everything my wolf isn't. My wolf would never hurt me like Hunter just did. My wolf has a heart, one that's synchronized with mine.

Which means my wolf is nothing more than a dream. It means I've been very, very wrong about a whole lot of things.

Holding myself as high as I can considering the weight of the agony, I turn on my heel and leave.

13

AVA

Waking the next morning I welcome the silence. I wish it was a balm to the wound my soul now has, but it isn't. The quiet feels like it has something to say, but it knows there're no words. Instead, it's crowded with emotion that has nowhere to go.

Today the silence is the sound of grief.

There's a knock on my door and I wipe my hands over my face.

Josh pokes his head around the door, his face not quite smiling. "You weren't there at dinner last night. You okay?"

No, I'm really not. "Yeah. I had stuff to do."

He walks in and sits on the edge of the bed. "To do with the vaccine?"

I push myself up a little more. I have an idea of how Josh is going to take this news. "I booked our flights home."

"Home?" Yep, there's the shock.

"Yep. We're flying out this afternoon."

"As in, today?" And the confusion. That's the hardest part. There's no way I can have this make sense.

I pick at the blue comforter. "Well, we've done what we came here to do. The vaccines have been delivered and the pack knows what to do with them." I shrug. "Doesn't seem to be any reason to stay."

He narrows his eyes. Dammit. There's his brain ticking over. "Something's changed."

My hand clenches around the material. Josh is the one person who's going to see past this. "Achak needs me. I left him to rush off and do this. Now that it's done, I want to head back."

"We literally just got here."

Flipping the comforter off, I clamber past him. Staying still is no longer an option. "There's no point discussing it. I've already made the bookings."

"But—"

"I need to get dressed, Josh. We'll have to go say goodbye to Dawn."

And if I'm lucky, I won't see Hunter again.

Josh holds himself there, and I know he's wondering whether he should push this. I hold my breath; my aching chest can't handle any more pressure right now. Josh turns and heads for the door, but his narrowed gaze and tight lips tell me this isn't over.

I sag once he's gone. How do I explain that I'd put all my hopes on a dream? A vivid, recurring, and truly realistic dream, but a dream nonetheless? I'd sound as naive and foolish as I looked yesterday. And as much as his words hurt, Hunter was right. That's not a mistake I'm willing to repeat.

I dress a little more carefully than yesterday. Both because I now know that I'm always being seen through the filter of the Prime Prophecy child, but mostly because I need some sort of armor. I choose a dark top, this one a little tighter than yesterday, like it will help keep me together.

Everyone is in the kitchen when I arrive. It's hard to work up a smile, but I manage it. Lauren has a bowl and the box of Mocha Munch in front of me before I've even sat down.

"Thank you." I pick up my spoon, knowing I need to get this over and done with. "We're heading home tonight."

"Oh." Lauren looks like I just killed her puppy. "Is there something wrong?"

"Oh gosh, no. You've made us feel very welcome."

Riley crosses her arms. "You were talking of disseminating the vaccine yesterday."

I look down at my plate. This cereal tastes worse than it did yesterday. "I'm sorry. I've discovered I need to get back to Jacksonville. There's a wolf that needs me. I've already booked our flights."

Lauren glances at Riley. "But..."

Riley shakes her head. "Looks like it's been decided."

Her mother turns to the sink. "Well, that settles it, then."

I look to Josh to see if he's going to ask what they're talking about, but he's staring at his bowl. His face as he eats the cocoa covered sugar cubes isn't comical today. His expression seems to mirror how uncomfortable this conversation is. And it hasn't finished yet. "I was hoping to go out to Resolve again today."

Lauren turns, that smile back on her face. "Of course. I have to work today, but Riley can take you."

I feel like I've just used a royalty card I never wanted to be dealt. "Thank you."

Riley rises from her seat. She dumps her bowl in the sink and walks out.

I shrink within myself even more.

I too, wish things had been different.

The buildings and fences of the Resolve program strike me with their familiarity again. It'll be good to go home and be somewhere that feels right but actually belong.

We've just walked in the door when Joshua and Riley disappear down the hall to the right. Neither bothers to let me know where they're going. I allow myself a moment to wince. I get that they're upset with me.

Walking straight ahead, I remember Dawn's offer to show me around. I would have liked to have seen the wolves here. Arctic wolves are unique not just in their snow-white coats, but their stockier ears and muzzles. They're an animal designed to live in some of the harshest climates Mother Nature could design. Even before—I mentally shy away from where my thoughts were heading—even as a child I admired and respected them.

I haven't gone far when I come to an open door. Inside is what looks like an office, and Dawn is sitting at one of the desks. Hers is the only one that isn't cluttered with paper and coffee cups. A smile lightens my chest a little. She always loved neatness and structure and outcomes. There was never a loose end with Dawn.

She turns to find me standing in the doorway. "Ava. I'm glad you're here."

I open my mouth to share the news that I'm leaving, but Dawn is already walking toward me. She scoops me in her arm and propels me back down the hall.

"We need to get the first vaccine in."

"Oh, I—"

"No time. I thought you understood how important it is that we do this as soon as possible."

Glancing at my watch, I figure I have time. And there's something in Dawn's voice that holds me back.

"Our breeding pair was in the first enclosure."

Was? Taking a sudden left, she opens a door and I find myself outside again, a tall fence in front of us. I'm about to ask what she means but I pause. Movement at the far end of the enclosure captures my attention.

Three arctic wolves have just stood up, ears erect, tails high. The sense of familiarity hits me again, but this time it doesn't make sense. It's logical that I'd recognize the enclosures and setup here. It's so similar to home.

But why would I feel like I've met these ones before? As much as I've loved arctic wolves, I've never seen one. Well, not in real life...

One white, thick tail starts to twitch, and like a Mexican wave, the others join in. Then all three start flapping about. These wolves are getting excited about something. Just as I think it, one jumps forward before the rest. I somehow know that the smallest one will hang back. The middle one will get overexcited and mouth the smaller one.

How do I know this?

Then I see what got them all hyped up. A person is entering through the gateway at the back. A person who has my breath hitching and my heart clenching.

The three wolves leap at Hunter, who has his arms open wide. They topple him like a soggy snowman and he goes down on his knees. Straight away he's inundated by a tidal wolf hug. They jump and pounce all over him, licking his face —the canine happy greeting that also communicates submission. What really catches my breath is Hunter's face. He's smiling.

At a distance, he looks amazing. At a distance, he's everything I thought he would be. Tall and strong. Deeply connected with the animals. A heart that I already recognize.

Like he's been stuck with a cattle prod, his head shoots up. Across this distance, his gaze connects with mine. The recognition intensifies and my chest fills with joy and pain all at the same time. It's a feeling that lifts and sinks simultaneously.

How could I have been so wrong?

"Shall we keep moving?"

There's an urgency in Dawn's voice that I don't understand, but she's already striding away. When I turn back, Hunter has gone back to playing with the wolves. Confused and hurting, I hurry to follow Dawn.

The breeding enclosure is at the far end. This is where wolves picked for their genetic fitness are paired together in the hope they'll breed. It's a choice made carefully, one designed to maximize genetic diversity, while being conscious that wolves mate for life. Once they choose, only death can undo the connection.

Dawn kneels, dropping the vet pack beside her. "I'll need to sedate her first. She's one of the first we caught and has always remained a little wild."

Looking in, I can only see one animal, and it doesn't look like it needs sedating. A white wolf is lying listlessly at the back corner. Even the sound of us approaching didn't have her moving.

I walk further down the length of the fence, wanting to get a better look at her. As our thread comes to life she sits up, looking around. When her canine eyes find me, she stands completely.

Without a doubt, I know we've met before.

The hand that was coming up to grip the fence stops. I was so sure about so many other things too…

The wolf rises, and steps forward. She studies me, an intense moment that has me captive. With slow, measured steps she comes forward. It's all so familiar. Her proud lines, her alabaster fur, the way she tucks in her chin when assessing something.

I crumple to my knees as my legs give out. Like it's what she was waiting for, the wolf approaches me. With a steady lope, she stands before me, the wire of the fence separating us. My hand lifts and presses into the metal. The wolf moves, her head pressing against my palm. For some reason, tears sting the edges of my vision.

I hear Dawn behind me. "I've never seen Sakari behave like this before."

Sakari. So that's her name. So many images are flooding my mind. Sakari wrapped around her pups. Sakari running over the snow with her pack beside her.

How can those images be a dream when she's right in front of me? Why do they feel so much like memories?

The last is the most vivid—Sakari with her mate.

"Where's her alpha mate?"

Dawn freezes, the syringe halting midair. "Do you think you can hold her there, whilst I give her the vaccine?"

She didn't answer my questions, but I suppose we need to focus. "Ah, I can try."

Turning back to Sakari I curl my fingers through the wire. "We need you to hold still, old friend."

Sakari's ears zero in on my voice. She holds there, and I know she's judging whether she should trust me.

I wait. Trust is born of respect and time, and I'm willing to give her both.

After long moments, Sakari turns, her body parallel to the fence. She would have had vaccinations before as part of her annual health check. But I doubt she's ever chosen to do it, or been awake for it.

Dawn leans in, her movements slow but sure. No doubt she'd be weaving her Fae magic, working to keep Sakari calm, and I wonder how much of it has played a part in what's happening. A quick pinch of the thick white fur at Sakari's shoulder and the injection is administered. With the same confident movements, Dawn administers the second shot.

"Thank you," I whisper. Losing such an amazing animal to such an awful disease would be heart-breaking.

With a last glance, Sakari takes herself back to her corner where she lies down. Why do I get the sense she isn't happy? Is she sick? Is it the captivity?

In that moment, with images that I don't know if they're fiction or real, I make a decision that I know doesn't make sense.

"I'll be here tomorrow."

"Of course you will be." Dawn states it like it's obvious. She looks out to Sakari, jaw tight. "You obviously haven't been told. We lost our alpha male to Furious last night."

14

HUNTER

18 MONTHS BEFORE

"The place looks like a bunker." KJ leans back, stretching his spine.

I shove the desk another inch to the left. "Seems fitting."

Six months of planning and hard work have certainly happened. Securing the old DEW Line building had been easy, almost seamless. On the days that hate morphs into loathing for this whole set up, I suspect Dawn had already started some sort of negotiations.

But then KJ points out the committed, passionate person Dawn is, and suggests that I'm spending too much time in the dark.

Setting up the fences had been next. As much as Dawn had explained that the enclosures were as big as was affordable, and we needed to be able to see the wolves on a regular basis to monitor them, they'd never seemed big enough. Watching those prison walls going up had been hard.

The last step was decking out the building. Lugging this desk, which I'm pretty sure came from an army barrack somewhere, a place designed to withstand a nuclear attack judging by the weight of it, is the last piece of furniture. KJ had called it a 'challenge' to try and get it through the front door, down the hall, then through another doorway.

I call it the cherry on this bittersweet pie.

KJ dusts his hands on his jeans. "It's almost ready to go."

A feeling, a familiar one now, stabs me in the stomach. "Yep."

"We had to do it, Hunter. You made the right call."

I sigh. "That's what I keep telling myself."

"This year when Sakari and Zephyr breed, their pups will have the best chance they can."

"I know."

His hand lands on my shoulder. "And they'll be safe from poachers and disease and all the other stuff that goes wrong out there."

I throw him a wry glance. "We've been over this."

He gives my shoulder a squeeze. "And we'll keep going over it until that frown gets turned upside down."

Shrugging his hand off I shake my head at him. "You'll have to flip me for that to happen."

KJ grins. "Challenge accepted."

KJ goes to grab my knees but he's forgotten I know his Achilles heel. I grab his beanie, hand scrunching up the wool so it starts to pull up. His hands instantly come up to keep it down.

"That's playing dirty!"

I don't relax my grip. "You know me. Nothing's sacred if it means getting the job done."

He elbows me and I release it. Stepping away, he readjusts the glorified tea cozy on his head. "I suppose the world should be grateful you use your powers for good then."

I shrug. "Now there's an assumption on your part."

KJ's double checking the placement of his beanie as Dawn

appears in the doorway. Her hands hike up on her hips as she takes in the office space. "It's looking good, guys."

Scanning around, I decide it depends on your perspective. As a prison for breeding an almost extinct species? Yep, it does look good. As a place where wolves can be free and happy? Not so much.

She smiles at us. "It's nice to find someone just as committed to this cause. We're going to make a great team."

KJ shrugs. "This is important." He walks over to the backpack he brought and pulls out a stack of papers. "This is the stuff you asked for."

Dawn heads to the mammoth desk and pulls up a seat. She takes a few moments to leaf through the data I've collected and KJ has collated since we started working with the wolves.

Those green tilted eyes of hers look up at us both. "This is quite comprehensive."

I can practically hear KJ blush. He steps over and shuffles a few pages. "This is what I could put together for their genetic history."

Dawn leans in closer, eyes scanning. "Hmm. This is exactly the sort of information we need." She looks up at us. "We can just about start breeding straight away."

KJ's breath whooshes out. "That's great."

Dawn's head is already buried in the papers again. "You have some extensive family lineages here."

There's the scratch under the beanie. "Yeah. I...ah...did some research. We want to create as much genetic diversity as we can with the matings. That way the wolves we release are increasing the genetic vigor of the wild population."

"Exactly. Who are these two?" She points to something on one of the pages.

"We brought Zephyr down from the north. And—"

"How?" Dawn looks genuinely surprised.

I answer that one. "Trails of road kill. He followed them like Hansel and Gretel and the breadcrumb trail."

Dawn weighs up the answer. "Smart move. And the other one?"

"My guess is that's Sakari. Zephyr was just as excited to see her as we were that he agreed with our match."

"They were a good match. You two have done well."

I put up my hands before she jumps to too many assumptions...like that I think this whole system is a good idea. "He's the brains, I'm the brawn."

KJ snorts. "More like I'm the data collector, and you're the one who has to make the calls."

Dawn smiles a gentle Fae smile. "Well, you're not alone now. Neither of you."

I don't smile back, but KJ sure does. It's something I've been watching over the past few months. I don't know if it's KJ's desperate drive to save the wolves, or the lack of a strong parent figure in his life, maybe it's both, but Dawn has become a mentor for him.

I'm actually glad. This work can be lonely and isolating. I've found someone who can share this with me, it's only fair he has someone in his own way.

Dawn is back to pouring over the pages. I cross my arms and lean against another of the desks. KJ is twiddling with the edge of one of his sleeves. Now the facilities have been set up, we need to start looking at our next steps.

Several pages have been read and flipped before Dawn looks back up again. She glances at her watch before looking at KJ. "You have an interest in genetics, don't you?"

Man, was that another blush?

"It's actually really fascinating. We can learn so much through what genes remain in the population. It tells us what's the next best step."

A sound comes from the hallway and Dawn looks like she's going to bust a happy bubble. "Well, you'll be excited to see these then."

She heads to the door and disappears down the hall. KJ and I look at each other. What is she up to now?

"This way," her voice carries back to us. "Be careful please."

She enters again, but this time there's someone behind her. A man follows, pushing a trolley. On it are two smallish wooden crates.

KJ practically leaps forward. "Microscopes?"

Dawn looks like a proud parent. "They most certainly are."

"No freaking way!"

"And that's not all…"

Another man follows the first, this time pushing a trolley with a much larger crate. KJ is beside it in a second, fingers tracing the label on the side. He looks up at Dawn, eyes the size of plates, mouth moving like he's forgotten how to speak.

"A thermal cycler?" His voice is filled with disbelief.

Dawn nods and I'm wondering if they should hug.

I step forward. "A what?"

In a blink, KJ is before me, gripping my upper arms. "We'll be able to do PCRs."

I wait for the translation. When KJ gets this excited, the words come all by themselves.

"Polymerase chain reaction is a widely used technique used in molecular biology to exponentially amplify a specific segment of DNA to generate thousands to millions of copies of a particular DNA sequence—"

I grip his arms right back. "English, KJ."

He grins so big it swallows his whole face. "We can sequence DNA. Heck, we can analyze it and even isolate specific sections if we wanted to. This will take the breeding program to the next level—give these guys a fighting chance."

His wonder and excitement are contagious. I almost start to feel good about this whole decision. "That sounds pretty cool."

He spins around and heads back to the crate. There's a possibility KJ will sleep with that thing tonight. He looks at Dawn, who's smiling as big as he is. "I'd love to learn."

She comes over to stand beside him, her hand resting on his arm. "Good news. I was recruiting for a lab assistant."

This time KJ actually stays still. He stares down at the crate, head nodding slowly. "You won't regret it."

I wonder if Dawn realizes the gift she just gave KJ. It feels like his lost soul not only found a direction, but someone willing to show him the path.

So far, it's the first good thing that's come of this.

A knocking on the front door has me looking up. Glancing at Dawn I head out to see who it is. Maybe more deliveries Dawn didn't mention? KJ is still communing with the crate so I head out alone.

Just before I open it, the knocking becomes banging. The impatience almost has the positive mood that was gaining traction losing its footing.

"Alright, alright. Since when was patience dead?"

The light that blasts me the minute I open the door has me putting my arm up in defense. It feels like shafts of pain just speared into my head. "What the—"

"We're here to speak to the organizer of this killing machine breeding farm."

"What?" I try to lower my arm but the light is still trying to burn through me.

"You heard me. I'd like to speak to whoever runs a program that has such disregard for human life."

When I feel someone try to push forward I start to get angry. Head down I step forward and hear a surprised shuffle. Didn't expect that, huh? I take another step. "You need to move back, sir."

"I need the person in charge."

Without whoever it is bearing down on me I find I can drop my arm. It takes a short second for my eyes to adjust, but when I see the asshat who's making the demands, it drops right to my side. "You've got to be kidding me."

Alistair Davenport is only a few feet in front of me, holding a microphone as a cameraman stands behind him.

"Turn that thing off."

"You'd like that, wouldn't you?" Alistair straightens, like he's found the fight he was looking for. "Move out of the way, young man."

Spacing my feet out, I cross my arms. "I'm in charge."

The man who's trying to single-handedly lead wolves into extinction looks at me in surprise. "I'm not someone to be trifled with, boy."

Alistair is reed thin, his barely-blond hair wisping from its combover. I think I could be taller than him.

"You can leave now, Alistair."

His nostrils flare. "So, you know who I am. That I lost my father to the very animals you want to breed."

"Last I heard, your father is still alive."

That has his water-colored eyes flaring. "He lives as a recluse, petrified of leaving his own house, with the constant threat of another heart attack. That's no way to live."

"True." I glance at the camera. "It's just that if you're insinuating he's dead, it starts to feel a little like you're touting propaganda."

Okay, now he's really angry. "Did you know there have been over 7,600 fatal wolf attacks?"

I tilt my head. "Isn't that since the thirteenth century? And most of those statistics were in the middle-ages?"

Alistair's face flushes bright purple. "And victims have largely been women and children? The most vulnerable targets."

Unfortunately, that part is true, but I'm not having this argument with someone who's already made up their mind. "How did you even know about this place, Mr. Davenport?"

Alistair's eyes slide to the side before returning back, a sudden flare in their watery depths. "Don't want to acknowledge it, huh? Is that because wolves are one of the most dangerous carnivores that exist in the wild?"

"Actually—"

Alistair steps in. "With jaws that can crush a human femur?"

I frown. This guy is starting to piss me off. "I think—"

"Who have killed and terrorized humans for too long?"

The irony of those words, as we stand at the door of a facility trying to save them from extinction after humans have terrorized and killed so efficiently that wolves hang onto survival by a thread, has me moving forward too. My clenched hands feel as hard as rocks and it's an effort to keep them by my side. I'm glad KJ isn't here. This isn't something he needs to see or hear.

It's people like Alistair who've meant I've had to make the decisions I have…because I lost my father to the culling laws he campaigned for.

"Leave, Alistair. Now."

Triumph has Alistair almost smiling. He's getting the fight he was looking for, but as I take another step forward, a sliver of something else slips across his face. Nervousness. Good, it means he's not a complete idiot.

"Got something to hide, do you?" He sneers.

His dead body if he doesn't back off. Just as I go to take one more step that will have me in Alistair's personal space, communicating quite clearly why it's in his best interest to get the hell out of here, the door behind me opens.

"Hunter." Dawn's voice sounds worried. "Alistair," then drops like a wad of wet snow.

"Hello, Dawn. I should've known you were behind this vile concept."

Dawn straightens then smiles. "I'm afraid you've come at the wrong time."

Alistair glances over his shoulder, checking that the camera is still rolling. "And why's that?" Smugness buoys his voice.

"Well, the wolves aren't here yet. You're missing a wonderful opportunity to appreciate what a magnificent animal they are. They're as essential to this planet as we are."

"They're dangerous," Alistair stabs his finger with each word, "Unpredictable, and deadly animals that threaten our very lives."

"They aren't what you should fear, Mr. Davenport."

Although Dawn says those words with a smile, they're as hard as ice.

Jeez, doesn't she realize she's inflaming him more than I was?

Alistair is spluttering, all he has to do is to make sure the camera is getting all this. "Did you get that? That was a direct threat!"

But Dawn looks at the camera, those Fae eyes of hers, her wise old face, full of nothing but innocence. "Hatred is what you should fear, Alistair. The very same hate that you peddle." She steps back and opens the door. "That's what will ultimately destroy humanity."

Before Alistair can retort, Dawn glances at me. "Shall we go in? We have work to do."

Feeling proud to be part of this, I follow her through. "Yes, we do. Damned important work."

Dawn half shuts, half slams the door behind us. We stand on the other side and I don't know how we're not panting. It felt like we just ran a marathon.

Dawn is shaking her head. "He's an idiot."

"But a potentially dangerous one."

"Yes. He's been trying to cause trouble for a long time now."

I glance at the door as I hear a car pull away. "As long as he doesn't have any ammo, then he'll continue to be the crazy that everyone ignores."

She nods, looking deep in thought. "You're right." She turns to me, green eyes serious. "It's time we got some wolves."

15

HUNTER

18 MONTHS BEFORE

I'm sitting at the desk that was allocated to me when Dawn walks into the office. It's funny that I've been given one considering I never use it. There's no computer on its flat surface, which is probably a good thing as it would be buried under all the empty takeaway coffee cups. The only stipulation I had was that it faces the monitors. If I can't be out there with the wolves, I want to be able to see what I can.

She heads to KJ's desk as he works at his computer. I've wondered every now and again what exactly could be taking up so much of his time, but then decided I didn't want to be bombarded with jargon. Dropping a sheaf of papers in front of KJ, she steps back.

It seems he doesn't have to go through them to know what's in there. "Figured it was time to make the call."

I stay where I am. I don't need to see what's printed on those pages either. I know what it is we need to discuss.

Dawn pulls up a chair, sitting across from KJ, but angled to face me too. "The decision at this stage is always tricky. Do we capture pre-breeders, or experienced breeders?"

KJ scans the pages in front of him. "Most of the pre-breeders are too closely related."

"Exactly. Nor do they have a track record as being successful breeders."

They look at me. Dawn looks resolute, KJ looks pained. The Fae Elder points to a place on the page. "We'll start with these two."

Something dark starts to grow in my gut, and KJ's expression is only feeding it. "Who?"

KJ swallows and it's not the most comfortable process I've ever seen. "Zephyr and Sakari."

I shoot up. "No."

Dawn's hand comes up in a conciliatory gesture. "Now, Hunter—"

"You're not capturing them and you're not containing them. Those wolves have grown up in the wild."

"Didn't they have a litter last season?"

I wince. "Yes."

"Then they've successfully bred. They're also the best match to create the most genetic diversity. It's their genes we want to spread through the gene pool."

"There has to be another way."

I can't even picture Zephyr and Sakari in one of those pens.

"There isn't." Dawn's voice has a thread of concrete through it. "Do you want another litter to die out there?"

Those words are a punch to the gut, one so violent I find it hard to breathe for a second. I look to my friend for a lifeline, but KJ's miserable expression tells me I have to face it.

It has to be them.

Dawn takes a step forward. "None of this is for the faint-hearted, Hunter. We've all made sacrifices."

I bite back my retort. I know about sacrifice.

She waits, and I know I'm being weighed and measured.

Capture the two wolves I've been following and protecting every night for so long. They thrive on the wildness and isolation of the tundra. And what will that mean for the pack they leave behind? Others will step up in their place, but inbreeding is going to be even more of an issue.

But I've already watched one litter die. I've seen poachers practice their aim just to hone their skills. I've been there as KJ created that ream of paper, tallying numbers that were decreasing year after year.

Straightening despite the weight that's just compounded exponentially, I lift my chin. "I'll get them."

※

SETTING the trap is simpler than it should be. First, find a spot where they're likely to frequent. Seeing as I've spent most nights with these wolves for over two years, I know their movements. I choose the stunted marsh bush that sits along the track they use for their border patrols.

Second, I scrape back the layer of snow, glad at least my hands are numb. I carve out a shallow hole, then hammer in the two metal stakes attached to the trap.

"They don't hurt when they close,' Dawn had reassured me. "They have soft rubber where they shut and they've been boiled and coated in wax to make sure they remain sterile."

Looking at the metal jaws, powered by tightly coiled springs, I hate myself a little more. They may not be hurt physically, but there's no way this is a stress-free process for anyone.

Next, setting the jaws open wide, I lay the trap in its shallow grave. Now all it takes is to gently push the soil back over and make it look as undisturbed as possible. Finally, I put the garnish on. A handful of twigs Dawn gave me. The moment she'd passed them to me I smelled it—the mark of another wolf. She'd obviously thought of every detail to have these urine-soaked twigs sent from Jacksonville. I knew exactly what they would mean.

The scent of another wolf will mean our wolf will stop to mark their territory. And when they do...*snap!*

I'll become their captor instead of their protector.

The dirty work done, it's time to sit back and wait. Retreating, I set off at a jog. Being as far away as I can whilst still in hearing range for when the moment happens is what I need to do. Even as Dawn suggested we check it in the morning, she knew she was wasting her breath. There's no way I'm leaving a wolf in that thing any longer than I have to.

Finding a spot on the lonely tundra, I start out standing up, but the wind quickly has me hunkering down. Winter has firmly established itself on the landscape, and it's looking to do the same with me. The wind slaps the cold in my face, trying to spear into any vulnerability in my layers. Wrapping my arms around myself, I grit my teeth. It's bloody cold out here, even for a Were. I could build a bit of a windbreak out of snow to protect me.

Or, I could shift...

I don't do it every night, the promise to my family winning out. The bottom line is it's dangerous to be a wolf out here. But after a few nights of being solo out here, long hours of playing our last encounter through my mind, and the temptation becomes overpowering.

Not to mention the cold that's trying to freeze my bones...

It barely takes a conscious thought and I'm a wolf. Straight away my sharpened senses smell the clarity of the snow and the whispers of the wind, but more so, I revel in being surrounded by my very own Gortex coat. My fur means the wind no longer feels like it's snarling and snapping at my bare skin. Now, my armor is so thick that I uncurl and arch.

Then she's here, the magical recipe of night and wolf making her appear. The wind rushes over her golden fur as she finds her bearings. Like I'm the center of her compass, she turns and finds me. I think I live for the moment when our eyes connect. It's like a live-wire has a line straight to my heart. It recharges me. Some days it feels like it resuscitates me.

She's a balm to my aching soul. What is it about her that has me believing that this will all work out?

I don't know and I don't care. All that matters is that with her, I have hope. Wanting to give something back, to show her, I step in a little closer. Those wintergreen eyes of hers widen, then warm.

Moving forward until we're eye to eye, I pause. Her breath seems to match mine—shallow and excited, a little quick and kinda impatient. Determined to make this something special, I don't give in to the temptation. This is going to be slow...and memorable.

A small step and my muzzle is parallel to hers. Ever so gently I stroke it against hers. Her fur is velveteen soft and I wish I could stroke it with my hands. Her breath hitches as mine snags. There's so much warmth, so much emotion. Ducking underneath her jaw, I head to the other side. I want to know every inch of this golden girl.

I breathe in deep, brushing up against her golden coat. It shimmers with depth, seems to tremble with anticipation. Coming around, we're eye to eye. The heat grows, the emotion multiplies. Our eyes drift shut as our foreheads come to rest against each other. How can something so laden with feeling not be real?

When I hear the snap, then the yelp, then the clank and shuffle of a struggle, I know it's happened. I also know it's cut our time short because this is something my golden wolf shouldn't see. She's always had a deep connection with the wolves we've spent time with, it's going to be painful for her to watch what has to happen next. I swallow. It'll be painful for me, but that doesn't mean I have to share the pain.

With a last brush of fur on fur, I shift, the decision to shoulder this on my own not one I regret.

She disappears in an instant, reminding me exactly how fragile this whole thing is. Real wolves, connections that can survive in reality, don't do that. I'm glad I don't have time to dwell on it, because I know I'm going to do whatever I can to keep seeing her, and I'm not sure what that says about my state of mind.

Jogging over, I find the wolf frantic; panic and rage driving it to yank on the metal holding its paw over and over and over again. The clanking of the metal only fuels its fear. Moving in I smell it's a male. Now I wish my armor extended to my heart. This is going to be one of the hardest things I've done.

As the wolf comes into sight I feel guilty about the relief that floods through me like an avalanche. It's not Zephyr.

The muscles of my legs feel like they've turned into a slushy.

It's not Zephyr.

Which means I can let him go.

16

AVA

"That's our soft release enclosure." Dawn points to the image of little more than flat earth. The biggest of the enclosures, and the one set up furthest from the building, it allows the wolves to live as independently as possible before being released into the wild.

"You have a lot of cameras set up," I observe. A total of seven screens line the wall, each rotating through about four or five images. Water troughs, shelters, the odd white wolf, rhythmically flicker over them. The security cameras here are definitely more numerous than the ones back home.

Dawn glances over her shoulder to where KJ is tapping away at a computer. "We had a computer whizz, so I thought why not?" She smiles at me, Fae eyes soft. "He took our system to a whole new level."

You can't help but smile back when Dawn gives you that look. "Sounds like there's a lot of talent here."

Dawn points back to the screen we were just looking at as three wolves lope past. "They're our first litter. They'll be ready for release soon."

I sense her pride and the glow grows to encompass me. I've

been part of releases back at Jacksonville, they're moments you don't forget. "It's a great feeling."

She nods, arm coming around my shoulder. "It's not a very big program, but the results show that it's worth it," she squeezes me like she did when I was younger. "Because it's working."

KJ's voice comes from behind us. "They're here." He's tilted his head to the side as he hears something we don't.

Dawn glances at her watch. "Excellent. They're on time."

Must be Riley and Joshua back from doing the rounds. I would have loved to go with them, but Josh had glared at me as I'd opened my mouth. And then I'd remembered that I could run into him...

So Dawn gave me the grand tour of the Resolve building instead. It'd taken all of fifteen-minutes to do the lap, but spending time with her and KJ in the lab had been fascinating. I think one of the microscopes is KJ's girlfriend. He'd practically stroked it as he talked me through what they've learned about wolf genetics here. Words like genotype and chromosomes and something about crisper technology had been enthusiastically thrown around.

He'd also used words like genetic bottleneck to describe what human culling had done to the wolf population. The drastic reduction in population size means there are two ways things can pan out—the downward trajectory will continue and mean extinction, or we'll turn it around and recover.

Dawn was quick to point out that we're making the second option happen.

She'd taken me back to the office then, talking me through the enclosures and how they monitor them. KJ had followed, saying something about wanting to analyze some results.

Just like KJ predicted, the door opens and Josh and Riley come through. They're doing what I'd hoped they'd be doing —smiling.

Like he's been here for years, Josh grabs one of the desk chairs, spins it around and plonks himself down, arms crossed over the back. Riley comes to stand beside me, her relaxed smile never leaving. I smile back, enjoying the more casual air our relationship has developed.

KJ has barely acknowledged their entry. He's leaning forward, eyes close to the screen as he studies it intently.

It's then that my cell vibrates in my pocket. Pulling it out I see that it's Mom, and I almost don't answer, until I realize this is unusual. We've spoken every day since I arrived, but it's always been in the evening. Why would she be calling me now? Stepping outside, I take the call.

"Hey, Mom."

"Hi honey. Do you have a moment?"

That has me frowning. No 'how are you?', no more questions about why I changed my mind in relation to staying for me to sidestep? "Sure."

"I went to check up on Achak today."

There's a pause I don't like. "Is there something wrong? Is he sick again?" Please don't let him be sick again.

"He's been a picture of health. His daily blood tests have come back clean."

Relief has my shoulders dropping down. "Good." Except then I straighten again. "But something's happened."

Images of poachers lining up Achak in their sights or poisoned slabs of meat being thrown over the fence zing through my mind.

"I'm really sorry, Ava, but Achak has escaped."

I flop back against the cold concrete wall. "He's what? How can that even happen?"

I can hear Mom's sigh. "He was there yesterday. When we went there today, he was gone. We think he found a rock near the fence and used it to jump the fence."

Achak has escaped? The wolf I helped raise is gone?

"Ava? Are you still there?"

"Yeah, I'm here. Just trying to process it."

"I know. We're all shocked too. We're going to have to review all our fences."

"Do we have any idea where he's gone?" I know it's a stupid question with no answer, but I ask it anyway. It's like my brain needs verbal confirmation.

"He could be anywhere. Probably headed for the wilds of the reserve."

"Probably." Achak was never going to be a passive participant of the breeding program. "Thanks for letting me know, Mom."

"Honey." Mom's voice is soft with compassion. "I know how much he meant to you."

I swallow as this finally starts to sink in. "Do you think…do you think this has anything to do with the Furious virus?"

There's a pause. "His blood tests came back clear, so it's highly unlikely."

I let my head fall back as my eyes drift shut. Mom isn't saying that we still don't really know what we're dealing with, so there's a possibility…

Dawn calls out my name and it has me shooting upright. "I've gotta go, Mom. Keep me posted if there's any sign of him."

"Of course I will. Love you, honey."

"Love you too, Mom."

I hang up and stare at the wall. Achak is missing. Escaped.

Something in the air shifts and a thread I wish didn't exist flares. It's enough to have me darting back in the office. We have a meeting to hold and I need to start ignoring that sensation. Technically, I can tap into any thread I want, so it doesn't mean anything. It will die off the less and less I see him.

Dawn takes her place at her mammoth desk. "Well, we might as well get started."

I take in the people in the room, wondering if we should wait a few more minutes, despite Dawn's love of punctuality. "Is everyone here?"

Riley looks around. "We're all here. Well, except Hunter, but he's always late."

I ignore the shiver in my chest that his name triggers. I'm here for the wolves. "So there's no one else?"

How is Dawn the only person in the room older than twenty?

Riley picks up a pen and starts to twirl it. "Dad wasn't real keen on the whole captive breeding thing. Lots of the older members of the pack still think like that."

Josh rubs his jaw, face pensive. "But Hunter went ahead with it anyway."

Riley tilts her chin, looking at Josh squarely. "Yep."

Josh nods slowly, never shirking her gaze. "That takes some serious cajones."

Humans opposed Resolve as well as Weres? And Hunter took all this on at sixteen?

"Dad would have come around eventually."

Everyone's gaze shoots up at the sound of Hunter's voice. Everyone's except mine. I'd sensed him a little while ago, but I couldn't judge how far away he was. Despite the minutes of awareness, I still don't feel ready to face him.

KJ walks over and slaps him on the shoulder in greeting. "For sure. He loved those wolves as much as you do."

Except Riley looks away, something in her face saying she doesn't agree.

Hunter enters the room and the space shrinks. I'm looking forward to this awareness dialing down and going extinct. Especially when he hasn't acknowledged I'm in the room. He heads to KJ's desk, the one on the opposite side of the room to me, and perches on the edge. With his arms crossed he looks almost relaxed.

Except then his eyes meet mine. They flash copper fire before he quickly banks it, something that just confuses me more. If we've never met before, why is he angry with me? If he's not my white wolf, then why does the thread between us feel like it could charge this room?

He blinks and looks away and now I'm angry with myself. Why was I the one to be looking first and now the last to look away? Surely I have more pride than that.

"Right." Dawn pushes herself forward so she can rest her crossed arms on the desk. "The good news is, we've vaccinated all the captive wolves."

Hunter nods. "Quick work."

KJ throws him a look I can't decipher. "We had double Fae power."

"You're right, KJ," Dawn adds, "I don't think I could've done it so quickly on my own. We would've had to sedate and monitor them all, one at a time."

As much as I hate myself, I watch to see what Hunter's response will be. All he does is grunt as he keeps a steady gaze on Dawn.

Josh's chair creaks as he rolls forward an inch. "Any signs of Furious?"

My attention zooms back to Dawn. Just like Achak, this program has just lost an alpha male. I yank in a breath. Is that the alpha I saw in my dreams? Would I have felt the same sense of recognition if I'd met him as I did with Sakari? But then the possibility whooshes straight back out. That was when I was with my white wolf. The one I'm not sure existed at all…For all I know, Sakari acted like she did because two Fae were in the same area as her.

"Not at this stage. We're waiting on the blood work for the last couple."

There's a collective sigh of relief around the room.

Josh rubs his chin again, a sure-fire sign he's deep in thought. "I wonder if it's too fast acting to spread very effectively."

Riley tilts her head. "As in it flared up but didn't have a chance to spread because the animals were killed?"

He nods. "Pretty much."

She glances at Hunter and KJ. "I hope so," she half-whispers.

KJ spins to face his computer. "That's my theory, but I'll get back to you on that one."

I swallow, I've been wondering about this next question all morning. "So, what's next?"

That seems to get Hunter's attention. With the briefest of glances at me he looks back at Dawn. "The wild wolf population is next. It'd be easier if two people go out."

KJ shrugs. "You're the best person, Hunter. You know these wolves and the terrain."

Hunter nods and I suspect that was obvious. He looks to Dawn again. "Your skills would be useful."

But Dawn's hand comes up like a stop sign. "Yes, some Fae powers would be helpful to keep them calm, but these bones creak out on that cold tundra."

Riley comes to stand beside her brother. "It's summer, Dawn."

Dawn is already shaking her head. "Your definition of summer fits my definition of hot-chocolate weather. I'm too old to be zipping around on a quad in those biting winds."

One by one, four sets of eyes turn to me. Everyone's but Hunter's. Oh crap, I'm the only other one in the room with Fae blood. "Ah, I can't, unfortunately. I...ah..."

"No need." Hunter's voice is firm with command. "You'll probably feel the cold too."

"Exactly." There's no way I'm heading out to the isolated wilds with the one person who pointed out everything I'm not. There's got to be other ways I can help these wolves.

"You're probably better off here, working with KJ."

KJ's eyebrows hike up. "It's going to be slower going if it's just you."

"It'll be fine." Hunter's arms are crossed as he pins KJ with his gaze. "You know I'll get it done."

After a moment where my heart seems to have jumped into my throat, KJ shrugs. "Fine. She can help me with trying to figure out what we're up against. We have time."

I sag as the tension drains. That I can do.

In the silence that follows I use the time to study my shoes. Mom had insisted I buy snow boots but I'm glad I won't have to use them. I'm actually relieved when the printer comes to life, the whirring sound pouring out a sheet of paper.

"Ah, I was waiting for that." KJ wheels his chair over and I figure that's the cue for the meeting to finish. I'm about to stand when KJ pushes back from the printer like it just exploded.

"Whoa." He's holding the piece of paper like it's the holy grail. "I had a suspicion, but now…"

Hunter has stood up as we all look at each other, wondering what's going on. "Finishing the sentence would be good, KJ."

KJ looks up at Dawn, then over at Hunter. "Buckle up, guys. This is gonna blow your mitts off."

Hunter sits back down, and I wish I didn't notice the tightening between his shoulder blades. "Explain it like we haven't gone to med school."

Josh leans back and crosses his arms in his classic smug pose. "Give me a couple of years."

I'd roll my eyes if I didn't get the sense that KJ has something important in his hands.

KJ is rapidly scanning the sheet from left to right, top to

bottom, before starting the process all over again. Dawn leans forward, her voice gentle in the silence. "KJ?"

He looks up like he'd forgotten we were there. He glances at the paper, then up again. "So you guys know that when first infected, rabies travels through the nerve endings?"

I glance around, relieved to see I'm not the only one who didn't. We turn back, waiting for KJ to continue.

"Well, normally that's what it does. It's why rabies can take up to a month to show symptoms after infection. It takes time to mosey on up to the brain."

Hunter straightens a little. "Normally?"

So he noticed KJ's use of the word too.

KJ glances at the paper. "Yeah, normally. The virus can't do anything until it gets to the brain. That's when it causes its havoc, then makes its way to the saliva to spread."

Dawn's eyes are narrowed as she watches KJ. "But this is different?"

"From the samples I took," KJ glances briefly at Hunter, "Furious was in the bloodstream." He looks at all of us. "And it had been for some time."

Josh's spine goes straight as a rod. "It traveled through the bloodstream?"

KJ nods. "Yeah. That's why this strain has worked so much quicker. It's found a shortcut."

In the silence that follows, I can hear my heart pumping a little too fast. This sounds serious.

Josh stands, like the rod just speared into the floor. "That must be why the immuno globulin worked! The added immunity dose went straight to where the virus is."

I gasp. "Then that's good news."

Riley looks around. "It means that if we get that vaccine around ASAP, we can nip this in the bud."

KJ glances at the sheet, his face pensive. "That makes sense.

The globulin provides immediate antibodies where the body needs it most—the bloodstream." He looks up at Hunter. "Getting this stuff out fast is going to be key."

Riley stands. "I'll go with you then."

Hunter frowns. "No. You know Mom couldn't cope with that."

Like he's just yanked out the plug, Riley flops back into her seat, muttering. "But she's willing to put me through The Bachelor."

Josh shrugs. "I've worked at our breeding program. I'll head out."

Hunter's glance my way is swift but there nonetheless. "Thanks. We'll get it done in no time."

Except Josh doesn't know these wolves. And they don't know him. Nor does he have the Fae ability to calm animals. These wild wolves are going to need two shots each, and the quicker and more humanely it can be done, the higher the chance of success and the less stress for everyone.

I glance at Hunter, who's already turned away. Why is he so familiar, yet nothing like what I'd imagined? Why is our connection so strong, yet one he doesn't seem to feel?

Surely I can't be considering the idea that's germinating like a weed. Still too confused and scared by what all this means, I'd just be making myself vulnerable.

My eyes shut for the briefest of moments. You've got to be kidding me.

"I'll do it. I'll go with you."

17

AVA

Meeting Hunter back at the Resolve Center early the next morning has my stomach feeling like there's a snowstorm going on inside it. The few words we've had have been terse. Never have I been so disappointed as I was in the moments after we met. Never hurt so deeply.

And yet, like I'm some sort of masochist, I've elected to spend time with him.

I know I've done it for the wolves. I'd told Mom last night what we'd learned about Furious—that it's a threat now here on Evelyn Island, but also the need for rapid release of the vaccine.

But is it possible I'm here for another reason? My white wolf had me believing that maybe I had the potential to be something more. His loss meant the foundations for that belief were annihilated. So am I trying to prove I'm not some half-breed prophecy let-down?

Or am I stupid enough to hope for something else...?

The blasting sound of an engine yanks me from my thoughts as a quad bike zooms around the corner of the building. I halt my pacing when I see who the rider is.

Hunter is in jeans and a t-shirt—no helmet, no jacket. Right now, my scarf feels like overkill.

He pulls up in front and kills the engine.

"Can you ride a quad?"

"Ah, no."

There's a half-sigh, half-huff. "Didn't think so." He keeps staring ahead, like even looking at me is distasteful. "You got the meds?"

I tap the bag hanging from my shoulder. "Vaccines and globulin, check."

When he finally does look at me, those copper eyes take in my scarf. "Man, I hope you're up for this."

Open hostility is not something I've ever had to deal with, probably because of who I am. It's a privilege I hadn't even realized I had. I'm not surprised it's unpleasant, but I am surprised at how much it stings coming from Hunter. I realize I have to decide how I'm going to respond to it.

I angle my head, grabbing his gaze with mine. "Why are you so rude to me?"

Hunter jerks back ever so slightly and I relish the sense of victory. Most people see my long blonde hair and sweet face and make assumptions. This is the first time in my life I've sought to really challenge it.

Hunter rises in his seat, legs pushing him upward. He leans forward and the breath I pull in is reflexive. Hunter this close is a challenge to my senses. All dark hair and angled lines and the smell of open plains, I know I should move back...but I can't.

Copper eyes tell me my honesty just triggered something. "Because you and something else in my life can't exist together." He shifts back, his hand slicing through the air between us. "And I don't want to lose that other thing."

I blink as I try to wipe away the sting of his words. For the most part, they don't make sense. But I get the general gist.

He doesn't want me here.

The hurt from the day we met flares like a banked fire, except this pain is cold and full of shards. It's the sort of hurt that has you breathing shallow for long seconds and you can't think straight. The first things that filter through the haze are two copper eyes, churning like a maelstrom. Hunter is watching and waiting and fighting some sort of battle of his own.

It's that realization that has me pausing. For someone so angry, he sure looks conflicted. And conflict means uncertainty. For some reason, it reminds me of Achak. A beautiful, wild animal who ultimately just wants to be understood.

And uncertainty and conflict are exactly what I'm feeling.

What is it I can't reconcile? This stay-the-heck-away guy with my hearts-beating-as-one wolf? My hope that the existence of some sort of magical connection made me special? The belief that at least the threads don't lie?

I realize I want answers. If I'm being brutally honest with myself, I'm hoping that maybe there's something extraordinary happening here. Dawn always did say I was a hopeless optimist.

I look away, needing a break from the hypnotizing effects of his intensity. I've already had a taste of the pain this boy can cause me. A smart, self-protective girl wouldn't even consider this. As I flick my hair over my shoulder I discover I'm neither smart nor self-protective.

I shrug one shoulder, feeling my hair shift around it. "I can respect that."

Hunter blinks. The storm in his eyes seems to settle for a second and I wonder what that means. But then he looks away, taking in the horizon. I wait long moments to see what he's going to say next.

He clears his throat. "We might as well get going then."

Why does that feel like a win? I know it's pathetic, but I decide to give myself a talking to later. "Let's do it." He holds his hand out and my heart hiccups again, until I realize he's waiting for me to pass the vet bag. I lift it from my shoulder and hand it over.

Hunter leans back and opens the compartment on the back of the quad. He pulls out a helmet before tucking the bag in. He seems to pause before he holds it up for me. I take it as I process what this means.

We're riding the quad. Two people. One bike. A whole lot of driving.

What have I done?

Hunter clears his throat again. "So, you've definitely never ridden one of these?"

I shake my head. "Ah, no. Shouldn't you have a helmet, too?"

Hunter's gaze is almost challenging. "I ride these things all the time."

Is that another dig about my fragile, part-human status? I yank up a smile. "Thanks for looking after my safety."

There's that blink again. For some reason, I like those blinks.

He turns around and faces forward. "We have wolves to vaccinate."

We certainly do. Pulling on the helmet, I brace myself. I hadn't banked on so much physical contact so soon. As my butt touches the leather seat I wonder whether I can hold myself back a little, maybe maintain some distance.

Hunter is very still as I settle myself down and I wish I could see his face. The thread between us shrinks as our bodies come closer. It feels like a rubber band tightening and pulling, but I fight it. Digging my feet into the pegs I push back, trying to secure a few inches between us, except I hadn't considered that thing called gravity. My knees brush his thighs. The Were warmth radiating from him is like a magnet. I'm not sure where I'm supposed to put my hands, so I awkwardly reach back and clamp onto the metal that the compartment is strapped to.

Long seconds pass and nothing happens. Hunter is like a statue, body tense, breathing almost nonexistent. Is it possible he feels it too? This heightened awareness, the sense of familiarity, the exhilarating newness?

I decide to take the opportunity to slip off my helmet. I grew up with Weres, living like a Were, and I'm not about to act like some fragile flower. I slip it behind me and strap it to the vet pack.

Hunter shakes his head and mutters something that if I had Were hearing, I probably would've been able to decipher. Reaching down he starts the engine and the vibrations instantly rise through me. Excitement and nervousness become my only thoughts.

With a contraction of his arm we roll forward, starting off slow. It still feels like a jerk as I tense my arms, using my hands as anchors. How in the world am I going to stay on like this?

Accelerating, the wind picks up and I discover my next hurdle—how to do this and not breathe. Hunter's scent is thrown straight back at me, and the deep inhale is reflexive. He smells of wild outdoors and spiced heat. If my wolf had existed, would he have smelled like this?

Picking up more speed, Hunter glances over his shoulder. He's about to turn back when he does a double take. He just realized I don't have my helmet on. He frowns and I do all I can do in that moment as the wind whips at my face and hair and clothes—I smile again. This time, as we zoom across the tundra, it starts to feel genuine.

Blink. He turns back and my guess is he's frowning again. Hunching down in a way that just emphasizes his shoulders, he accelerates again.

Summer in the arctic tundra is a place of contrasts. It's so bare and vast, but as I squint I notice the beauty in the details. In the distance are the harsh snowcapped peaks you associate with this area, but here on the flatlands, it's green. Actually, it's shades of green layered with bronzes and reds and flashes of yellow—all grasses and wildflowers blooming as quickly as they can in the short summer season. It's known as one of the driest places on earth, but intricate little streams trickle in any crevice they can find, trapped on the surface by the permafrost not far below. It's a place of life and light, but also a place of endurance and extremes.

I find my head moving from side to side, trying to take it all in.

I've lived a loved and protected life, and for that I'm grateful. But this, riding across the landscape I feel so connected to, whether in my dreams or not, is a taste of freedom. A taste of freedom that I'm relishing.

"Faster," I say quietly, but with anticipation. I know Hunter will hear me, but what's he going to do about it?

To my surprise, his glance back almost looks like it's been sprinkled with a smile. "You're not wearing a helmet."

I release the tight hold I had behind me and lean forward. "Neither are you. Plus we have wolves to vaccinate, remember?"

Another raised eyebrow glances back and I wish I could have held that look longer. I can't tell if there was a challenge in those copper depths or unimpressed frustration.

All of a sudden, the quad spears forward. My arms instantly shoot out and grasp, straight onto Hunter's waist. I feel the jolt, but I can't tell if it's me or him or the air between us, but there's no way I'm letting go. We gain more speed and I discover I may have unleashed more than I bargained for.

In seconds it feels like we're flying over the rutted ground. My hair is a sail behind me, probably becoming a tangled mess, but I don't care. It's like this sense of excitement and exhilaration is bigger than me, like it comes from both within and without. I shake my head—the cold air is probably freezing my brain.

As the ground begins an irregular rhythm of sloping up and down, an arctic hare startles from behind a rock. It darts away with amazing speed. I mentally apologize for frightening it just as I notice the faint thread that connects it to Hunter. They must have come across each other before.

When Hunter reaches out to point I follow where he's indicating. I gasp and push up a little off the seat—it's a herd of bison! Big and burly, they look like hunks of moving fur. Their heads rise as they hear the quad, and they're on instant alert. Like a consensus has been reached, they turn and head for the horizon.

"Wow," I breathe, not sure if Hunter can hear me but it doesn't really matter. He wouldn't know what I'm amazed at anyway. It's the gossamer network of threads that just came to life that has me wowed. Despite the isolation, they're everywhere.

Hunter can't see them, but threads show how deeply and irrevocably he's connected to this area. The bison run, but they're still part of his fabric just like everything else around us.

He heads east and I hunker down. Intensely aware of the heat and muscles playing under my hands, my excitement contracts as I try to get my head around this. There are too many contrasts and contradictions.

How can the frowning, silent guy who doesn't want me here, be the same person who's a lifeline to this island?

18

AVA

We drive over rocky hills, across plains of deep greens and stunted shrubs, progressively climbing higher. When we reach a mesa-like plateau, Hunter comes to a stop. Killing the engine, we sit in the strange new silence.

I clamber off, head spinning with everything I'm learning, but somehow sensing that Hunter's strange defenses are going to be on high alert. "This is where we set the first trap?"

Climbing off the quad, he barely glances at me. I'm not sure if I should feel disappointed or pleased that I predicted that correctly. "I set the traps last night."

"Oh, right."

Which means there could be a trapped wolf nearby.

Hunter strides away. "I'll check. Wait here."

I do exactly what he says, for as long as it takes him to power several feet ahead. He looks like he's heading toward the center of the plateau where some scrubby bushes have sprouted up. I grab the vet pack and sling it over my shoulder, heading out after him.

He hears me within moments, spinning around to face me. "I told you to wait by the quad."

"I may not have Were hearing, but you said it loud enough."

He takes a deep breath, trying to get something under control. "Go back, please."

I walk forward, closing the distance. "If there's a trapped wolf, we'll need to vaccinate it."

"I'll let you know. The wolf is going to be angry and scared. It may not be safe."

I roll my eyes as I walk straight past him. "Which is why you need a Fae."

"I'd prefer a Were who can get away if they need to."

As much as I wish those muttered words don't have an impact, I still falter for one step. It's the slightest pause, a stumble of my center of gravity, and I recover quickly, but it's there nonetheless. Hoping he didn't see it, I keep going.

Changed or not-changed, I can still do my bit.

Hunter quickly catches up but I don't look at him as he walks beside me. If I'd met this wolf before, there would be a thread that would appear once we're close enough and I'd have a sense of where it is. But I haven't, so I realize I'm walking without knowing where I'm going. I slow a bit, glancing at Hunter.

He's staring ahead, eyes pensive, lips tight. For some reason I feel like he's sad, which isn't what I need to see right now. Empathy and anger can't exist simultaneously, and anger is far more self-protective.

"The trap's just up ahead."

"Where the sura bushes are?"

He glances at me before looking away. "Yeah, the sura bushes." He frowns. "But I can't hear anything."

I cock my head like I have some sort of Were hearing. "Is that a good thing?"

"I'm not sure."

We're both quiet as we approach the diamond-leafed willow,

its fragile, stunted branches losing the last of its fuzzy flowers. Hunter stops several feet away, releasing a breath. "It's empty."

I look at the soil around us. "I can't see it."

Hunter points to an area at the base of one of the bushes. "It's buried over there."

I squint, seeing two rods of metal just jutting from the ground. "A leghold trap?"

Another glance. "Yeah, a leghold trap."

"I've been involved with captive breeding most of my life, you know." I've seen my own share of trapped wolves.

"What about knowing the name of the bush?"

I shrug, although there's a smile wanting some air time at the understatement I'm about to deliver. "I've studied this area a bit."

"Why?"

I pause, I'd banked on Mr. Antisocial ending the conversation at that. Turning, I start walking back to the quad, but Hunter is by my side like he can feel the thread that ties us together. I hoist the vet pack, giving myself even more time to come up with an answer. Because I wanted to learn the names of all the plants and animals I believed I'd already seen? Because for the past two years, I'd felt this area was my second home?

I still haven't responded by the time we're back at the quad, and I focus on strapping down the vet pack.

"Why, Ava?"

I look up to find Hunter watching me, arms crossed, face unreadable as always.

I shrug. I could say I did some quick research before I headed up here, but lying isn't something I see much use for. "The area fascinates me."

I tilt my chin as I stare back, wondering what he'll make of that.

But Hunter looks away, and I'm not afforded even the effort

to try and disentangle his look. He swings a leg over the quad and climbs on. "Come on, the second one isn't far away."

I climb on without answering, deciding it's pointless trying to figure it out. Right now, we need the next trap to have a wolf, even though I always hate seeing them caught in one. For a wild animal, being captured like that is a deep violation.

Hunter was right, the next trap is only on the next hill. We must be deep in the wolves' territory if they frequent here.

I hear it the minute Hunter kills the engine. Growling driven by fear and anger. I climb off and unstrap the vet pack. He'd better not try the whole 'stay here' thing again. But all he gives me is a warning glance before taking the lead. I catch up quickly, even though it means half-skipping to get there. Hunter's going to learn that we're in this together.

This trap is in a rocky outcropping, one that feels far more familiar than any place we've been. I don't have time to wonder about it though, because I can see the wolf. Snow white like they all are, the male frantically yanks over and over at the metal jaws holding its foot. I ignore the sense of recognition that slips through my consciousness.

There's no time to wonder whether it's real—we need to do this as quickly as possible so we can release it.

Stopping yards away from the wolf I open the vet pack. The tranquilizer gun is sitting on the top, just like I packed it. Loading the pre-prepared syringe, I look up at Hunter. "You a good shot?"

"I'll probably be able to do it from further away."

Thanks to his better eyesight, but I don't think that was a dig. Hunter is focused on the animal desperately trying to escape the trap. The yanking looks like it could dislocate something if he keeps going.

I pass Hunter the gun, we need to do this as quickly as possible, and without stressing the poor animal any more.

I find myself holding my breath alongside Hunter as he holds his arms out, braces himself, and lines up the sight. The single shot spears out with a pop and embeds straight into the wolf's chest—close to his heart for maximum effect. It leaps, only to be yanked down by the chain holding it to the ground.

Hunter lowers the gun. "Now we wait."

I flick my hair over my shoulder. "Good shot."

There's the briefest of blinks before he frowns again. "You always so positive?"

I glance back at the wolf, who isn't showing any signs of slowing down, not realizing that all that movement is just going to pump the tranquilizer faster around his body. I'd always considered myself an optimist, someone powered by hope, but in the face of someone who defines me by my flaws? "I'm learning more about myself out here in just a few days than I have in seventeen years."

I don't get to see if that prompts a blink because I'm watching the wolf. The tranquilizer is working quickly. He's already slowing, shaking his head, legs a little wobbly. Hunter's shot was a good one, and despite all these weird 'don't come near me vibes', I'm glad I acknowledged that. It makes me genuinely like who I am, which I hadn't realized was a feeling I'd been missing for quite a while.

"You're very honest."

I smile. "I kinda am, aren't I?"

Hunter grunts, turning back to watch the wolf. "You get along with my sister, don't you?"

My smile does something I didn't expect—it grows. "We bonded over Mocha Munch."

The edge of Hunter's lips twitches, like a teeny-tiny thread is trying to pull them up. Of course, they don't, but Achak didn't let me see his smiles for the longest time either.

Well, not until I'd shown him that we had more in common

than he realized.

The wolf's hind legs collapse and he struggles to stay upright. But he can't fight the chemicals in his bloodstream and a few moments later his front haunches drop too.

I pick up the vet pack. "Let's do this."

Hunter's arm shoots out but stops before it connects with me. "Hang on, it's too early."

Glancing back, I raise a brow. Watch this Mr. I-Have-No-Idea.

It doesn't matter whether the thread between myself and this wolf was born the minute our eyes connected, or whether it had already been seeded long ago. I tap into our universality, finding his fear and his anger. Sending him soothing tones I keep walking forward.

"We just want to help."

My mother and all the Fae I've ever met talk to animals in their head, using the threads like a telepathic link. But I've never seen the point in keeping it hidden. I believe anyone could achieve a fraction of this if they tried because everyone has the threads.

The wolf's head raises from where it's lying, canine eyes watching me approach.

"We need to look after you." I put out my hand. "Will you let us?"

The wolf glances at Hunter, but I can see they already have a connection, and it's one built on trust. He looks at me for a long breath, then drops his head, eyes closing. I send my thanks through the connection, sensing his tiredness and capitulation.

Hunter joins me as I kneel down. "You do know it was the sedative, don't you?"

I grab out the vial. "Of course it played a part. The sedative allows me to get past their innate fear and anger. Those emotions are like a shield that keeps them safe."

Hunter holds out his hand and I let it drop into his palm. He glances at me ever so briefly. "Good thing I'll never get stuck with one of these."

What in the world does that mean?

I pass Hunter the syringe. "You do it."

He focuses on drawing the clear liquid through the needle. "Queasy?"

I shrug. "Not keen on inflicting pain."

"Fair enough."

I keep my surprise hidden. Did Hunter just miss an opportunity to have a dig at my very un-Werelike squeamishness?

He squats and injects the vaccine into the wolf's thigh. There's a twitch in the animal's fur, and I feel his psyche register the nip of pain. I send soft, soothing vibes through our connection and feel him relax again.

Quickly filling up the next syringe, I pass it to Hunter. "We need to inject the globulin at a site away from the vaccine."

He pauses the downward trajectory he had. "Why?"

"Because otherwise the shock to the immune system is too localized. It will compromise both their effectiveness."

Hunter nods and looks at the wolf. "We're going to have to turn him over."

We move around to the legs, planning on using them like levers to roll him over. Hunter is about to grab the front paws when one jerks back. We both still. When nothing else happens Hunter reaches out again. This time the foot kicks out.

Hunter instantly shifts forward, a barrier between the wolf's head and myself. "He's going to need a second shot."

"No. It'll take longer to wear off which just makes him more vulnerable to poachers."

"It's too risky."

I wonder if he'd be suggesting this if it were only him out here doing this. Nor do I know whether he's suggested this because he sees me as a fragile half-human, or if he's just being protective.

It doesn't really matter, because this wolf isn't going to have another shot of tranquilizer. Hunter doesn't realize how little the wolf was under anyway.

Standing, I move around to the head of the wolf. Hunter opens his mouth but I hold my hand up. "You need to understand something."

Kneeling, I bring my face close to the wolf's. His golden eyes open, his gaze slightly unfocused, but also unwavering. Stroking his head, this fur thick and amazingly soft, I whisper, "One more."

The wolf pulls in a giant breath, and I'm pretty sure Hunter isn't breathing at all.

Hand sinking into his ruff, I feel our thread grow. "But we need to do it on the other side."

The wolf groans—a half-growl, half-grumble—before half pushing himself up. It takes some effort on his part, but he tucks in his back legs and pushes his back haunches to the side. The bottom half his body topples to the side, exposing the left thigh for Hunter.

I nod at Hunter, letting him know to hurry up and get it done. There's the biggest blink I've seen so far, but I'm too focused on the wolf to even begin to process it. Surely he's seen Dawn do something similar with the wolves.

The wolf's eyes flare when Hunter injects the globulin but I soothe him. It's hard for an animal to understand that we're helping them when we're causing them pain. That's why trust and respect are so integral. It's why trust and respect are what the threads are made of.

The moment the needle is out we both retreat. Standing side by side, we watch as the wolf lies there for a few panting breaths. With a blink that's familiar enough to make me smile, he looks up and around. Registering that we're no longer beside him, he tucks his legs in and pushes up. It's a wobbly, slow process, but within seconds, he's standing.

He looks at us, taking our measure, and I send our thanks through the connection. The wolf raises his head and launches into a great big shake, one that starts at his head and ends with a flick of his tail. He stumbles to the side as he does it, but when he's finished his white fur has thrown off the dirt and memory of the touches he just endured.

Not waiting until he's completely sedative-free, he lopes away, no doubt off to find his pack.

Feeling satisfied in a way I don't really understand, I pick up the vet pack. "One down. Three more to go?"

"Yep." Hunter looks at me curiously. "There were six in total until we caught Sakari and Zephyr."

It's my turn to blink. How did I know how many there were?

Hunter glances at the wolf who is now a moving white form in the distance. "Thanks. That went smoother than I expected."

My eyebrows shoot up. Did Hunter just thank me? But I decide to act like that word wasn't the first sign of good grace I've seen from him. "He trusts you. I don't think this would have looked the same with someone else."

Hunter shrugs. "That's because I've spent a lot of time with him. That was Taima, Sakari's younger brother."

I follow his gaze. The wolf has made good time and is about to disappear over the horizon. I don't ask the question because I already know the answer. The sag in Hunter's shoulders suggests he's thinking the same thing. The last members of this pack are all related.

I walk over and stand before him, hoping to lift some of the burden. "You're one of them, Hunter."

But he looks away. "I was."

HUNTER

18 MONTHS BEFORE

Driving the Ski-Doo through the night, I'm not sure what I want to find. After the first trap with Taima, who I had to tranquilize to release, the last two nights have come up with nothing. I can't help the sense of relief.

But I know we need to capture Zephyr and Sakari. The future of these wolves depends on it.

So, as I near where I set the trap, I slow. Cutting the engine, I wait for the silence to become absolute. There's no sound coming from the rocky outcropping, which is a good sign if you don't want a wolf to be trapped, but less so if you want a captive breeding program to get started.

Walking forward, the icy air swirling around me, I strain for the sounds of movement or frustration.

But there's nothing.

Which probably means the trap is empty.

But at the next crunch of snow beneath my boot, there's a yelp. I rush forward, coming around the scrubby, rocky edge to find that a wolf is most definitely trapped in the jaws of the trap. My breath sucks in and icy air stings my lungs.

It's Sakari.

On seeing me, she jerks, then yelps. She immediately moves forward again, taking any tension off her clamped foot.

And she's injured.

Leaning forward without putting any weight on the injured limb, she zeroes in on me and growls. Her muzzle serrates and her teeth flash white on white. Everything about her says back the hell up.

I stop, hands coming up as if in surrender. I wish I could.

Her furious eyes don't leave me, nor does the growling stop, even though I don't move another muscle. It doesn't matter that she knows me, that she's seen me most nights hovering on the horizon. She's a cornered animal; a hurt, cornered animal.

A wild wolf who's been trapped is dangerous. An injured one is far more likely to be deadly.

With slow steps I back away, knowing what I need to do. The minute I've created a little more distance I jog back to the Ski-Doo. The trailer on the back has everything I need.

Ignoring the big-ass cage on the back that's about to have a body in it, I tear open the vet pack. I need to be quick. Grabbing what I need, I head back.

Sakari jerks and yelps again when she hears me approach and it makes me wince. I'm the one who set that trap. I'm the one responsible for her injury.

Clicking the syringe into place, I hold up the tranquilizer gun and start moving forward. I need to get close enough to be accurate.

With each step closer, Sakari steps up the growling. It starts as an ominous thunder, but within a few moments it detonates into a violent explosion. Barks and snaps have her jerking forward over and over, no longer paying attention to her injured foot. Sakari looks feral and angry and I don't blame her.

Heart hammering, I need to get this over and done with as quickly as possible so she doesn't do herself any more damage. As much I hated it, I'm glad I spent the hours upon hours working on my aim. Dawn had insisted on it.

Waiting for the space between breaths, and without flinching, I pull the trigger.

The pain of the needle slamming into her throat has Sakari leaping so high that her foot, as good as impaled to the ground, jerks her back down. The yelp is all pain—the physical discomfort of whatever torn tissue the trap has inflicted, along with the mental anguish of helpless fury.

I back away, swallowing hard, chest aching.

I wish I didn't have to do this alone. I wish someone could carry this with me.

But no one else deserves to have this weight in their chest, this responsibility to carry for the rest of their lives.

Which means I do it alone.

Sakari struggles even harder, and I flinch with each yank on the chain. Please let it work fast.

I'd like to pace, give my anger and frustration some freedom, but I stay still. Sakari has enough to worry about without trying to keep an eye on the one who's hurt her.

Minutes pass, my breath misting in the cold, and I wonder if it would be better if I shifted. My wolf form is something that Sakari would be less threatened by.

But then *she* will appear.

And this is not something she needs to see. Selfishly, I wonder what she'd think of me if she saw what I'm doing. I'm certainly not okay with it.

So, I wait, pretending the cracks aren't starting to show as I hold myself still. It's not long before Sakari slows, then becomes as motionless as I am. Her gaze holds mine, laden with warning. I don't move, giving her what space I can.

Two minutes later she drops down, eyes no longer looking quite so sharp. Then she begins to lick her paw, tending the site of her injury. The area is already wet from when she must've been doing this earlier.

Not long now and I'll be able to inspect the damage.

The first long blink has me holding my breath. The second follows just after. The tranquilizer is working. I take the first step forward when her eyes close and stay closed. At the sound of snow compressing, Sakari forces them open again. I freeze, but like they're weighed down, her lids droop again. Another step and she doesn't move. A handful more and I'm only a few feet away.

KJ said tranquilizers are all about timing. Too soon and you risk the animal not being sedated. Leave it too long and they may wake up before you're ready. And that's all assuming you've given them the correct dose.

This isn't something I ever saw myself doing, so I have no idea whether I've got it right. Urgency has me stepping forward again. Sakari doesn't move. She's a big mound of regular breaths and little more.

Kneeling down, I keep my eyes on her face. Relaxed, it's lost its fury, and is the Sakari I know. Regal, gentle, fierce.

The metal of the trap is cold on my fingers. Sakari has mostly trodden and melted the snow around it. My hand creeps up to touch her fur and I pause. Her breathing hitches but nothing else.

Scooting so I can move in closer, I wrap my fingers around her leg. Gently, I feel around and relief washes through me. I can't feel any broken bones nor is there any significant swelling. From the looks of things, it's a sprain. Maybe a nasty one considering how much she's pulled on it, but nothing we can't treat back at Resolve.

When I move my hand back down the trap, Sakari's leg jerks. My eyes fly to her face, my body coiled and ready to move away. KJ's words float through my mind as he'd read over the ins and outs of sedating wild animals. Effectiveness will depend on body size, site of injection, the animal's health, and the circumstances of the shot. We'd been very careful in our calculations, but he'd pointed out there were a heck of a lot of variables. He'd said that if there was too much adrenalin, a single dose probably wouldn't cut it.

But Sakari's eyes stay shut. Maybe it was a reflex or something.

I wait, just in case. Opening the trap always involves noise and movement. If it wasn't for the injury, I'd do it once I had her in the cage. But there's no way I'm moving her with those pounds of metal hanging off her foot.

Knowing there's a clock ticking over us, I feel around for the release mechanism. With a last check to confirm she's still out of it, I press the lever. There's a clank and the jaws release. Sakari's foot falls to the soggy snow.

I'm so relieved I don't see the snap coming. Razor teeth powered by a powerful jaw flash by my face in an uncoordinated grab. I fall back on my butt, watching as Sakari struggles to her feet—all four now that she's released from the trap.

Shifting is reflexive; a protective act. As a human I'm vulnerable. As a wolf twice Sakari's size I stand a chance against her anger and pain. If I'm lucky, I can get away without either of us being hurt.

Sakari leaps back as a massive white wolf appears before her. I watch the wince as she lands on her injured paw and I wonder how the hell I'm going to stop her from doing any more damage.

What's more, if she gets away like that, she'll be at risk of poachers picking her off.

Sakari shakes her head and her body wobbles, but she holds her ground. There's no way of telling how she's going to react. She's in pain, the fear of capture was very real for her only a moment ago, and I just shot her.

Relax, girl.

I shift my center of gravity, but that's enough for Sakaris' eyes to blaze. Her head drops and the growling becomes a constant rumble.

How do I tell her I'm moving away? That despite it all, I've never meant her any harm?

When I feel a presence beside me, it takes everything I have not to leap away. But my heart rate stays the same frenzied speed when I see who it is.

My wolf, golden wolf, looks at me with her soulful wintergreen eyes. She looks over at Sakari, taking in that she's on the offensive, noticing the open trap by her foot. Sakari steps back, probably aware she's now outnumbered, and the limp is unmistakable.

Golden wolf looks back at me, and those eyes I know so well are calm and determined. She brushes her nose against my cheek, the softest caress against my fur that always makes my heart warm, before turning back. She takes a step forward.

She's moving towards Sakari?

I thought she'd figured out what was going on here. There's no way I'm letting her get near an injured, wild animal. Realizing I have to shift back to human, still this close to Sakari, has my body tightening, but there isn't a choice. Her safety comes first.

Feeling the compression of muscles that's the beginning of morphing back to human form, I wish our time could have been longer. She's so graceful, her movements sure and confident. She loves these wolves as much as I do, but I'm not letting her put herself in danger.

Except Sakari straightens, heck, practically relaxes. Surprise has the change stopping before it really started. Sakari is looking at golden wolf, face probably looking like mine when I first saw her. Shock robbing her of the ability to move, eyes taking in the glory that an animal can look like she does.

Golden wolf approaches like they're friends from way back, and I'd swear I can feel calming waves rolling off her. Sakari's teeth are no longer visible but I still tense when I see her take a step forward. Except golden wolf isn't the least bit scared, in fact, I think she welcomes it. Almost expected it.

They meet and Sakari sniffs the air. She must like what she smells because her tongue lolls out, her face lighting up in a canine smile. I feel my ass hit the snow as they greet each other and I'm not even sure why I'm surprised. Of course this glorious wolf could calm a furious animal who's been backed into a corner.

The moment my wolf is within her personal space Sakari leans forward, her tongue coming out in greeting. With tentative licks of golden wolf's jaw, she welcomes her. I can't see my wolf's smile, but I can feel it. She nudges Sakari with her head, a sign of affection and thanks. Golden wolf moves forward, encouraging Sakari to sit.

She wants her to take some weight off her injured foot.

Sakari glances at me but I haven't twitched a muscle. Will she be comfortable enough to take such a vulnerable position?

Golden wolf nudges her again and Sakari sits back, no doubt enjoying the relief it provides her injured leg. Golden wolf turns and sits beside her, then drops into the snow. She looks up at Sakari who joins her a moment later. Straight away, Sakari begins licking her injured paw again, impressing me that she's comfortable enough to do that, but also showing exactly how much it's bothering her.

Golden wolf looks back at me, and I know now it's my turn to do what needs to be done. She calmed Sakari, now I need to help her.

I'm glad I have to shift to human to do this because it means she won't see what I'm about to do. Shame pricks at my conscience because golden wolf probably believes I'm something I'm not. She probably assumes someone else set that trap, that someone else is responsible for Sakari's pain.

I know I need to do this quick, like a Band-Aid. Shift then shoot. I'm beside the tranquilizer gun before I'm ready so I let myself have one last glance. Golden wolf, the glorious animal that's my anchor, is curled around Sakari. Sakari has stopped licking, her head now resting back on her new friend. It leaves her throat wide open for my shot.

Golden wolf's eyes meet mine. For the first time, I can't keep her gaze. I shift, and in the moment where I'm neither wolf nor human, but somehow both, she disappears. Teeth jamming down, I pick up the gun.

Down the sight I see Sakari jerk upright. Knowing I can't afford to flinch, I squeeze the trigger, knowing as I do so that these were Sakari's last moments in the wild.

20

HUNTER

18 MONTHS BEFORE

Dawn's grainy image on the camera as she tends to unconscious Sakari's foot isn't the win it should be. Sakari wouldn't need medical help if it weren't for us in the first place.

KJ's hand comes to rest on my shoulder. "We're giving her the best chance we can."

I sigh. "I know."

"And for her future pups."

"I know that too."

This time, it's KJ's sigh that fills the empty office. "I'm just not sure when the last time I saw you smile was, that's all."

That would've been when I was last out with the most amazing, impossible wolf I've ever met.

I hold up my cup full of wakeup juice like I'm toasting him. "Every cell smiled when you brought me this."

"Well, we're screwed if there's ever a shortage of that stuff."

Or if golden wolf turns out to be nothing but a figment of a brain that snapped under too much pressure.

I go to grab his beanie. "Or if sheep go extinct and there's no more wool."

KJ ducks, his hands holding down his protective head covering, a cheeky grin flashing over his face. "Except I could easily live with a substitute."

He's talking about the times Riley tried to sneak in chicory, chai, and mushroom coffee—what special snowflake came up with that awful idea?—makes me shudder. All those alternatives are like hairless cats; they exist, but that doesn't make it right. "Man, siblings are overrated."

KJ looks away, the grin gone, and I could kick myself for mentioning siblings. One of the side-effects of lack of sleep means I tend to speak before I think. Nor can I take it back, no matter how much I want to. KJ is very clear that we don't talk about his past.

He heads over to his desk where his bank of computers now sit. He moved all his tech stuff to Resolve not long after we set it up. It meant he could work more closely with Dawn while still being the digital watchdog he assigned himself as.

He flicks the mouse and the screens come to life. "Alistair has been quiet."

I walk over, knowing going along with the change of topic is my best form of apology. "Which may or may not be a good thing."

"Exactly."

"You think he's waiting?"

KJ nods as he opens a new tab. "He's looking for ammo. I think Alistair scans for info about as intensively as I do."

I draw out a whistle. "Whoa, do you think he has a thing for millinery too?"

KJ's arm whips out, aiming for my coffee. "Shut up."

But I dodge the familiar move, relieved I can see the grin he's trying to suppress. "Although that guy would probably spend fifteen minutes using the torch on his cell to look for his darned cell."

KJ rolls his eyes, looking at the next screen. "You don't need brains. You just need passion."

Which Alistair has plenty of thanks to his father. Grabbing a chair, I sit next to KJ. "Lucky for us, you have both."

KJ looks at me, eyes still and serious. "You know I need to fix this."

I nod, meeting him at the place where truth speaks. "We'll do whatever it takes."

We hold our gazes for a long moment. The commitment to saving the wolves brought us closer together far more than our familial bonds ever did.

The door opens behind us. "Are you two settling the debate about whether tacos or pizza are better with a staring contest again?"

KJ turns back to his computers, throwing a wry glance back at Riley. "I see what you mean. Totally overrated."

I pick up a pen and throw it at my sister. "We were eight."

She catches and throws it right back, just like I knew she would. "And macaroni cheese wins, hands down."

I'd smile, except I know it will be short-lived. The first thing Riley will do is walk over to the screens lining the wall to see what I've been up to during the night.

I can tell the minute she sees Sakari in the pen because her whole body tenses and stills. She spends long moments watching the screen where the female wolf now lies alone.

She turns back to me, and her whole face is taut with sadness. "She's here."

I hide the wince the yank on my chest inflicts. "Yeah. She's here."

"I was kinda hoping you'd be unsuccessful."

I almost wasn't successful. "Me too, to be honest."

KJ wheels around. "You both know this is their best chance."

Now I'd like to kick him for talking before thinking. Those words were just what Riley doesn't need to hear right now.

Riley strides forward, the stillness of sadness shattered by the force of anger. "Because it's no longer safe for them to live in the wild? Because Were and Fae have to protect them from humans?"

I walk over, understanding her pain. "Some humans have helped fund this program."

"But the fact is, we need to have it in the first place because of them."

"We all do."

"We have to do this because of them!"

I pull in a deep breath. I figured we'd have to go through this now. "You know it's not that simple."

"They get scared so they kill. It's pretty simple for them." Riley glares at me. "I hate them, Hunter. I hate them."

I'm already shaking my head. Riley's personality has always had bite, but she's never been one to hold a grudge. But that was before humans killed our father. "You don't mean that."

Riley crosses her arms and looks away, her tense jaw stopping any more words from coming. My fists clench because I can't tell whether that means she agrees with me, or whether this has gone further than I thought.

There's a ping from one of the computers and I hear KJ wheel back over. I know it's a vain hope, but maybe there's something to the staring thing and if I stand here long enough, she'll answer.

"Ah guys," KJ types rapidly, "Something's come up."

We're by his side in a second thanks to Were speed. The screen is Evelyn Island's Facebook page. Last time I looked at that there was a Ski-Doo for sale and someone warning drivers to slow down around the library. "What's up?"

"There's been a wolf sighting."

Riley leans over the other shoulder. "Where?"

KJ pulls in a gasp. "At Mount Hearne."

Alarm has me shooting back up. Mount Hearne is the closest peak to the town. It's the spot the oldies use as a scenic lookout and the teens use as a make-out point.

He scrolls further down. "Crap. Alistair has commented."

KJ was right. He is trolling, looking for any mention of wolves.

Riley leans forward. "They never come in that close."

KJ scrolls back up and we discover another post was just made. This time it's a photo of a wolf, still in the distance, but close enough to zoom in on. The caption has me frowning; 'should we be worried?!?'

Alistair will undoubtedly reply that they should be more than worried.

Riley gasps, saying out loud what I've registered. "It's Zephyr."

KJ curses. "He must be looking for Sakari."

Riley narrows her eyes as she studies the image. "He's probably had enough."

I'm pretty sure Riley is talking about herself rather than the lone wolf who's standing in the snow, but I'm not waiting around to find out. Picking up the vet pack that I only just restocked, I head for the door.

"He's not trapped, Hunter." Her voice is full of worry.

"I probably never needed them."

Zephyr and Sakari would have let me close enough to shoot them. Maybe I was avoiding the ultimate betrayal—getting close only to shoot them. And at least this way we don't risk Zephyr being injured like Sakari was.

"But—"

I hold my hand up to stop the next sentence. She's going to

point out that shooting him is only going to anger him, and there's always a gap of time before the sedative starts to work. "You know I can take care of myself. I won't get hurt."

I started this when I called Dawn six months ago. Now I need to see it through.

Zephyr and Sakari will be reunited by tonight, in the home that will keep them safe.

21

AVA

When I enter the office for our next update meeting I'm surprised to find only KJ in the room. He's leaning over a microscope, totally absorbed in whatever he's checking out. I stand in the doorway, wondering if I got the time mixed up or something.

I'm about to step back, figuring I can go see some of the wolves, when his hand comes up, waving me in. "Just in time."

He must've heard me. KJ looks up, his face warm and grinning in welcome. "I was just confirming something."

"Oh?" I slip my hands into the pockets of my jeans. It's nice to have a guy happy to see me for a change.

He pushes his desk chair back and he zooms across the room. "But I should probably wait till everyone else gets here."

"Well, I should be glad my Dad is Noah Phelan. Mom says he's patented patience."

KJ's eyes are still twinkling when he looks at me, but they take a curious tilt. "What's it like, growing up with them?"

I shove my hands further in my pockets. "Pretty amazing, actually. They're practically each other's air. I got to grow up surrounded by that sort of love."

"Sounds...amazing."

"Yeah, it is. Everyone's really close. Both with our pack and the neighboring pack."

"The Channons."

It doesn't surprise me that he knows the names. Every Were knows of the Phelans and Channons. Every Were knows of me.

"They're all amazing people who've achieved amazing things."

He tilts his head, the grey wool on his head shifting to the side as he studies me. "All waiting to see what their legacy will be."

I swallow, also not surprised that KJ gets it. I sensed a kindred spirit in this guy the moment I saw him. It's like our threads were already woven before we even met. "Yeah. All waiting."

"Well, if you can be nice to Hunter, then someone should consider sainting you."

I bite my lip. "He's very...taciturn."

KJ snorts. "Or they can give you an award for using the word taciturn in a sentence. I think Hunter's spent too much time out on the tundra alone. Somedays he's more wolf than human."

"I thought it wasn't safe to shift. That you guys don't spend time as wolves."

"That's the rule." KJ shrugs. "But Hunter is Alpha, he can do what he wants."

I'm not sure that makes sense. "Isn't it important that he stick to the rules, seeing as he's the Alpha?"

KJ's gaze shifts to the window, becoming introspective. "It's the fact that Hunter is willing to question the rules that's made him the Alpha he is, even when it was thrust upon him so young."

For some reason, Hunter spending time as a wolf has stolen my attention. "So, he shifts when he's out with the wolves?"

"I'm not sure how, but I think it's kept him sane through all this craziness. His mom and Riley wouldn't be happy, but if it's helped him, then I say it was a good thing." KJ looks back at me like he's just realized something. He yanks up a smile. "Anyway, less about boring stuff, more about exciting news!"

That's the least bored I've been since I got here, but I get that KJ feels like he's said too much. His bond to Hunter is obvious by the thick thread that connects them. "Which you say you can't tell me." I pout, willing to take his lead and change the subject.

KJ glances over his shoulder, as if checking that someone hasn't snuck up on him. "Well, if you can keep a secret..."

I thought I had for two years, until my wolf turned out to be the stuff of dreams. "Ask Josh why my parents never found out where the scratch down the side of their truck came from."

KJ grins. "Impressive." He glances over his shoulder again and I almost roll my eyes. He's a Were, no one can sneak up on him without him hearing or smelling them. "Well..."

I wait with bated breath. Is this about Resolve? Or the wolves in the wild? Is it something that explains why Hunter has me on the probably-has-leprosy list?

"Sakari is pregnant."

It takes several seconds for the words to sink in, process, and then explode with implications. "No way!"

"Totally way!"

My eyes are wide with disbelief. "But her mate, he—"

"Obviously got in just in time."

"KJ, that's..." I'm lost as to how to finish that sentence. If Sakari is pregnant, then that's another litter of pups that will increase numbers. Not only that, they will have the genes they've so carefully chosen to boost the genetic vigor of the vulnerable population. There won't be time lost trying to find a mate, waiting for them to bond, then waiting to see if a litter would even happen.

KJ's face is alive with joy and excitement. This is a really big moment for them. It's so monumental, the emotion is so infectious that I throw my arms around him in a great big hug. His arms wrap around me and we give the joy free reign as we pull in tight.

"I'm so happy for you, KJ."

He pulls back to look at me. "It's a really important step forward."

KJ stiffens and then I hear it too. A clearing of a throat from behind me. I release KJ, already sensing who's there.

I turn to find Hunter in the doorway. His arms are crossed, his face remote and unreadable as it always seems to be.

KJ scratches under his beanie. "I have some good news."

"Awesome."

The word falls flat in the center of the room. Emotions mill about within me that I don't understand. Anger that doesn't make sense. Guilt that I shouldn't be feeling. And attraction that I wish wasn't there. Dark hair, muscled arms, intense copper gaze, looking at Hunter seems to have a direct connection to my heart rate.

Hunter stays in the doorway, the lone wolf that KJ says he isn't. Why would he care if I'm hugging KJ? From the way he's been treating me, he wouldn't care if I'd been kissing KJ when he walked in.

"So, what it is?"

"Ah, I was waiting till everyone was here."

Hunter arches a brow, obviously noting that's exactly what KJ didn't do with me.

I summon a smile—KJ and I have nothing to hide. "You're going to be really happy with it, Hunter."

Hunter turns his copper gaze towards me. For some reason,

his name seems to hang in the room longer than it should, then his gaze holding mine does that same thing. Our thread pulses, a swirling mix of glorious color and I feel my chest inexplicably lighten. This sense of connection and lightness doesn't make sense. The guy has never smiled at me, there's no indication right now that he feels this.

But the knowledge remains. It's what keeps driving me despite the roadblocks.

KJ clears his throat and we both look away. The Lino floor becomes fascinating. Hunter pushes away from the doorjamb and walks in. "So where is everyone?"

Is there a huskiness to his voice, or is that more of my wishful thinking?

KJ shrugs. "Last time I saw Dawn she was in the main lab. She hasn't surfaced from her microscope for most of the day."

Hunter nods. "Probably double checking the last of the Furious blood samples."

"As for Riley and Josh—"

"You rang?" Riley strides into the room, bubbling energy a stark contrast to the aftermath of whatever just happened, shutting the door behind her.

"You're late," Hunter says.

Riley flops into a chair, flicking her fringe back. "Ah, hello pot, kettle here."

"What were you doing?"

The door opens again, and Josh peeks his head in. "Sorry I'm late."

I have to hold in my smile. Hunter glances between his sister and my cousin, eyebrows ever so slightly raised. He looks to KJ, but he's already reading something on his screen. When his gaze meets mine, I allow my eyebrows to raise just a little too. What do you make of that, Alpha?

I don't know why I expect another frown, but it means I'm

even more surprised when I see Hunter's lips twitch. I'm too shocked to respond, but it doesn't matter, because with a fast blink, he turns away.

I've really got to stop reading so much into this stuff.

He walks to the head of the room, beneath the line of camera screens. "It looks like it's just us then."

KJ spins his chair to face him. "Well, now that we're pretty much all here…"

Riley leans forward, obviously knowing him well enough to hear the hint of something in his voice. "Yeah?"

It's infectious, because Josh straightens. "No more signs of Furious?"

KJ grins. "Well, as a matter of fact, we haven't seen any signs of that angry little bastard."

Hunter nods. "All the captive wolves have been vaccinated." He glances at me, the connection brief but there. "And all the wolves in the pack have been vaccinated."

Riley reaches out to high-five me and I slap her palm, loving her enthusiasm. I can see why Josh ran late today. She grins. "Good job, guys."

"Thanks." I know I shouldn't say this next bit, but I can't help myself. "We work well together."

Riley's eyes widen with surprise as she turns to her brother. "That's great." Then I swear her eyes take on a mischievous glint. "You guys should do the northern pack then."

The northern pack?

Hunter glares at his sister. "We're not talking about the northern pack at the moment." He turns to KJ. "So looks like Furious may have run its course?"

KJ picks up a piece of paper from his desk, nodding. "I think Josh's theory has some merit. It burned too hot, too fast. The infected animals never got a chance to infect others."

I wince, thinking of Achak's mate and Resolve's alpha male. The virus didn't spread because they were killed.

My chest tightens for a moment. I've spoken to my parents every day, and there's been no sighting of Achak. I choose to believe that's because he's taken himself to the depths of the wild somewhere, far away from human contact.

KJ places the paper down. "It's still early days, but with the vaccinating, it's certainly looking promising."

Riley claps her hands. "That's definitely good news!"

Hunter is looking at KJ closely. "Except that's not it."

I look to KJ, impressed that Hunter noticed the twinkle in his eye. Apart from that, you wouldn't know that KJ is sitting on a giant surprise. Excitement tingles along my spine—this is just the news these guys need.

KJ points at his friend. "Remind me not to play poker with you."

Hunter snorts. "You'd probably card count."

"Hey, need to keep the neurons firing." He taps his temple.

"KJ." Riley's voice is heavy with warning. "If you don't get to the point..."

Josh's eyes widen, making me giggle. The irony that Josh has connected with someone that reminds me of his younger sisters isn't lost on me. "I'd get to the point."

KJ nods slowly. "You're a wise man, Josh. Well, I ran some tests today." He looks around at everyone in the room. "And Sakari is pregnant."

Riley's squeal is ear-splitting as she leaps from her chair. "You legend, KJ!"

KJ laughs, the sound loud and light. "Well, it wasn't me working the magic exactly."

Riley bursts into her own peals of joy, and when she finds Josh standing beside her, grinning like he's the father, she throws her arms around him. She's quick though, because she's already released him and turned to KJ before he can hug her back. She gives KJ the same whirlwind hug before running to her brother.

I'm so caught up in this overflowing happiness that it takes me a few seconds to register Hunter's face. He's wrapped his arms around Riley, obviously quicker than the other two, but there seems to be far more shock than anything on his face.

She moves away, chattering about whether there may be four in the litter this time, oblivious to what seems to be morphing across her brother's face. KJ and Josh are already pointing out that smaller litter sizes are far more common in arctic wolves, but Riley is shushing them, saying they should take a leaf out of my book of optimism.

I'm the optimist?

I suppose if an optimist believes in the power of hope, then I guess that label is appropriate. I remember Hunter's words, 'Are you always this positive?'

I turn back from the gaggle of happy friends who are now laying bets on the size of the litter—Riley stating Sakari is a Pisces, which means she's highly fertile, whilst Josh and KJ decide to look up the average litter size of all births from the wolves—to find Hunter gone.

I look around, maybe he's just moved to a computer and sitting at a desk or something, but Hunter is definitely not in the room. The others are too excited to have noticed, so I use the moment to slip out the door after him. Why isn't he celebrating with the others?

In the hallway, I pause, tapping into the threads that are far more mystical than physical, sensing that he's headed towards the enclosures. Without giving myself time to think, I turn left.

I find him standing at Sakari's pen, fingers threaded through the wires as he watches her. She's just stepping out of the artificial den that's been built from rocks. This will probably be where she gives birth to the litter she's carrying.

I know Hunter has sensed my presence because there's a tell-tale tightening between his shoulders. He straightens, releasing the fence and gives me his usual greeting—a frown.

I smile right back. I doubt Hunter would want to know that I can just about follow him anywhere. "Congratulations."

Hunter half-snorts, half-huffs as he turns back to watch Sakari. I have no idea what that means. "You aren't happy?"

He glares at me, but for some reason I don't take offense. Maybe I'm becoming immune to his glares, or maybe I can sense it's not me he's angry at. "Why are you here, Ava?"

Now it's my turn to blink. Talk about a confronting question. Is it because Hunter's hurting and I can't stand anyone hurting? Is it because I can sense so much turmoil? Yes and yes.

But it's more than that.

I've been nothing but honest with Hunter, and I'm not going to stop now. "For some reason, it's hard to stay away."

Hunter's head snaps to look back at the wolves, except his eyes are shut. It looks like breathing is taking a whole lot of concentration. The fact that this is so hard for him makes me smile inside. There's no disputing Hunter feels something.

And finding out what that is has become very, very important.

Sakari's head perks up when she sees me and I sense her welcome. At least she's happy to see me.

I step forward, the awareness of his body increasing as the space between us shrinks. "She's lucky to have you all looking after her." I hear the three pups, almost adults now, playing in the adjacent pen. "They all are."

"There are some good people fighting for them."

Why do I get the sense Hunter hasn't included himself in that? I watch him, hoping he'll turn that copper gaze my way, but he continues to watch Sakari. I decide to say it anyway. "Yes. There are."

"They've all made some big sacrifices."

"You've worked really hard for these wolves, Hunter. They owe you their lives. All those hours out alone on the tundra was your sacrifice."

His jaw works, and when he finally turns to me, there's anguish in his eyes, but also challenge. "I wasn't always alone. I thought there was someone with me."

Oh. I hadn't expected that, nor for it to hurt so much. Except I hear the catch. "But there wasn't?"

"Apparently not."

Then why all the stay away vibes? I frown. "I don't understand."

"Because by losing her, I had proof of exactly who I am."

He lost her? No wonder there's such a sadness in his soul. "Hunter—"

"No, Ava. I'm not the person you seem to think I am. There are things I've done—"

"Hard choices have to be made." Hunter had to adult far younger than most people, even Weres who tend to mature young.

"Stop, Ava." He looks tortured. "Don't you see I'm trying to make this as painless as possible? I'm not the one who's part of your legacy."

The legacy. The one I've never fulfilled anyway. That's why I don't get to explore something I've never felt is more right? That felt like maybe I could be someone who could fulfill whatever it is I'm supposed to do?

Sakari must sense something, because instead of hanging back and watching whatever tug-of-war seems to be happening, she trots over. Hunter goes to step back but I grasp his hand. "She's coming to say hello."

His muscled body freezes and I wonder if he can feel the heat and electricity between our palms.

"Sakari hasn't come near me." He swallows. "Not since I killed her mate."

My chest aches at the pain in Hunter's words and I'm at a loss of how to heal it. But just like Achak taught me the power of patience and connection, Sakari shows me that I don't need to do anything.

She slows as she approaches us, but never falters. Stepping up to the fence she looks Hunter in the eye. Like that one look just leveled him, Hunter drops to his knees. Eye to eye, they take measure of each other. Hunter is so still I'm pretty sure he isn't breathing.

This is so beautiful it hurts. "It looks like your bond is stronger than that."

He shakes his head ever so slightly. "It's because you're here," he says softly.

But I can see their thread, alive and invigorated, growing strong again. "It's not me she's saying hello to."

As if to prove me right, Sakari takes the final step forward. She presses her nose to the fence, eyes bright and focused. Hunter raises his hand slowly, as if worried he'll break the moment and she'll move away. But he doesn't realize how strong their connection is. Sakari sits, like she's happy for this to take as long as it needs.

Hunter's breath whooshes out as his finger slips past the wire and brushes her nose. Sakari closes her eyes as he strokes her muzzle and I can't help my smile.

When Hunter finally breaks the moment to look up at me, I've already retreated several steps. I would love to stay and watch this reconnection, a part of me wishes I was part of it. But I instinctively know that Sakari is telling Hunter something.

He opens his mouth but I shake my head. Sakari needs this just as much as he does.

And although it hurts to walk away, I know I can't make this about me.

I turn and make sure I don't glance over my shoulder as I leave. Hopefully Sakari has shown Hunter that he's more than he realizes.

22

AVA

When Hunter comes to a halt the next afternoon, his long-legged pace stopping like he just hit a brick wall, I almost laugh. Even in the gloom of the shed, I can see his surprise morph into a frown.

Instead, I bedazzle him with a smile as I push away from the quad bike. "Figured this was the time we'd go out." I amp it up a lumen or two. "Even if you forgot to tell me."

He recovers quickly, straightening. "We've got some territory to cover, which means it's going to be a long night."

"Thought so." I pat the bag on the back of the quad. "Which is why I packed sandwiches."

"And the further we go north, the colder it gets."

I tap it again. "And hot chocolate."

He opens his mouth but I hold my hand up. "And coffee."

You only need to spend about fifteen minutes with Hunter to know it's his first food group.

Hunter narrows his eyes. "You remind me of my dad."

I flick my hair back over my shoulder. "I'm going to take that as a compliment."

When Hunter shakes his head, those lips of his tipping up

ever so slightly, I suck in a breath. He walks over to the quad, checking the gas. "Well, we might as well get going then."

The breath races back out. I never expected it to be that easy. I'd had images of climbing on the quad and not getting off as we argued that I was most certainly coming. It seems Hunter has learned how single-minded I can be.

Or he wants me to come...

I push that thought away. There's optimistic and then there's just delusional.

Hunter climbs on and I feel my heart rate pick up as I swing a leg over behind him. The sensation of our bodies touching is about to be experienced.

As I sink down, I don't bother fighting gravity as I slide toward him. My legs touch his as my hands find his waist.

Oh my...

There's a rapid pulse but I don't know whose it is. It seems to start where our skin touches and finish deep in my center.

"Ready?" Hunter's voice is husky and low, a sexy vibration that has me thinking things I've never considered before. Images that include skin and heat and lips. I'm glad he didn't turn around to ask me that question because my face feels like it's on fire.

If I were thinking straight, I'd give an answer with words longer than a syllable, but right now, my mind is mush. "Ah, yeah."

Clearing his throat, Hunter starts the engine.

We power out over the landscape, Hunter accelerating steadily. Within a minute we've hit enough speed that I can feel my hair whipping back behind me and the cool air nip at any exposed skin. And even though it's cold and I know brushing the knots out is going to be painful, I revel in the sense of exhilaration.

"How far?" I call into Hunter's ear.

He flashes me a look over his shoulder. "Get comfortable."

Which is exactly what I do. I settle in, hunker down a little behind the powerful, warm body in front of me, and take it all in.

Hunter avoids the puddles and bogs as we zoom over the landscape. It means the odd yank to the left or right, but I don't mind. It's only normal that I'd need to tighten my arms around his waist in those moments. The feeling of muscles moving, often tightening, beneath my hands, soars my heart-rate far more than the delight of traveling at speed.

It feels almost natural to chew through the miles with Hunter. We head deeper and deeper into tundra territory, the landscape becoming harsher and wilder, every inch sculpted by Mother Nature's extremes. The cold tries to make itself more and more known, but it's like there's a cocoon around me. I relax into the ride, outwardly enjoying the view, secretly loving the feelings that are slowly evolving within me.

It's about an hour later when Hunter glances back at me. "We've just crossed into their territory." He accelerates again. "Now we need to get a sense of where they've been hanging out to set the traps."

I start to look around a little more closely, trying to catch a glimpse of flashing white fur.

The terrain is even wilder this much further north, the air colder. We power up and down rocky hills, the ground rough and jagged. I hold on tight, but my focus is on trying to spot the wolves. But there's nothing. No movement, no wolves.

I start to sense Hunter's worry when we haven't come across them a while later. He slows down, head scanning left to right. I find myself doing the same, eyes squinting, trying to find a glimpse of movement.

When I see a flash of white, I gasp and straighten. Hunter stops immediately, but I deflate when I realize it was an arctic fox. It darts away through the low shrubs and I exhale in disappointment.

"Sorry," I mumble.

Hunter shrugs, the movement shifting beneath my palms. "Good spotting."

I know I shouldn't blush at that off-hand compliment, but I do. Hunter is already focused on scanning again, so I tell myself to get my head back in the game. These wolves need to be vaccinated.

As we keep going, I start to get a sense of how big this island is—these wolves could be anywhere. What's more, I'm struck by how alone we are. The odd flash of wildlife has been the only living beings we've seen for hours.

And yet Hunter has spent most nights out here, alone.

No wonder his social skills leave something to be desired.

As we reach the flattened top of a hill, Hunter slows and comes to a stop. He climbs off and I realize he's using our vantage point as a lookout. I do the same, wishing I had the same eyesight he does. The landscape reaches out for miles around us, stretching to the horizon.

Still, there's no movement, no wolves.

I'm wondering where we'll head next when Hunter closes his eyes, breathing in as he turns slowly in a circle. I freeze where I am. The thread that connects him to the earth looks like a fire that has just had oxygen drawn into it. It flares and brightens, gaining life and strength.

At home, seeing this web between every living being is overwhelming. It's something I struggle to take in, to understand what I'm supposed to do with it. But out here, everything is simpler, purer, more primal. I take a deep breath too. This is what people need to see. To know.

Hunter stops, and my heady moment is fractured by the frown that blooms across his brow.

"What's wrong?"

Hunter is facing east, the buffeting wind hitting him straight on as the frown deepens. "I'm not sure."

I step forward. "You've smelled something."

His eyes narrow as he zeroes in on the terrain before us. "It's probably nothing."

"Probably." I shrug. "There's only one way to find out."

Hunter finally looks at me, his copper eyes still and serious. "I think you should stay here."

My hands shoot to my hips. "We're not starting that again."

"I'm serious, Ava. We don't know what we're going to find."

I may not have shifted or inherited any Were traits, but I've grown up with them. Hunter has sensed something I can't. "What did you smell, Hunter?"

His gaze slides away. "Blood."

Bloody hell. Why did it have to be the one thing that curdles my gut?

Hunter walks back to the quad bike. "Wait here, I'll check it out and come back. A wolf or a fox has probably caught themselves dinner."

Why would it feel like a step backward if I were to stay here? I don't know, but I don't give myself time to analyze it. I'm striding over and climbing on in the space of a breath.

Hunter lets out a long breath before turning back to me. "You know there's a point where stubbornness becomes stupidity, don't you?"

Like I always do, I smile in the face of his frown. "How many times has Riley said that to you?"

This time there's a half-chuckle as Hunter turns back and twists the key. The engine rumbles to life beneath us.

My smile is still on my face several seconds later when we hit level ground. Hunter drives due east, the quad steadily picking its way through the mosaic of puddles. We've only reached the next rise when Hunter stops again.

My smile fades. It's closer than I realized.

Hunter climbs off and looks down at the foot of the hill. "It's not far."

I nod, his seriousness deeper than I've ever seen it.

"Wait here." His glare is full of warning. I consider rolling my eyes. What's he going to do? Frown at me? Be rude and antisocial?

Instead, I nod. Now isn't the time to argue.

Hunter walks away, stopping three times to check that I haven't moved from where I'm standing. Each time, I simply stand there, brushing away the stray hairs that keep flitting across my face.

Seeing that I'm actually doing what he's asked me this time, he strides away. Pausing several times to scent the air, he heads to the right where the land dips down.

I try to scent the air myself, even though I know it's pointless. All I smell is earthy soil with a hint of vegetation. Why couldn't I have been born more Were than Fae?

Hunter pauses once more, but this time he fails to start again. Instead of tilting up his head to taste the breeze, now his head is scanning the terrain.

Then he stops. Stock still, he stares at the ground.

He's yards away, but something has me freezing too. I could call out, but I don't and I'm not sure why. I wait, figuring Hunter will move any second.

Except he doesn't. He stands and stares at whatever he's found.

23

AVA

Without realizing it, I'm running. Something about the slant of his shoulders, like they've drooped or caved in or something, injects me with speed.

Within moments I smell what Hunter must have. The scent of blood isn't one I've experienced often seeing as I tend to avoid it. I don't eat meat, I don't visit Mom's vet surgery very often, and I'm not around for any procedures on the wolves in the captivity program. But you only have to smell it once to know it. Then you instantly recognize it the second it hits your nostrils.

The wolves must've caught a bison or something because once I smell it, it's strong. As much as that makes my stomach roil, at least it means we know where they are now. Maybe that's why Hunter hasn't moved.

When I'm only feet away, Hunter turns. His hands come up as if to stop me. "Ava, no!"

"Hunter—"

He takes swift steps forward. "You need to go back."

There's an urgency in his voice that I don't understand. A half-eaten chunk of animal isn't going to be pleasant, but I'm made of stronger stuff than that.

He meets me a few feet away from where he was standing, and when my momentum goes to take me past him, he reaches out and grabs me. The shock of his strong hands clasping my arms has me looking up at him in confusion. Since the moment we met, Hunter has avoided physical contact whenever possible.

"I'm not some weak half-human, Hunter."

Except his gaze isn't frustrated or frowning. "This isn't about that."

Not understanding what I see in his eyes I tear away, but he's fast, and his hands are back on my upper arms. "You don't want to see this."

But it's too late. The smell of blood is overpowering now, and my eyes seem to follow the scent to its origin. Animal bodies, several of them, are lying in the bog. They're half-submerged in black water, limbs taut with rigor mortis, their faces open in silent screams.

I bury my face in Hunter's chest, but the image has already seared into my brain. "Oh, god." Even with eyes held tightly shut, I can see what's there.

Hunter's arms clamp around me, anchoring me to him. My hands come up to tangle in his shirt, holding on tight. "They were..."

I can't finish the sentence. I didn't realize what they were straight away because they weren't white. The things lying in the ditch were hues of red.

They were shades of blood.

My whole body tightens with revolt as my brain figures it out and I feel Hunter's arms tighten. "I know."

They were wolves, but they were wolves who've been skinned.

I bury in deeper, needing the warmth and comfort that Hunter's offering. I feel his head tip down to mine as he curls even tighter around me. Anguish erupts in my chest, too much for me to know what to do with.

Oh, god. These were Hunter's wolves. He would be feeling this pain far more acutely that I am. I reach up to brush his cheek. "Are you okay?"

He blinks, then blinks again. "I...ah..."

It seems Hunter isn't used to being cared for. I cup his face, feeling bold seeing as he hasn't pushed my hand away. My heart is ricocheting in my chest. "You've protected these wolves for a long time."

His heart must be aching far more than mine.

"Ava."

He says my name in a way he never has before. He says it like it's a safe haven yet a source of torment, full of unrestrained emotion but riddled with the struggle for control. His copper eyes seem to brighten and deepen at the same time. It's a mesmerizing process that pulls me in.

His hand comes up, brushing a stray hair from my face. Heat tingles across my skin, following his touch like the tail of a comet. When his gaze flickers down to my lips my breath ceases to exist.

He pauses, and his eyes seem to be asking a question. All I know is my heart is hammering yes, yes, yes. I want this. I want Hunter.

I lean in, glorying in the sensation of all of me pressing against all of him.

This time when he blinks it's like windscreen wipers have just cleared the fog from his eyes. His breath pulls in with a stab and his hand drops. Before I can find my bearings, he's stepped back.

I have to lock every muscle to stop me from crumpling, or worse, following his heat like some lost puppy. The cool air douses me like a bucket of ice water.

Hunter clears his throat. "We need to get out of here."

Wrapping my arms around myself, I make sure I don't look down. "Do you think we're in danger?"

He shakes his head. "I doubt it. Whoever did this is long gone."

I shudder. Along with the pelts of these poor wolves.

Oh no, the wolves!

I step toward Hunter, but then stop. Neither of us is up for a repeat of whatever just happened. "What about the others?"

Hunter swallows, his gaze moving to the horizon, looking like he's holding onto it with all his strength. "There were five wolves there. There are no others."

My throat constricts. My chest fills with pain.

Those bloody bodies were the last of the northern wolves? That means that Sakari and her pack…

"Hunter…"

He crosses his arms. "We need to get back."

I nod. Hunter's walls are back up and now isn't the time to chip away at them. He's hurting at the loss we've just been dealt and arguing from me is the last thing he needs.

Without looking back, trying not to smell the crimson in the air, I start walking. Falling into step beside me, we trudge back to the quad. Silence is the song that captures the loss of the lives we leave behind in the tundra. It's fitting, because there really aren't any words.

Keeping my movements quicker than Riley and her hug, so fast that Josh would be surprised, I grasp Hunter's hand, squeeze, then release it. There aren't any words, but I let him know he's not alone.

Without glancing at him to see what he thought of that, I climb onto the quad. Hunter takes his place at the front without speaking.

When he starts the engine, the roar feels sacrilegious somehow. Five animals lost their lives, their threads cut and disconnected, their naked bodies exposed and defenseless.

I don't realize my forehead has dropped to Hunter's back until I feel his muscles flex. I hold there, not wanting to move, but waiting for the tension that will tell me I have to.

I feel him pull in a deep breath. "Thanks, Ava."

I draw in my own breath, one full of the heat and essence of Hunter. What do I say to that? You're welcome? Anytime? My heart is thumping one word, a word that is confusing, inexplicable, but undeniable.

Always.

Instead I let out the air I'd been holding. "Sure."

Accelerating, we leave the place where these animals will never roam again.

This tundra no longer has wolves in its ecosystem. It feels like a hollow, horrible, cavernous hole has just been torn open.

As I hunker behind the wall of muscle that protects me from the cold wind, I try to push away the horrible images I just saw. It's a long trip home and we're going to have to tell the others what's happened. There will be enough time to rehash everything we just saw.

Instead, I focus on the body I'm holding. Muscle contracting with each bump, dark hair ruffled by the breeze, his heady scent a mantle around me. I close my eyes, the memory of the moment we just shared holds just as much emotion.

Yes, Hunter pulled away.

But he also held me and comforted me and found it darned hard to let go.

What's more, for the briefest of moments, I comforted him.

It seems there's some hope in this time of blood and uncertainty.

24

HUNTER

12 MONTHS BEFORE

"They're growing fast."

Dawn's voice is full of pride as she watches the pups leap and tumble over each other like they've been thrown in a dryer.

"I think KJ has been feeding them growth hormones or something."

Dawn chuckles. "We both know you're the one who keeps slipping them the little extras."

I figure I'm better off not answering that seeing as it's true.

Not far away, Sakari lies in the sun, probably enjoying the break from her rough-housing brood. Zephyr has taken himself to the opposite side of the enclosure, reminding me of my dad. Deeply traditional, he'd let Mom deal with Riley and me squabbling over the last pizza slice or trying to see who can do the most tumbles across the sofa. At the same time, Zephyr's gaze, just like Dad's, stays sharp and ready. No one will get past him to his pack.

It turns out Riley's prediction was right. Against the odds, four pups were born, meaning Dawn pointed out exactly how successful captive breeding is. All the pups have Inuit names, each capturing their unique personalities. Desna, the firstborn, means boss, and he certainly likes to act like the CEO of the enclosure. Then there's Miki, or little, which captures his height, but is the exact opposite to the size of his appetite, and Kayuh, which means mountain. The last is a female, small, sprightly, and aptly named Pakak—one who gets into everything.

Dawn makes some notes on her clipboard. "And they're strong and healthy."

I nod, wondering when the band of tension around my chest will loosen. These pups have been textbook captive breeding participants. Sakari's birth, which we all watched on the screens was quick and complication-free.

Riley, my tough, smart-aleck sister had rested her head on my shoulder, her eyes moist. "They're our future, Hunter."

I'd stayed at Resolve for the days after. Sometimes inside, watching the screens with the same focus Mom gives The Bachelor, but mostly patrolling the enclosure. I was going to do everything I could to make sure this litter survived. If it meant even less sleep than before, then it meant I just needed to drink more coffee.

And survive they did. Growing into the tumble of white that's romping around. Soon they'll tire and curl into their mother for their next nap.

But despite the good news that's growing day after day in the form of four wolf pups, the tension won't abate. I'm probably going to give myself a heart-attack before I turn seventeen, but I can't get it to budge. It's like someone welded this belt of fear around my chest with no intention of taking it off again. Maybe it's my penance for losing the last litter.

I've wished I could show golden wolf these bundles that hold the future of arctic wolves more times than KJ has said the words 'genetic diversity'. Our time spent out on the plains continues to be magical, my thread of hope. But I can't shift so close to Resolve, mostly because it's too close to humans, but also because then she'd appear. I'm not ready to find out whether her gossamer colors would appear on the screens.

If she does, then she's no longer just mine and there are a heck of a lot of questions to be answered. How can a golden wolf even exist? Where is she from? What does any of it mean? And I don't know the answers to any of them.

If she's not...then I lose something very precious—my ability to believe in a future I want to be part of.

With so much hanging on it, I don't care if it makes me crazy because I'm the only one who sees her. I'm happy to never put it to the test.

We're about to head inside to get their evening meal ready when the sound of a car has me turning toward the parking lot. Dawn straightens and focuses when she hears it a few moments later. We're all here—Dawn, Riley, KJ and me—and as far as I know, we weren't expecting anyone. Looking at Dawn confirms that suspicion. Arms crossed, lips tight, she's on the defensive as much as I am.

Walking over I go on even higher alert when I recognize the car. It jerks to a halt and Alistair climbs out, the wind catching his sparse blond hair. Dawn and I glance at each other and I don't know whether I should frown or roll my eyes. What does this douche bag want?

We meet him beside his car, intercepting him before he gets too close to Resolve. Crossing my arms, I look him up and down. "No cameras this time?"

Red flushes across Alistair's cheeks. "I hear you've managed to breed more of these killers."

I clench down on my retort. Giving Alistair any information is just going to feed his obsession.

Dawn stands beside me, a barrier between Alistair and the building behind us. "Is that why you didn't bring the cameras? Cute wolf puppies aren't going to help your cause, are they?"

Alistair's watery eyes flash with victory. "So, the rumors were right."

Dammit. Not information I wanted Alistair to have.

Dawn shakes her head, her face soft and relaxed like she's talking to a child. "We have nothing to hide here, Alistair. These wolves are as important to this earth as we are."

Alistair's hand slices through the air. "Don't give me that new-age hippie rubbish. These animals need to be exterminated like…like smallpox! They pose too great a threat."

He's likening wolves to a deadly disease? Anger peaks through my body. "You need to leave, Alistair."

He looks at me, derision curling his lip. "You can try to use your size and strength to intimidate me. It's exactly what they," his finger points to the enclosures behind us, "would do."

Images of me shifting to a wolf to show him exactly what he's up against flash through my mind. This guy who hides behind cameras and hyped-up hate would crumple to his knees. There's a reason wolves are at the top of the food chain.

Dawn steps forward, her Fae senses probably picking up my anger. "If you're here to discover exactly how little you know, Alistair, then I welcome you. Otherwise, I'm going to ask you to leave."

A door opens behind us and Alistair glances over my shoulder. I scent what just caught his attention—Riley and KJ have joined us. I can practically feel Riley's furious gaze trying to impale Alistair.

I cock my head to the side. "I'd get going if I were you."

Alistair's eyes narrow, probably weighing up his options. Leave and lose face? Or stay and face the four guards of this program.

He didn't think quickly enough, because Riley is already by my side. She doesn't stop there but keeps striding forward. Alistair's eyes widen as she closes in on him. "If you're looking for a fight, Alistair…"

Showing that he's not completely stupid, Alistair takes a step back. "You guys don't intimidate me." Holding his ground, he tilts his chin. "What I stand for is too important."

Riley's arms explode out. "Killing? Death? The taking of lives because you can?"

I'm beside my sister in a second, knowing what's fueling her anger. The murder of your father isn't something that you ever come to accept, which means the pain can never ebb or diminish. Anger is a natural outlet.

Alistair must figure he's got a chance against the girl striding towards him because he doesn't move. "The protection of those we love will always come first."

My arm shoots out, grabbing my sister before she detonates again. This time there will be no containing the explosion. She tries to shake me free, but I don't let go. Keeping my voice low, I don't take my eyes off Alistair. "He's a douche-bag. We're better than this."

Riley pauses, energy pulsing through her body. She stares at him. "He stands for everything we're fighting."

"Yep. And he's here because we're winning."

My words diffuse some of Riley's anger, which is what I was hoping for. Not enough for the waves of hatred to stop being generated, but enough for me to know that she's not going to do something stupid.

Riley shakes off my hand again, and this time I let it drop. Her gaze never leaves Alistair as she replies. "He better not come around here again."

There's so much venom in Riley's voice that Alistair steps back again. Spine looking like someone jammed a javelin down it, he spins and takes the few steps to his car. He opens the door and stops, holding it like a shield. "This is exactly what I'm talking about. You people are as dangerous and violent as they are."

The four of us stand where we are, no one responding. Alistair stands there for a few more moments, waiting for us to prove him right. When nothing but the breeze shifts, he climbs in and slams the door. If this wasn't such a tense situation, I'd smile. Our silence and inaction was far more humiliating for him than all our words put together.

With a petty spray of gravel, Alistair drives off. He glances in the rear vision mirror and I catch his gaze. His icy glare is full of warning, telling me we didn't win anything today. As long as humans like Alistair hate, then we have a war on our hands.

Dawn lets out a breath. "I don't think he'll ever give up."

Riley spins on her heel, jaw working. I don't step forward, I don't touch her even though my chest feels like it's splitting. Riley wouldn't want that right now. She's barely holding it together as it is.

Instead I hold her gaze, letting her know she's not alone in her pain or anger. These are two emotions we will always carry.

Hands clenching and unclenching, she bites her lip. And then she's striding away, heading toward the enclosures. I watch her leave, getting that she needs some time alone. Sometimes sharing space with the wolves is the only thing that will heal your soul.

That's what golden wolf has meant for me.

Dawn, green eyes strained, turns to the building. "I'll keep an eye on her from inside."

I nod, grateful that she understands.

Then I realize there's someone else who'd be deeply affected by Alistair's words. KJ has moved away from the entry and is leaning against the wall of the building, hands shoved in his pockets. That has me clenching my teeth. KJ's hands are never in his pockets—they're either on a keyboard or making sure his beanie is where it should be.

I join him, welcoming the dig of the bricks into my back. "They're not all like him."

KJ keeps his gaze on where Alistair drove off. "I know."

I do the same. We probably look like two guys discussing sports or the latest music video, rather than what's eating away at KJ. "And we already know that sort of rhetoric doesn't win."

The desire for blood and retribution and dominance may have started this, but it certainly didn't win.

KJ's sigh is almost invisible. If I weren't a Were I probably wouldn't have heard it. "I know."

The pups must've woken up, because I can hear the faint sound of their growls and yips as they play. I listen, knowing KJ can hear them too. They're the proof of what Alistair is up against. "We'll win because we'll do what it takes."

Finally, KJ moves. He turns to look at me as he nods. "I know."

25

HUNTER

12 MONTHS BEFORE

By that evening Alistair's visit has me so agitated that I decide I might as well use the energy to patrol the enclosures. The darkness, after a summer of light, is welcome, as is the silence. There's so much talk about how to save the wolves—who to breed, when to feed, how to save them. I think that's why I prefer being out here. When the uncertainty of the future becomes too much, it's easier to feel like I'm doing something when I'm out patrolling and protecting.

Not to mention I get to see her...

I reach the corner of the soft-release enclosure. The biggest of them all, it's the one enclosure that hasn't been used yet. But with the birth of the four pups, in a year's time, it will be preparing them to live back out in the wild. Seeing those four white wolves survive and thrive has meant the choices I've made may actually have been the right ones.

Heading back down the fence, I stop. The wind has taken a break for a change, and the night air is still. All that intercepts the silence is my breath. It's so quiet I'm pretty sure I can hear my own heartbeat. With the fence behind me, I take in the darkness. My Were sight can make out the shadows of undulating tundra and little else. Nothing moves. Nothing else breathes.

This is what the nights were like before my wolf of gold appeared. I can see why KJ was so worried. Spending all that time alone, doing nothing but protecting our wolves from the threat of hate, would have snapped something in my brain.

At the same time, the absence of anything means it's going to be another uneventful night. KJ has pointed out many a time that we have cameras to keep an eye on the wolves and the enclosures. He says my evening walks are more to feed my inner control-freak than anything.

Running my fingers down the wires, I guess he could be right.

Not that I'd admit that to him.

Whether I walk these fence lines or not, quiet is good in our corner of the world. It's probably why Alistair was trying to stir up trouble. The past few months have been muted on the wolf-human front. No close contact. No over-reactions. He wouldn't want people becoming complacent in their unfounded fear.

Except he came up empty handed whilst learning exactly the level of determination he's up against.

I've just reached the edge of the breeding enclosure when I decide I'm going to go for a run. Not because I have to, but because I want to. It's been days since I've seen golden wolf, and there's some sort of metaphysical ache in my chest because of it. Maybe I could introduce her to the northern pack. It's not too hard to scent them out when I'm in wolf form.

Having reached a decision, I step up my pace. Her patience, her mischievousness, how she seems as drawn to me as I am to her, have me considering breaking into a jog. A run with her is just what my soul needs.

As I near Sakari's den I slow down, not wanting to alarm her. She doesn't need a happy, possibly delusional, Were disturbing her much-needed sleep. But as I slow, something has me stopping.

There's a scent. A scent that doesn't belong. Holding still, I breathe it in letting it register. My eyes open wide. It's the smell of a human.

Squatting, I squint as I survey the ground. The smell is stronger here, laced with others. As my fingers find the divots of a boot mark I catalog them. Rubber from the sole of the shoes. A vague trace of sweat. The tang of male aftershave.

Someone else has been here, and recently. Someone who isn't part of Resolve.

Foreboding, heavy and slick, settles around my shoulders. Breaking into a jog, I head for the part of the fence where the den is. Within seconds the sound of pups growling and tussling are unmistakable. Except it's night time, when they should be asleep.

And someone was just here.

The smell of meat and blood hits me seconds before I'm there, and the foreboding spreads down my spine like cold, black tar. We don't feed the wolves at night—too likely to draw their wild cousins in.

Reaching the den, I press myself against the fence, scanning the enclosure. The pups are out, and I quickly see why. A slab of meat sits in the center of the clearing before the den, and they're fighting over it.

I've heard of baiting captive wolves, but we haven't come across it. It's one of the reasons we kept Resolve quiet.

Until tonight.

I don't need a run up, adrenaline is jack-knifing through my veins. It propels me over the fence and I land in the enclosure. Two of the pups scatter when I land, but two have their jaws clamped around the bloody chunk, each yanking in a game of tug-of-war.

"No!" I roar, jumping forward and yanking it from their mouths.

One pup manages to tear a shred off as the meat is snatched away whilst the other falls back on its rump. I throw the meat over the fence, disgust roiling in my gut. I look down, hoping I got here in time.

Zephyr and Sakari are have come out, faces alert as they take in the intruder. Breathing heavily, I'm thankful Zephyr has mellowed in his time in captivity, otherwise I couldn't focus all my attention on the pups. I need to make sure they're okay. They pad over to their mother and I watch carefully, not that I know what I'm looking for.

Does Miki look like he's walking a little stiffly? His body, smaller than the others, looks like his legs have been splinted. Another pup bumps into him—Pakak. Which wouldn't be unusual if they didn't both fall over.

Then struggle to get up again.

Moving with all the speed I can muster, I scoop them up. Sakari startles and I hear Zephyr growl. But there's no time. I'm certain these were the two pups playing tug-of-war with the meat moments ago. There's no telling how long the meat has been in the enclosure.

Meat that was undoubtedly poisoned.

Tucking them into my chest, I run. Please let someone be monitoring the screens.

The banging of the gate slamming shut triggers a seizure in Miki. His small, white body starts to convulse in my hands. Every spasm feels like it's directly connected to my heart, every writhe and twist is a stab in my chest.

They need medical help and they need it now.

Relief joins the urgency when the door swings open and

Riley reaches out for one of the pups. I pass her Pakak, her face telling me they've seen what's happened. "They're in the lab."

We rush in to find Dawn there, KJ standing beside her. I lay Miki on the steel table and they contract around him. Riley has Pakak beside him a second later. We step back, giving them room.

Dawn leans close over the two pups. Miki isn't moving whilst Pakak looks petrified. "Symptoms?"

"Miki was walking pretty stiff legged, then he went into convulsions when the gate shut."

Dawn's lips flatline. "Strychnine."

Jesus. The stuff used in rat poison.

Opening Miki's mouth, she holds out her hand. "Activated charcoal." She barks, the first time I've seen her be curt.

KJ passes her something and they lean in to administer it. It looks like they pump the two pups full of it.

Reaching back, KJ brings several syringes around. "Anticonvulsants and muscle relaxant."

Dawn takes them, barely glancing at him. Miki begins seizing again, and they both hold his fragile, young body still. I don't know medical jargon, but it's obvious they need to get that stuff into him as soon as possible.

Riley's hands slip around my arm, holding onto me as her face presses against my shoulder. I reach over to squeeze her hand, wishing there was something I could say.

Dawn looks up. "We need to make sure the other two are okay."

We're at the door and down the hall before she can finish.

Inside the enclosure, the wolves are both standing on alert at the mouth of their den, the pups curled up by Sakari's feet. My heart surges into my throat and I grab the wire, trying to get a closer look—neither of them are moving. Zephyr steps in front of them, blocking them from view. Dammit. We don't have time for this.

Double dammit. I'd probably do the same thing if I were him.

Riley strides up the fence. "They're not moving, Hunter."

I go the other way, hoping another angle may help. I almost trip on the hunk of meat I threw over the side. I stop, nudging it with my foot. It barely looks touched, which has got to be a good thing. I turn toward the den. "They may not have got to the meat. We just need a better view."

Now that we're divided, Zephyr has to choose who he's going to keep an eye on. He picks Riley, the one who's least familiar to him, which works for me. As he turns to keep her in view, the two remaining pups come into sight.

They're wrapped around each other, looking so much less with only half of the litter there. Please let them move...

I hold my breath, as if by stopping my own that'll mean I'll see their chests move, but I don't see anything.

Again, a wolf obstructs my line of vision and my hands clench in frustration. Sakari moves over to her pups. She glances at me before looking down at them.

Is this what she did when she found her last litter dead?

She nuzzles one, gently nudging it with her nose. Desna's whole body shifts on the ground, a limp ball of fur.

My whole body sags, my fingers in the wire the only thing holding me up. Oh god, they're...

Sakari nudges her pup again, and this time Desna opens his eyes to look up at his mother. With a yawn and a mewl, his head drops down again. The sound wakes Kayuh, who shuffles closer to his brother.

"They're asleep." Riley's voice rushes out with relief.

I look at her on the other side of the enclosure. "They were asleep."

We both grin, the expression powered by relief, and watch as Sakari curls around her pups. Zephyr returns to her side, standing as a sentinel beside his family.

I let myself pull in a shaky breath. They didn't eat the meat.

We both head back at the same time, meeting each other at the gate. Riley studies me. "I think you got to them in time."

Wrapping an arm around her shoulder, I turn us toward the building, 'I hope so' rushing through my mind. "It looks like it."

I'm about to open the door when it pushes open. We jump back to find KJ there. He looks pale and drawn, and I don't know if that's a post-adrenalin rush look, or if there's bad news.

He comes outside, rather than bringing us in, which straight away puts me on edge. "Pakak looks like she'll be fine. We gave her some charcoal to absorb any contamination from the poison, just in case. Dawn is just preparing some mince with it for these guys."

I nod. "There's no sign or symptoms in the other guys."

"Good." He pauses, and any relief or joy at the good news is quickly extinguished by dread.

"Miki didn't make it. Dawn said his body was too small for the amount of meat he'd eaten."

"Dammit." My hands tighten into fists. We've just lost another wolf.

Riley gasps then strides straight past KJ. Opening the door, she heads inside without looking back. She'll want to go see Miki, say goodbye.

I don't think I'm ready for another farewell, so I step back. I'm not surprised when KJ follows me. We're both Weres who prefer to digest this stuff away from others. We head around the front, both silent.

Staring out at the horizon, I try to find some words. Hope is what we need right now. "Three still alive. That's good news."

Except KJ is too smart for platitudes. He turns towards me,

his frown tight with tension. "We're hanging by a thread here, Hunter. We have two packs left. These guys and the ones in the north."

The reality of where we're at is a punch in the gut. "We're doing everything we can."

"What if it's not enough?"

Frustration explodes through me. What the hell else am I supposed to be doing? But I reign it in. KJ tends to take enough responsibility for all of this as it is. "It's going to have to be enough."

KJ pulls down his beanie, and I recognize the gesture for what it is. That woolen hat is like a security blanket for him. He tugs it again. "There's something else we can do."

There's an undercurrent in KJ's tone. He says the words low, almost under his breath, like it's a secret or taboo. KJ likes to think outside the square, but there's something about those words that make me uneasy. "What?"

He pulls in a breath, which only increases the edginess. "It's called genetic rescue."

The band around my chest loosens a little. That doesn't sound too much different to what we've been doing. "Which is?"

KJ turns towards me, eyes alight. "So, you know that the biggest threat right now is the genetic bottleneck. Because there's so few of them they're vulnerable to any changes—disease, change of environment…losing even more lives."

I nod. None of this is new.

"For these guys to survive, we need to ensure genetic diversity just as much as keeping them alive long enough to pass on those genes."

Yep, also common knowledge.

"Well, why not go straight to the heart of the problem? Why not increase their genetic options?"

I narrow my eyes. "Why are you telling me this and not

Dawn?" Dawn is the one with all the medical know-how. She would be the one who would know whether this is a good idea.

Another breath in, this one he takes the time to let out. "Because I'm not talking about just wolf genes."

The tone is back. The words heavy but placed down with caution. "What are you talking about, KJ?"

"I'm talking about adding Were genes."

I shoot like I've just been pumped with electricity. "No!"

KJ leaps to his feet too. "Hear me out, Hunter. We add small sections of Were genes, the ones we actually share with them. They actually have a chance."

"We're already giving them a chance. We started the captive breeding program—something my father never would have wanted."

"We're talking de-extinction here, Hunter."

"Things aren't that desperate. What you're suggesting..."

Is...is...wrong.

"Think about it, Hunter. We have what they need, the mix of genes that will keep them alive. We don't have to select wolves, catch them, hold them in cages."

"No."

But KJ is a Were in motion. "There are so many more of us, we carry the blueprints they need to survive."

Holy crap, he's thought about this. Probably for a while now. "Stop, KJ. This is wrong."

"It's what needs to be done."

"No, it's not. We have Zephyr and Sakari. They still have three healthy pups who we're going to make sure survive. There are wolves in the wild."

KJ opens his mouth but I step forward, getting into his personal space. "KJ!" His eyes, fervent and bright, seem to take ages to connect with mine. "No."

He finally stops, my words getting through his zealous fog. "But—"

I don't back down. "It's too far."

He deflates, eyes sliding away as he steps back. I wait, not sure what that means.

Flopping back against the wall, he runs his hands down his face. "I just can't watch them disappear, Hunter. I can't."

I move in, grasping his shoulder. "We don't need to do this to make sure that doesn't happen."

He looks up at me, eyes full of pain. I make sure I hold his gaze. He needs someone to believe for him.

After long seconds he lets out a breath. "Okay."

Tension unwinds from around my chest, making it easier to breathe. I step back. "Good. We've got this, okay?"

"Okay."

"Now don't you have blood tests to do or something?"

KJ pulls up a crooked smile. "We did a double check on the other wolves to make sure there were no more traces of strychnine."

I roll my eyes. "That doesn't surprise me."

KJ reaches up, grasping my shoulder like I just did to him. "Thanks, Hunter. You ground me when this all feels like it's getting out of control."

The irony that I feel the most out of control strikes me, but I grin as I grasp KJ back. "Anytime." Stepping away, I turn back. "Although that one came out of left field. Genetically modified wolves? Using Were genes?"

He narrows his eyes at me, his lips twitching. "It's called genetic rescue. They've used it quite successfully with the Florida panther and the greater prairie chicken."

Shaking my head, I turn back away. Did he just say chicken? "I think your beanie's shrunk and is messing with your head."

"Hey, they were down to forty-six prairie chickens before they saved them with this strategy."

I roll my eyes. "You need more coffee or something."

Once I'm at my truck, I glance back to double check KJ has gone inside. Confirming I'm alone, I lean back against it, everything inside feeling exhausted. A wolf-Were hybrid? KJ is more desperate than I realized. Thank god everything I said was true. We have Sakari and Zephyr. The northern wolves are so isolated that no one bothers them. And our pups are proof the captive breeding program was the right choice.

He just needs time to see that.

Jumping in the truck, I put it into gear. Maybe I can get in a couple of hours' sleep before tonight.

My chest warms, like a certain golden wolf has taken residence in there.

Right now, I'm counting down the hours till it's night-time again. Then nothing is stopping me from heading out and seeing the one soul who makes this world okay.

26

AVA

"O.M.G.!" Riley is bounding from foot to foot. "I can't believe this is actually happening."

Her excitement makes me smile. The first release of wolves you've bred and raised in a captive breeding program is definitely a special one. "You guys have worked really hard towards this."

My words are just as much for Hunter as they are for Riley, but he's too busy inspecting the three big metal crates that now house an adolescent wolf each. In fact, he's barely glanced at me since I've arrived.

Riley flutters around her brother like a bee on speed. "You have no idea, Ava. We lost one as a pup when someone tried to poison them, then we lost their dad."

Hunter's shoulders tense, and I know those words struck a chord. "Well, it's all paid off. These guys are heading out to the wild."

Riley has bounded over to stand beside Josh. She grasps his arm and squeezes it. "I know."

Josh glances down at her, a look in his eyes I've never seen before. "We have twice as many people doing this back at Jacksonville. This is quite an achievement."

Riley turns her gaze back to watching Hunter, and the blush creeping up her cheeks is adorable. She releases Josh's arm like she hadn't realized she'd grabbed it.

Dawn ties back her long hair with a band, a sure sign we're meaning business. "Let's get these guys out there."

I can feel each of the wolves' fear as they struggle to understand what's going on. I'm surprised Dawn doesn't seem to be focusing on calming them more. Peering in through the small holes in the side of the metal crate, I see Pakak's yellow eyes in the gloom. They're wide and feral as she pants.

I never really inherited the Fae ability to calm animals the same way they do. Mom says it involves connecting through a melody, but it's not one I've ever heard. The threads are something I see and feel, so I use them. I've spent time watching these guys in the soft-release enclosure. I've been there when Riley feeds them and when Dawn did their final health check. We have enough of a connection for me to be able to tap into them.

Feeling the gossamer thread that reaches from me to each of them, I pull in a breath, then push it back out with controlled slowness. Infusing the air with all the reassurance I can, I send it to them.

"It's going to be okay, guys," I whisper.

Pakak licks her nose, a sign of nervousness, but she sits nonetheless. I lean over to the adjacent cage, doing the same. It's not much, but it's something considering how stressful this whole process is going to be for them.

When I look up, I find Hunter watching me. I don't know why, but I blush. It could be because he just saw me do something no-one here but Josh knows I'm capable of. Or it could be the intensity in his gaze that has my skin heating. There's so much emotion in those molten eyes that I don't know where one starts and the other finishes.

How could he look at me like that if there isn't something pulling us together?

My mouth parts, my breath disintegrating as the second draws out. But then he blinks, frowns, and looks away.

I start a little when Josh leans in. Looking up, I pretend I don't see the glint in his eye. "You always were an overachiever."

I shove him with my shoulder. He's pointing out that even he's noticed Hunter's antisocial tendencies. But it also means Josh noticed the look Hunter and I just exchanged. "Coming from the guy who read medical texts as bedtime stories for his little sisters."

His face sobers a little. "You know what you're doing?" His hazel gaze flickers to Hunter and back. "There's aiming high and then trying to achieve the impossible."

He's talking about Hunter's loner reputation. But he hasn't seen what I've seen.

Plus, I think he could be my wolf...

"Technically, I was impossible."

My parents, and their amazing connection, defied the rules everyone believed were set in stone by bonding and then having me. Maybe that's why the possibility of something existing between Hunter and me feels more than hypothetical.

It's why even the surreptitious glance Hunter just took is enough to have me believing.

Josh sighs. "Is this like the time you were determined that a certain litter of pups was going to survive despite the loss of their mother?"

The mention of Achak tugs at my heart. There's still been no sign of the wolf I raised and released. I lower my gaze, my voice dropping to a barely-there whisper. "It could be more."

Josh sucks in a breath. "You could be really disappointed, Ava."

What he means is I could be really hurt. I look up to find him looking down at me, concern, maybe fear pinching his face tight.

And he's right. I've led a safe, sheltered existence as the world of Were and Fae wait to see whatever it is I'm supposed to do. Well, I've found something, someone, who has me wanting to be someone who can fulfill that.

I shove my shoulder into his hard chest again. "You'll have to practice doing stitches just in case this all falls apart."

In case I fall apart.

Josh wraps his arm around me, tugging on my hair like he always has. "I'll always be here."

I hug him back. "I know."

Hunter stalks past us, his frown deeper than usual. "Let's get these guys loaded."

Josh grins down at me. He leans in so he can whisper in my ear. "If you can get him to smile, then maybe you've got a chance."

I narrow my eyes at him. "You know I have enough unrealistic expectations resting on my shoulders."

With a chuckle, Josh releases me. "They've never been unrealistic."

"Now, people." Hunter is standing at the truck, arms crossed.

I sigh. I reckon I could do a dodo impersonation and Hunter wouldn't crack a glimpse of a smile. Oh well, no time to ruminate on whether I have my hopes too high—we have wolves to release.

It takes all five of us to lift each crate onto their respective vehicle. Two slip side by side on the truck, whilst a third—the one containing Kayuh—we load onto the trailer behind the quad. We strap them down, all silent and serious, aware of how monumental what we're about to do is.

Riley sighs as we step back to check out our handiwork. "I wish I was going with you."

Hunter squeezes her shoulder as he strides past. "The less people the better. This is their first taste of the wild."

She sighs again, this time deeper and louder. "I know. It's just hard saying goodbye, you know?"

Josh walks over to stand beside her. "It's totally worth it when we get to see a glimpse of them out there." A lopsided grin tips up his lips. "Although we have trees for them to hide behind."

Riley flicks back her fringe, rolling her eyes at him. "Pfft, they'd drop leaves in our nonexistent pool." She brightens. "It would be pretty awesome to see them out there, though."

Josh shifts in a little closer and their hands brush. "We'll head out tomorrow."

The smile that graces Riley's face seems to suck the air straight out of Josh. I don't blame him, that girl seems to do everything at a hundred-and-ten percent. "It's a date."

Dawn smiles as she climbs into the truck. I wonder how Hunter feels about his little sister making that proclamation, only to find him shaking his head as he climbs onto the quad. "We need to get them there first."

It seems he's either happy for Riley to have found love...or this isn't unusual behavior for her. Surely she's not a girl to hook up with whoever catches her fancy, is she? Glancing at Josh though, I realize it won't matter. Josh has his heart set and there's nothing I could say to change his mind. I feel myself flush. Those words seem a little too close to the conversation we just had about me.

Striding over to the truck, I climb in the passenger side without glancing back. Maybe it's time I had some pride.

Dawn turns on the ignition, the old engine rumbling to life. "Let's get these guys out there."

The truck unhurriedly accelerates and I know this is going to be a slow trip. The tundra tends to be rocky and bumpy, and the less we stress the wolves the better. Glancing in the rear vision mirror I see Hunter right behind us. The wind whips at his face and t-shirt, touching his skin in ways I haven't. I have to look away and remind myself that handsome face has never smiled at me.

As we drive past the enclosures, I see Sakari standing at the fence. She watches the two-vehicle convoy and I wonder if she realizes who's in the three crates we carry. Her ears erect, her gaze intense, I can't help but feel she does. She's watching her babies leave her.

Or maybe it's because she's watching her three pups head out to a life beyond the fence she stands behind.

As we head due north, I take in the uninterrupted space around us. In a couple of short months, this vista will be covered in snow. "This is different to how we did it at Jacksonville, isn't it?"

Dawn nods. "We had more resources. These guys will have a hard release."

I look out the car window; today the tundra looks lonely and harsh. "We have acclimation pens."

"Exactly. Our wolves got to spend a couple of months there before we let them go out into the wild." Dawn brushes her grey hair back from her face. "We also had more wolves."

Which means there's less room for error. And in captive breeding, that means you can't afford to lose a life.

Glancing over my shoulder, I check the crates. They haven't moved. Hunter is still behind us, maintaining the same steady pace. His face captures the significance of what we're doing. Focused gaze, every muscle tense, he has the look of someone who's willing to do what it takes. I settle back into the seat, feeling that same determination settle in my gut.

When Dawn pulls over, I notice again the sense of familiarity. There are certain places out here that have me feeling like I've been here before, but this is the strongest. I climb out, pulling the air into my lungs. It doesn't smell familiar, but the rocky ground, the low shrubs…I know this place.

I've been here with my wolf.

Hunter parks beside us. Climbing off, he moves to the trailer. "Let's get these guys unstrapped."

Not how my wolf would have spoken. That beautiful, white Were was loving and fun and everything was…easy. He never looked like he wished I were anywhere but here.

And I haven't seen him since I arrived on Evelyn Island. The past couple of weeks have been the most dreamless I've had in two years.

I move to the back of the truck. "I've got Pakak."

Dawn is already undoing Desna.

There's a growl from within Desna's crate telling us the sedatives are wearing off. The timing is just right, except I can feel how scared they are after the drive out here. Just like I did when we left, I send calming energy through our threads. Their terror dies down a bit after a few seconds, but they all remain on edge. That's a good thing. They're about to fend for themselves.

One by one, we lift each crate off—Dawn and me at the front, Hunter and his Were strength at the back. We line them up like blocks, each next to each other, all facing towards the tundra.

Dawn takes her place behind the first. "Get behind one each."

I take my place behind the center crate, Hunter takes the last. I've done this a few times before, and there's always such a sense of being part of something important. I glance at Hunter—this is his first time.

He's staring down at the crate, his perma-frown in place. I get his unease, so much is riding on these three arctic wolves. But it also means he's missing out on experiencing the hope these guys carry.

I lean over a little. "They're about to get the best surprise ever."

Hunter's gaze shoots up and connects with mine. "They are, aren't they?"

I nod, letting the excitement of this moment show on my face. "This is what you've been working towards, Hunter."

He glances down at the crate, out toward the horizon, and then back at me. His copper gaze is a little wide-eyed as he opens his mouth to speak.

Dawn undoes the bolt on the top of her crate. "Let's give them what they need, guys."

I snap back, knowing we need to get this done as quickly as possible. Sliding back my own bolt I hear Hunter do his.

Dawn looks at us both. "One, two, three."

We all lift the door of the cages up and they slide with a whoosh. The three crates now stand open, the wolves inside free to leave. There's silence, my guess everyone is doing exactly what I'm doing—holding their breath as we wait for the first wolf to step out. All we need to do is wait for curiosity to overtake caution.

Quicker than I expected, Desna's head pops out. He scents the air for the wealth of information it can provide him—the current weather, who and what are nearby, how many of them, whether he should be ready to fight or flight. Like he sensed the movement, Kayuh is next, his big, white body emerging from the cage. Last, and the most cautious, is Pakak. She spends long seconds scanning the horizon, acclimatizing like Dorothy would have when she landed in Oz.

Dawn's hand is on her chest as she watches. I glance at Hunter and find him watching them just as intensely. I wish I could move closer like Josh had with Riley, brush my hand against his to show him he's not alone. These three beautiful animals are about to leave. As exciting as it is, Riley was right. It's hard to say goodbye.

One by one, the three wolves leave the safety of their crate, a metaphorical birth from captivity. Who will be the first to leave?

When Achak went through this, he took two steps, sniffed the air, then loped off. There was one glance back over his shoulder, his canine gaze catching mine, before he broke into a sprint. Dad had figured we'd hardly see him from then on, but I hadn't been hurt or worried. Our thread had always been strong—I didn't need him to be something he wasn't for us to stay connected. In fact, asking him to stay would have weakened our unique bond.

The three wolves contract together, seeking safety in each other's familiarity. I'm not surprised when Desna is the first to make a move. Like the leader his name implies, he starts trotting forward, eyes set on the horizon. Kayuh takes his lead and falls behind. Pakak, on the other hand, isn't ready to follow blindly.

She takes a few steps, but pauses, looking back at us. She retraces her steps, coming in closer.

I feel Dawn tense. There's always a small chance that a wolf will take the opportunity to attack, but I know that's not what's happening here.

This is the worry with captive breeding—the familiarity with humans. Wolves in the wild understand that humans are dangerous. Naturally shy, they prefer as much distance between themselves and humans. Wolves who've been fed by humans become confused. These animals have been raised by those who love them and are fighting for their survival. They've never seen the threat we can pose.

Pakak stops again.

Dawn tsks, and I'm surprised at her annoyance. Hunter looks to me, and for the first time, I realize I'm more of an expert than he is.

He thinks it's because I've been involved in captive breeding. But he doesn't realize that I know Pakak is torn, and it's her thread to Hunter, the one that is glowing the brightest, that has her wanting to stay.

"You need to tell her it's okay to go." Hunter does that blink of his and I jut my chin towards Pakak. "She's finding it hard to let go."

"I've barely even touched her."

Which is exactly what should be done with a wolf you plan on releasing to the wild.

I shrug. "Connections are built on more than touch."

KJ and Riley told me the stories of the sibling pup they lost, and how Hunter had stayed around, practically on twenty-four-hour watch, as Pakak, the other pup who was poisoned, slowly recovered.

Turning back, he takes a few steps around the crate. Dawn takes a step forward but I put out an arm to stop her. Glancing at her, I wonder how she can't see it. "He just needs a sec."

It's then that I notice how thin her own thread with Pakak is. Learning to ignore the threads is something I've managed to do in this isolated corner of the world. It's a skill I know will come in handy when I head back to civilization, one I've been practicing. Except now as I tune into it, I see Dawn's thread, a Fae Elder's, is almost emaciated. Thin and spindly, there's barely a hair-width connecting her to the white wolf.

Dawn glances at Hunter, who's slowly moving towards Pakak. "He needs to be careful."

She really doesn't see it. Maybe this is her way of dealing with the loss of the pups she coordinated the birth of. "She only needs one thing."

Hunter walks around the crates and stops a few feet away from Pakak. She looks at him, tail high and alert, eyes not leaving his. He stands there for long seconds and Dawn shifts beside me. But I'm already smiling. Hunter knows what he needs to do.

Turning, Hunter takes in the wide expanse of landscape before them, then takes a step forward. Pakak watches as he takes several more. "Remember? You're that one who gets into everything."

Pakak's tail twitches. Although the words wouldn't make sense, they'd be familiar, and they capture her essence. Then it wags just a little.

And then she's bounding forward, straight past Hunter, and out into the wild. With a last look back, she lopes after her brothers.

A sigh slips past my grin. Their thread stretches and stretches as she moves away, but I know it's one that will never be broken. Hunter watches her leave, his back straight, arms by his side. He looks like a general watching his unit disperse now that the war is over. I half expect him to salute her.

When he turns to look back at me, I see something I haven't seen before and I catch my breath, startled. Hunter is smiling. It seems to short-circuit my brain. Flashing white teeth, lips molded into a gorgeous arch, it's his eyes that have my heart stopping. Glowing and copper, they're alive with light.

I find my grin morphing into something else. A gentler, happier version that can only be a mirror of what Hunter is holding on his face. A feeling that only seems to add to his.

I vaguely register Dawn stepping around me. "Well done, Hunter. She just needed a nudge."

For the first time, it's my turn to blink first. I yank my gaze away from the beauty that is Hunter smiling, glancing at Dawn. She's making it sound like she knew that all along.

Dawn wraps an arm around my shoulder. "Ava was right."

I flush, one, because of the praise, but two, for thinking like that about Dawn. This is the woman who has dedicated her life to wolves the minute they were threatened.

Hunter strides back to the truck, throwing me a glance that still holds traces of his smile. "Hope she doesn't get like Riley when you say that to her."

Dawn squeezes my shoulder. "You wouldn't quote that every day for the next six months, would you?"

With a cheeky grin at both of them, I shrug. "I think four months will probably be enough."

There's a chuckle from Hunter, but I don't get to see his face because he's already standing beside the crate that Pakak left not long ago. "Let's get packed up then, shall we?"

Muscles bulging in a way that's hard to look away from, he lifts each of the crates singlehandedly back onto the truck. This time, he stacks the third onto the other two. I'm so gobsmacked at the show of strength that he's done it before I get to offer a hand. Rushing forward, cheeks pink thanks to more than just the cold, I grab the straps and pass them to him.

"Thanks." His glance is brief, and I get the sense the word is loaded.

I bring back the smile that had bloomed just a moment ago. Remembering I'm trying to have a little pride, I swallow the 'anytime' that was just born on my tongue. "Sure."

Next, Hunter unhitches the trailer from the quad and attaches it to the back of the truck. Dawn looks at him questioningly.

Hunter scratches the back of his head. "I'm going to stay here for a bit longer, just to keep an eye out."

Which is exactly what I did when Achak and his litter were released. Not seeing them was just as reassuring, because it meant they hadn't returned.

I wonder if he's going to look at me—even the briefest glance I'd take as an invite to stay with him. We even shared that smile only minutes ago.

But Hunter turns his back and heads to the quad. Leaning against it, he crosses his arms as he gazes out in the direction the wolves disappeared.

Dawn climbs in the truck and starts the engine, but Hunter doesn't turn around.

The Ava of the past few days would stay behind, despite the signals Hunter is giving off. Ava who has some pride and a whole lot of sense would climb in that truck too.

I walk over to the door and pull it open. The metal creaks and crunches. Still, Hunter stays where he is.

Well, I have my answer. The smile meant nothing. The progress was imaginary.

I decide there and then, to be the Ava I want to be.

27

AVA

It's only when the truck is rumbling away that Hunter turns around. I see him glance at first, surreptitiously, but then he turns around, arms falling to his side.

I smile at him. "I decided to stay too."

Blink. Blink again.

I hold my hand up. "There's no point frowning now."

Hunter's lips twitch as he shakes his head. "With that sort of tenacity, I'm glad you're on the wolves' side."

I walk around to the other side of the quad bike, leaning against it and crossing my arms just like he did. "I stayed around after we released the last lot at Jacksonville."

Hunter stares out ahead. There's no longer any sign of the three white wolves. "Just to make sure they don't come back."

"Exactly."

He glances back at me. "How did they go?"

I feel my face soften as I remember. "They were a wonderful success. They acclimatized beautifully."

Hunter looks back out again. "So they all survived?"

"They did." The pang twists in my chest again. "Except for one who escaped after he was cured from the Furious virus."

Hunter moves closer. "He escaped?"

"Yeah. Jumped the fence somehow. My parents think he may have used a nearby rock to launch himself."

Hunter seems to still for a second. "That's one determined wolf." He leans on the other side of the quad. "No-one's seen him?"

I look away, deciding the tundra is probably safer to look at right now. "Nope. No one."

"He was important to you."

I shrug. "They all are."

"But this one, he was special."

Surprised at his perceptiveness, I glance back. "I helped raise Achak after their mother died. He was the sweetest, wildest wolf I've ever met."

Hunter arches a brow. "But you bonded because you didn't give up?"

I narrow my eyes at him. "I'm known to be patient."

Hunter snorts as he looks forward again. "Poor guy never stood a chance."

I have to stop my breath from sucking in. It's words like that, the fact that Hunter is standing right beside me like we have these casual chats all the time, that makes me glad I chose to stay.

Silence settles between us, but it's not an awkward one. It feels comfortable, natural…familiar.

Could Hunter, despite it all, be my white wolf?

I stare straight ahead as I decide it's time to get some answers. "There's something centering about being out here. It's so isolated, but you don't feel alone."

I sense him glance at me, but I don't look at him. There's a pause and I wonder if he's going to answer.

"There's nothing like it."

I nod. "I can see why you love it." I shoot a glance from the corner of my eye. Hunter is looking at the horizon again. "I would imagine staying awake night after night would be hard though. No company, no distractions."

This is the question I've been wanting to ask for so long. Maybe Hunter saw me in his dreams too. That would explain his look when we first saw each other. He looked like he recognized me.

I swear I sense him tense. "You don't sleep when you're on patrol."

Oh. "You never dozed off without meaning too?"

"No."

Right. That one word hurts more than I expected. "Did you ever get lonely?"

Hunter frowns. He's definitely not relaxed anymore. "Not really."

"But everyone needs someone." I haven't met a person who doesn't have threads tying them to another.

He pushes away, dusting down his jeans in short, sharp movements. "Apparently my imagination was able to keep me company."

What in the world does that mean? Despite the we're-done-here vibes, I decide I'm not going to let this go. This is too important.

I open my mouth to ask—

A *crack* stings through the evening air. It has my heart leaping and my body freezing. Hunter is beside me before I've had a chance to blink.

I look around. "That was—"

Hunter is scanning the horizon, eyes narrow, body on high alert. "A gunshot."

The images of the northern wolves, naked and bloody, flash through my mind.

Poachers.

My hand flies to my mouth. "Oh god, the wolves!"

Hunter is on the quad in one swift movement. He turns to me, eyes fierce with determination. "Wait here."

I'm already shaking my head. "I'm going with you."

"I'm not taking you closer to where that came from, Ava."

My mouth snaps shut on the retort that was ready to go. It's because I'm not a Were. Right now, with a poacher out there, I'm little more than a fragile human. I look away. For some reason, that's always been an inescapable fact.

He spears his fingers through his hair. "Dammit. Why didn't you leave with Dawn?"

Like his body language told me to. If we had time, those words would probably sting, adding to the prick of pain that has already established in my chest. I take a step back. "To be honest, I'm not really sure."

Jaw working, Hunter looks away. With a growl of frustration, he leaps off the bike again. "I'll be back."

Before I have time to respond, Hunter breaks into a sprint. Disappearing down the rise, he shifts. In a blur of white I don't have time to process, he's off in the direction of the released wolves.

I wrap my arms around myself, watching him run. Please let them be okay.

The second gunshot has me ducking reflexively. I'm pretty sure it came from the east and my hunch is confirmed when Hunter turns right. Gosh, he's fast. Powering over the tundra, he's a machine of muscle and speed. Even at a distance, you can see the determination etched in each powerful stride, in the unwavering direction. Within moments he's disappeared around the base of a hill, just like the others did.

Although what's he going to do when he finds them?

Oh no. What if he comes across the poacher?

I'm on the quad, desperately scanning the control within a

blink, I've turned the ignition before I can draw a breath, then I'm frantically flicking switches to the same rapid beat of my heart as I try to get this thing going. I've seen Hunter do this. I've studied his movements like a girl trying to get some answers. Surely I can figure this out.

When the bike lurches forward, I almost lose my grip. Instead, I tighten every single muscle and accelerate. The quad jerks again and speeds up. I can feel my hair fan out behind me as I angle the machine in the same direction as Hunter.

Jolting over the terrain, my heart thunders and my eyes scan the horizon. We can't afford to lose these wolves, and I know without a doubt that Hunter will do anything to keep them safe.

Well, he's not going to do it alone.

Powering forward, I can't see Hunter, nor have I heard any more gunshots. I don't know whether that's a good thing or not.

The land slowly creeps up hill here, rounding around the mountain. The cold stings my face making me catch my breath, but I don't slow down. I need to find them.

As I scan for wolves or people or Were the quad bounces as it hits a depression, then spikes as it hits a rock. It's a battle to keep the bike steady as I land with a jolt and the bike swerves. My already thundering heartbeat becomes a roar in my ears. The closer I come to the mountain, the rockier and more uneven the ground. But Hunter got here moments ago, and so much can happen in a moment. I can't afford to slow down.

Except I have no idea where I'm going. I followed a Were and a sound that are now gone. I have no Were scent that I can track with, no Were hearing to pause and listen with.

But I do have the threads.

The moment I think it, they appear. Two gossamer connections that disappear around the mountain base. Which means they must be together. Like I'm some adrenalin junkie, I accelerate some more. I don't have time to be worried about crashing.

I head a little more north, following the ribbon of light. The land dips down, probably into a bog, so I finally slow. As the landscape appears I brake hard. Hunter is in human form, kneeling just a few yards away.

Kneeling over the body of a wolf.

The quad squeals and slides to a halt and I leap off, heart lodged high in my throat. Please, please, please…

Hunter doesn't say a word at my arrival, and when I tumble to my knees beside him, I realize why. It's Kayuh laid out before him, and Kayuh is no longer all white. Crimson red spreads across his snowy fur. Hunter is leaning over him, his hands deep in the ruff of his neck, the place where the blood seems the most concentrated.

My stomach pitches in my chest and the taste of bile stings my throat. Not Kayuh.

"You need to do something." Hunter's voice is hoarse. Desolation has wiped his face of any other emotion as he stares at the wolf he protected from before he was born.

I collapse to my knees beside him. Kayuh is motionless, but then I see the feather-light panting that flickers over his chest. "He's alive?"

"Barely." Hunter looks up at me, eyes pleading so hard it breaks my heart. "You need to help him."

Oh god. Hunter thinks I can heal him?

I reach out shaking hands, fingers hovering over the blood-soaked fur. "I don't…"

"The bastard shot him. Twice." Hunter's forearms flex, his hands trying to stop the bleeding. "I got here just as he was about to…"

Hunter looks away, his head coming down to wipe his forearm on his sleeve. I have no idea how I'm going to tell him this.

"Hunter, I can't—"

"Just try, Ava!"

The anguish and agony in Hunter's voice slices through me. I know I have to give it a shot.

Tapping into the thread that connects me to Kayuh, I close my eyes. My hands move down of their own volition, sinking into warm, sticky fur. In the dark behind my eyelids, the thread is a shimmering, fragile being that takes my breath away. I blend into it in a way I've never been able to explain, feeling how weak it really is.

It confirms what I saw on Hunter's face—Kayuh is close to death.

I push as much life as I can into our connection. I channel it with every fiber of my being. Tensing my whole body like I can somehow hold onto him, I strain to concentrate. I'm not letting this one go.

"You can do this, Ava."

Hunter's words filter in, a mantra that I hope is true. Wanting to do this for him as much for Kayuh, I hunch down, pouring everything I can into the barely breathing body I'm holding.

The thread blooms with life and my heart lifts. I feel Kayuh pull in the deepest breath since I found him and Hunter. It's working?

But then the thread thins and thins again, like its being stretched and stretched and stretched. No! I feel like I'm going to explode, I put so much intensity into feeding life into this wolf.

Except it doesn't help. It does nothing.

I know the second he's gone, because the stretched-thin thread snaps, all the precious life-force flowing out without a body to hold it.

My eyes shoot open. "No!"

"No, no, no." Hunter's words are a chant of pain as his shoulders cave in. He sits there, like the grief is too much to carry.

I watch as the shimmery fluid that no-one else can see seeps out and sinks into the ground like a vein has been severed. My shocked brain watches it be slowly absorbed.

Not Kayuh.

Not another one.

My bloody hands fall to my sides. "I'm so sorry, Hunter."

Hunter pushes back so fast, I startle. He takes a few steps to the puddle of melted snow not far away and starts to wash the blood from his hands. I wait, but he doesn't say anything.

With no more words, I stand too, suddenly sick at the sight of my red hands. The smell of copper, the sight of crimson, the feel of it tightening my skin as it dries becomes overwhelming. I'm beside Hunter in a flash, scrubbing away the harsh evidence of my failure.

When I'm done, Hunter is back standing beside Kayuh, staring down at the bloodied body. I stay where I am, my legs lacking the strength to move. I don't need more irrefutable proof of the loss of life. I just got to see and feel it.

Curling my legs up, I'm about to sink my head into my arms when a flash of light catches my gaze. Frowning, I look closer. Silver is an alien color in the muted hues of the tundra. I pick up the knife, taking in the wooden handle and the stunted, curved blade. I lift it up to find Hunter watching me.

"The coward dropped it the minute he saw me."

My frown deepens. "He was going to finish him off?"

"No, Ava." Hunter's ferocious gaze pins me. "That's a skinning knife."

The knife drops from my numb hand, clunking to the ground. A skinning knife. He was going to skin Kayuh before he was dead?

Bile, hot and bitter, hits my throat, but I swallow it down. I've shown enough weakness today as it is. Denial tries to gain some momentum, but Hunter must see it on my face because he's already shaking his head.

"He would have done it and the bastard wouldn't have blinked." His hands spear into his hair. "It was the same guy, Ava."

"What?" I stand, confused.

"The guy who shot Kayuh was the one who shot my dad."

"But, that was almost two years ago."

"He was wearing the exact same parka as the guy who shot my dad."

I gasp. Stepping forward, I want to touch him, but know that I won't. Hunter doesn't need me pushing his comfort zones right now. "Are you sure?"

His eyes are burnished pools of anguish. "It's not something I'm ever going to forget. Not many people wear red out here. He was there for one reason."

To kill wolves.

My hand flutters by my side, yearning for contact. "He didn't know, Hunter." There's no way that man would have shot the wolf if he knew Weres existed.

Hunter licks his lips, eyes narrowing. "I'm not sure it matters anymore."

This time my breath sucks in and stays there. I know he's lost so much, but surely he's not saying what I think he's saying. What would have happened if he'd come across this poacher? "Hunter…"

He turns away. "We need to get back."

And tell the others. Dawn and her unwavering commitment. Riley and her barely contained enthusiasm. KJ and his deep-seated drive. Even Josh, who has adopted this cause as his own. This news is going to cripple them.

I turn to leave. What's there that I can do anyway? Today I learned exactly what my limitations are. I couldn't save Kayuh. Why would I think I can change Hunter's mind?

"What about Kayuh?"

Hunter's gaze flashes to mine, and I'm taken aback by the anger. "I'll come back for him. He deserves a grave that's deeper than a few inches."

I can't hold his gaze, not sure what it's communicating. Frustration at the injustice, or fury at my uselessness?

I walk over to the quad, waiting. Hunter climbs on and I slip behind him. His back is knotted with tension, his sides hard and hot as I clasp them.

Hunter is holding on by a thread himself.

The drive back to Resolve is a jarring, silent one. I don't know who Hunter is punishing more as he doesn't bother to dodge ruts or rocks, but it doesn't really matter. The crushing and smashing of my joints will never be enough penance.

We just released three adolescent pups, and within a short space of time, we're down to two.

Hunter pulls up at the front of Resolve and I slide off. I expect him to drive off but he kills the engine.

Staring straight ahead, he sighs. "Why don't you go wash up? You don't have to be here for this."

I wait for him to turn and look at me. "I didn't have to do anything I've done here."

Hunter's mouth pulls in, and I know that wasn't the response he was expecting. The thought brings a glow to my chest despite everything we've just been through. He shakes his head. "I don't think I've ever met anyone like you, Ava."

And the glow dies like it just got slammed into a bog.

I turn to head in, wishing I hadn't said anything.

Maybe he's right. Maybe we've never met and I'm just drawn to a pretty face and tortured heart.

Maybe I'm wrong.

28

AVA

Collecting the paper off the printer, KJ hands a sheet to Riley and Josh. "This is the roster. We're going to be patrolling these guys twenty-four-seven."

After everyone had gotten over the shock of our news, Dawn had gone into drill sergeant mode. She'd started planning out a patrol roster. I hadn't even pretended my name would be on there. What would I do if I came across a poacher out there? Ask him to please put his gun down?

KJ passes me a sheet too. "You're doing the Resolve perimeter, making sure we don't get any visitors."

I nod. Everyone in the room knows there are enough cameras in this place monitoring all the places that count, and I appreciate the pretense that my being here makes a difference.

Josh frowns down at the paper. "Have you guys had to do this before?"

KJ shrugs. "No. We've seen the odd poacher before, but..."

"But it's always been one here and there?"

KJ nods. "They've always been opportunistic bastards."

Josh looks at me and I know he's thinking of Jacksonville.

We've had the odd wolf shot, hunters proving a point, idiots looking for a challenge. But nothing like this.

Riley combs back her fringe with her fingers. "This feels different."

The northern wolves, their muscles and sinew exposed, feel like they'll haunt me forever. "They've never been this systematic, have they?"

KJ picks up the knife we found beside Kayuh. "Never an entire pack." He holds the blade up to the light. "The other questions is, why are they skinning them?"

I wrap my arms around myself, suppressing a shudder.

The door opens and I tense, knowing exactly who it is. Hunter has been out collecting Kayuh's body. His face had practically been emotionless as he told everyone of his death. Riley had cried as Josh held her. KJ had stared at Hunter like he was trying to imprint something on his brain. Dawn had walked out.

"He's buried. KJ, we're going to need another plaque."

Josh frowns. "You should've told us. We could've helped."

KJ passes Hunter his sheet of paper. "Save your breath, Josh. He works alone."

Hunter seems to ignore the jibe. In fact, he seems to be ignoring the room. He scans the sheet like it holds all the answers.

Looking away, I study my own piece of paper. Essentially, I need to do a few laps of the compound during the night. I consider whether I should wave to the cameras as I pass each one. I mentally shake myself. At least it's something—it's not like I'm going to sleep anyway.

Silence fills the air, but I don't look up. What do I have to say, at any rate? I'm sorry—I thought a bunch of dreams meant I wasn't just a bunch of left-over genes?

There are footsteps, and I hate that I recognize they're Hunters.

Riley stands up. "Where are you going now?"

Hunter taps the sheet. "I'm going to take over from Dawn."

I don't look. For the first time, I don't want to know.

There seems to be a pause, one long enough for me to realize I can't hold my breath forever, but then the door opens and shuts.

I let out the air I'd been holding. It's time I started being more of a realist.

I just need to figure out how to let everyone else know.

"You okay?"

Looking up, I find Josh beside me. I nod, not sure if it's the truth.

Pulling up a chair, he moves in close. His hazel eyes crinkle with concern. "I know how hard it is for you to see the loss of a life."

I glance around the room, but no one seems to be paying attention. KJ and Riley are looking over something on the computer. "It was so unnecessary, Josh."

He sighs. "It always is. Do you want to talk about it?"

"Kayuh held so much potential..." And I couldn't save him. I go back to studying the page, knowing I can ask Josh the question that's camped in my mind, but not having the courage to see that answer on his face. "Am I totally useless, Josh?"

He tugs a lock of my hair and waits. Fortifying myself, I raise my gaze to his.

Josh's face is serious, maybe even a little angry. "Don't let anyone have you thinking that, Ava." He leans forward, hazel eyes intense. "You're compassionate, determined, and strong. You inspire me every day."

I swallow, wondering how in the world I'm ever going to believe that. I thought I was something special. There were glimpses that maybe I am...

My white wolf had me believing that.

I slam down on those thoughts before they can gain momentum. That sort of thinking got me where I am now—confused and hurting. That sort of thinking gave Hunter false hope, and that's not something I'm going to do again.

I stand. "I might go check out my route."

Josh rises too. "Do you want company?"

But I'm already shaking my head. "I'm going to go solo."

I head out the door without looking back, knowing Josh's concern would be dialed up to worry. I'm hoping a bit of a walk will mean I can come back with something that will reassure him.

Outside, the afternoon cold hits my cheeks and I snuggle down into my scarf. It's probably a good thing I won't be around for the cooler months. I head for the fence line, planning on doing a lap, glad it will warm me up.

I've just come to the corner of the first enclosure when I discover Sakari standing there, almost like she was waiting for me. Seeing as she's only a few feet away, I pause. If she doesn't want me around, then I'm happy to give her some space.

She watches me through the wire, those intelligent eyes of hers assessing me. My shoulders drop as she stands there, obviously not intending on moving.

"You're not making this any easier, you know."

Why does she have to feel so familiar?

Sakari sits, ears and eyes alert. I can feel that she's inviting me closer.

Moving forward, I settle myself beside the fence, head and shoulder leaning against the wire. Maybe she can sense that we have something in common right now. We're both grieving—Sakari has lost her mate and her pups, I've lost something I never had.

Without hesitating, she comes and settles beside me. She sits so we're facing the same way, staring down the fence line, and rests her shoulder against mine. I suck in a breath and feel her do it at the same time. Simultaneously, we sigh.

It must be my connection with animals that means I can do this, some product of the threads. Not to mention Sakari has spent two years in captivity now—she's used to humans. Instead of getting back on that merry-go-round, I decide to just enjoy the closeness of such a majestic being. Her shoulder is warm beside mine, her breathing matching mine. I wish everyone could feel this with some part of the animal kingdom.

When Sakari rises, I know our time is up. She looks at me, golden eyes level with mine, for the longest moment. Then she pushes her head forward, pressing it against my shoulder before trotting off to her den.

I exhale, grateful for whatever that was, not sure exactly what it was. I wonder if the others have seen this on the camera and if so, what they think of it. To be honest, I don't know the answer to that one either.

"There you are."

I startle and jump to my feet as I recognize the voice. Dawn is coming up behind me, a tired smile on her face and a vet pack slung over her shoulder.

I summon a weak smile. "Hi, Dawn."

Her reply smile is broad and full of the Fae serenity that humans are so drawn to. "Waiting to see if Sakari would come over?"

I glance back but Sakari hasn't surfaced again. "She was just here. She seems...quiet."

Dawn drops the vet pack to the ground. "She's adjusting to life without her mate." And her pups. It's probably a good thing she doesn't know what happened to Kayuh. "She's actually the safest out of them all right now."

Because of the poachers. "At least we got on top of Furious. That's one less battle we didn't need right now."

"Oh gosh, Furious." Dawn's eyes widen with alarm.

I'm instantly on alert. "What about it?"

"Hunter just took over the patrol shift." She glances down at the black bag by her feet, "But I forgot to hand over the vet pack."

I look at it too. "Wouldn't he have one on the quad?"

"I took this one off to restock it."

Oh. For a second I wonder if he can just do without it for this one shift, but I instantly quash that down. We've discovered too many times how unsettled things are at the moment. "Someone will need to drop it off."

"Can you bring it to him?"

I have to hold myself in place as every cell in my body wants to take a step back. "I can't."

Dawn's eyes fill with something that's very close to sympathy. "I know things have been...rocky between you two."

I blink, not sure what to say to that.

She raises her shoulders in an apologetic shrug. "But you're the best person for the job."

I shake my head. "I'm really not."

"My guess is you can locate him, Ava. The tundra is a big place—he could be anywhere."

My jaw slackens but I catch it in time. Have I been that obvious? "Josh could—"

Her hand comes to rest on my shoulder. "It's the Fae in you, maybe the splash of Were. But my guess is you could probably find anyone if you wanted to."

I've been able to track Hunter through the threads. I've never needed to use that skill over large distances before now...

But it doesn't mean I'm willing to go see Hunter. There's only so much punishment this little mixed-breed can take. "Maybe you're right Dawn, but I don't think I'm the right person to go out and see Hunter."

Dawn sighs. "I know he can be grouchy, but it's only because he's spent so much time out there alone, looking after those wolves." She throws me a wry glance. "I wouldn't be surprised if the rebel in him meant he spent more time as a wolf out there than human."

I straighten and the pressure on my shoulder increases. A wolf.

Hunter was a wolf. A white wolf.

A white wolf who ran to save Kayuh.

A white wolf who I've seen before but was too frantic to recognize!

I'm grabbing the vet pack before I can give myself time to think about the decision I just made. "You know what? Maybe I will take this to him."

It's time to trust my gut.

Dawn beams a smile whose glow spreads across her face. "Thank you, Ava. I knew I could depend on you."

I kiss her cheek on the way past. "Thank you."

It's time to get some answers.

Inside the shed, I strap the vet pack to the second quad. Deciding it's time to mold my own fate, I jump on and start the engine. Like I've been driving these things all my life, I nudge it out of the shed. As the weak sunshine strokes my face, I almost smile. This feels much better than apathy.

Driving out over the savage landscape, I tap into what Dawn realized intuitively but I've never shared. The thread that connects me to Hunter stretches out like a homing beacon, a line of light for me to follow. Hunkering down against the wind, I narrow my eyes. Without a muscled, warm Were body to shield me, this trip is going to be a little less comfortable.

When I see a white wolf in the distance, my heart does a little hop in my chest. Have I found him already?

But I soon realize the body isn't big enough. Which means it's one of the pups.

I slow. One of the pups far closer to Resolve than it should be.

Bringing the quad to a stop, I frown as I watch him. The wolf is moving fast. He's running across the tundra, a blur of speed that has me narrowing my eyes.

He's heading straight towards me.

He comes in closer and I realize it's Desna, he was the only one left that had that size. He's the wolf we all assumed would become an alpha of his own someday. He disappears into a dip in the landscape and I kill the engine. Something has me on edge.

When he rises again, he's slowed. He sniffs the air, confirming that I'm here. He's obviously deciding what his next step is, and knowing wolves, that'll be to turn around and keep a safe distance. It maintains a buffer, a comfort zone of sorts. I'm happy for him to dictate it—he'll probably head back to the safety of the wilds in a moment.

Desna shakes his head, and I frown when he starts moving again. There's an energy about him that's familiar. He's pacing, like he's patrolling a border. It means his approach has a zig-zag trajectory—left to right, right to left.

And that zig-zag motion is slowly bringing him closer.

The land dips again and I push myself up on the quad, straining to see if he's going to appear where I hope he doesn't. He breaches the slope and my heart-rate picks up. Desna's erratic energy has brought him closer.

Close enough for me to see his face.

Eyes bright with an inner fire, his tongue lolls out of his mouth. A mouth covered in froth.

No...

Slowly, carefully, I reach behind me, feeling with my fingers for the zip on the vet pack. I don't find it straight away, and my fingers scrabble along the edge. I need to get it open, but I can't take my eyes off Desna.

There are two more rises between me and him. His erratic zig-zagging changes. Now he runs and stops. Paces and stops. There's no rhythm, no pattern, which only increases the agitation shivering up my spine. I tell myself this gives me more time to get what I need.

My fingers connect with the metal of the zipper, and I tug. Desna seems to stop in that second, so I still. His eyesight, so much better than mine, is probably taking in every one of my movements. He hasn't taken his gaze off me since he started this trajectory.

Desna doesn't move, so I tug again. A low scratch fills the arctic air as it starts to undo. Desna's head spikes higher and I stop.

I just want to help you.

Then I hear the growl—a low, ominous grinding of rage. Without the obstruction of trees, it spears across the distance between us. It's a sound I've heard before. Images of Achak, a wolf I hold a deep connection with, rabid and frenzied for blood above me, has pure fear pulsing along my nerves.

Furious.

Don't do this, Desna.

Like he heard the words, as if they were the green light he was looking for, Desna launches forward.

I yank at the zip and the vet pack opens. Taking my eyes off the missile who has me in its sights I grab the tranquilizer gun. Desna has covered more distance than I'd hoped in those few seconds, the growling is now a threatening sound that feels too close.

I grip the gun tight, willing the trembling in my fingers to stop. I don't have much time.

Scrabbling, I grab three darts and jam one into the bolt. When I lift it, I find Desna is only yards away. I line up the sight with the rabid animal who has violence in his eyes, but my hands are trembling as adrenalin peaks through my body.

My mind already knows that by the time Desna is close enough for me to shoot, there won't be enough time for the sedative to take effect. My only hope is it kicks in before he's done too much damage.

I pull the trigger desperately, but the red dart haphazardly slices through the air above him.

I whimper, registering the ice of tears on my face. All I needed was a little more time.

Taking a deep breath, I lock my muscles. My hand is barely shivering as I line up the next shot and pull the trigger. A split second later the dart embeds itself in Desna's shoulder.

And the instant it does, he rears and roars. As the pain hits him it feeds the fury.

Oh god.

He howls his anger one more time, his intention clear. You hurt me, I hurt you. His head drops as his trajectory becomes an arrow—straight at his target.

I've already loaded the last dart, I raise and shoot, knowing there's no time to aim. By the grace of fate, it slams into his throat. This howl of pain, the shake of his head, doesn't slow his momentum.

With the heaviness of inevitability a rock in my chest, I huddle down on the quad, knowing there's no protection it can give me. Within a blink, Desna is on the last rise. As I feel my heart rap out the staccato of its last beats, he covers the remaining feet between us.

As I raise my arms to defend myself, he launches into the air. His eyes are luminescent with violence, his teeth covered in lather, and I know the virus is powering his strength.

All I needed was a little more—

The rush of air behind me blows my ponytail in my face. There's a roar and a collision of bodies, and I wait for it—the power of the blow, the pain of the landing feeling like a scratch compared to what will come next.

But I feel nothing.

Scrabbling my hair back from my face, I freeze.

A massive white wolf has just leaped over me and crashed into Desna. The two bodies, both the color of snow but one so much bigger than the other, slam into the ground. They tumble over the rocky soil, white on white, melding and tangling.

Even before they've stopped, the larger wolf has righted himself. He slides back on his paws, already looking to gain forward momentum. Completely focused on Desna, he's all raw power and determined strength.

I know without a doubt that it's Hunter.

Desna's body skids to a stop and before he has a chance to right himself, Hunter leaps. Mouth open, teeth bared, he aims for Desna's neck.

I jump off the quad, arms reaching out as if I can stop what's going to happen next.

Hunter's jaw clamps around the white wolf's throat. Desna struggles, growling and writhing, and Hunter's mouth tightens then stops. Desna, wild and rabid, fights the hold pinning him down. Hunter growls, a deep, low sound of warning, and I almost trip at the threat it holds.

As I right myself I prepare to run again. Except I slow. Hunter could have killed Desna in any of the seconds that just passed.

Desna goes limp, his whole body passively submitting. One red dart is still in his neck, the other must have been knocked out during the tumble.

Maybe it was enough…

I see Hunter's nostrils flare and his eyes dart back to me. I stop.

As I watch, Desna's body slowly goes limp, his furious eyes closing. Hunter relaxes his hold but doesn't let go, watching and waiting to see if Desna is really out of it. Several breaths later he steps back. Desna's unconscious body stays where it is.

I race back to the quad and grab the vet pack. With hands that want to shake, but knowing I don't have time, I administer first the vaccine and then the globulin. Hunter stays beside me like a bodyguard.

Stepping back, I look at the still form of Desna. He was infected. He was infected and almost died.

Oh god. I almost died.

I look up to find the white wolf watching me.

Something shifts in my chest, a sweet, aching feeling. He's looking at me in a way I've seen so many times before.

It's my wolf.

Walking forward, I come eye to eye. His copper gaze is a glorious mix of familiar and unfamiliar. There's no doubt in my mind that he's the one I've seen before.

"Hunter. For two years I've been having dreams." I suck in a breath. "Dreams of a white wolf."

Hunter shakes his wolf head and steps back.

But I close the distance again. "They were so real. The wolf and I were so connected."

When Hunter shifts back to human, it startles me. I notice the flash of bare chest, his wolf tattoo, and then look up into his eyes again.

He looks like I'm torturing him. "Ava. You need to stop."

"No, you need to hear this. It's why we feel drawn to each other."

"Please, Ava. This isn't the time."

It's my turn to shake my head. Hunter, my white wolf, just

saved my life. "Have you always been alone when you've been out on patrol?"

Hunter pauses. His mouth closes, his lips thin.

I take a step forward. "Someone has been with you."

"Ava."

Hunter's voice is strangled with pain, but he needs to hear this.

"It's why you recognized me."

Our souls recognized each other.

"You're Ava Phelan, it was inevitable that I be drawn to you. What Were wouldn't?"

"It's why —"

"Stop!"

I freeze at the violence in the one word Hunter just shouted. I swallow, confused.

Hunter's hands spear through his hair. "The only bit you've got right is that I wasn't always alone." He stares at me, copper eyes ferocious. Why does it feel like he's telling me I brought this on myself? "There was someone with me. It was a wolf, Ava. A golden wolf."

The words are a wrecking-ball to my chest. They collapse my lungs, making breathing impossible. I blink through the pain, feeling the sting of tears.

A wolf?

A golden wolf?

I struggle for air, equilibrium, hope. "But—"

"Exactly." Hunter steps back. "There's no such thing as a golden wolf."

And I've never shifted. I've never been a wolf.

I accepted long ago I never would be.

My gaze drops, scanning the ground as if I'm looking for answers. I was so sure...

Hunter's fingers are in his hair again, so hard and rough he almost looks like he's punishing himself. "I'm not the person for you, Ava. I tried to tell you."

Which is the truth. Hunter has communicated from the beginning that this, us, isn't meant to be.

I look up, trying to find some sliver of pride so I can speak again, when my eyes widen as I glance over his shoulder. "Hunter!"

Desna has woken up. Faster than he should have, and he's looking far more alert than I'd expect.

Hunter spins around and he's instantly by my side, standing slightly in front of me.

Desna shakes his head, flecks of spit flicking out. Slowly, he raises his head. I go to step forward but Hunter blocks me. I let it go for the moment. My parents didn't believe Achak would recover either. Hunter just needs to see it for himself.

As Desna's eyes connect with mine my hand flies to my mouth. Oh god...

The yellow of his gaze is filled with fury and malice. His muzzle serrates, revealing teeth shiny with saliva as it drips to the ground.

"Hunter..." My voice is a horrified whisper. "He's still..."

"Don't move."

He's still Furious.

Without any warning, Desna leaps. As he launches into the air, his jaw opens, a deadly trap seeking blood.

Hunter shifts and his wolf form meets Desna midair. Desna yelps as they crash and collide. By the time they've hit the ground, Hunter has his jaws around Desna's head.

"No!" My scream is the agonized cry of someone who knows what has to happen is inevitable.

One flex of his powerful jaw and there's a crunch as Desna's skull collapses. His body falls limp, its thread severed and bleeding as Hunter releases him.

Hunter shifts back to human, chest heaving, shoulders defeated. He doesn't look at me, doesn't seek to comfort me, and I'm glad.

I stand there, shattered slivers of hope that feel like they've cut me all around.

Slain by the truth. Slaughtered by reality.

My dreams were nothing but the imagination of some girl wishing she was special.

And the lancing pain doesn't stop there.

The dead, broken body of Desna is unshakeable proof that the therapeutic vaccine didn't work.

HUNTER

THE DAY BEFORE

"Yes, sir." My hand clamps around the cell phone a little tighter. I keep my voice level and low, hoping I sound mature.

"Noah, remember? As you know, my daughter is someone we're very protective of."

Yeah, because she's the child of the Prime Prophecy. I'm sure she's lived a life lined with cotton wool. I haven't seen any photos of Ava Phelan apart from that one a couple of years ago, but there isn't a Were that doesn't know about her. Personally, I've seen too much to believe that one person can be what we all need.

The gob-smacking thing is that she's being sent here.

"We'll take good care of her, Noah." I use his first name like he's asked, even though it feels alien. I feel about sixteen right now. I keep my voice low and sure. "Dawn is here. I'm sure those two will have a lot to reconnect about."

"It's the only reason we agreed to this crazy idea."

Yep. Cotton wool. Probably organic, hand-picked by virgins, cotton wool. "She'll be safe here, sir—ah, Noah."

A sigh carries through the phone. "Well, we need to make sure this rabies, Furious as it's now been named, doesn't get a foot in the door."

This time my hand tightens again, but it's with determination. "The wolves don't have the numbers to fight it."

"Exactly. Which is why Ava is arriving with the vaccines."

The vaccines. I've already heard the story about two of their wolves being infected. One was cured, but the other killed before they could help it.

"At least we have a game plan." Which is more than we've had for wolves as a whole.

There's a humph of agreement. "You seem like a sensible guy, Hunter. Mature for your age."

Becoming Alpha at sixteen will do that to a person, but I don't say it. I can hear that Noah's trying to convince himself his precious only child is going to be okay. "Rendell means protector of the wolf—we've made that our mission here on Evelyn Island."

Except there are two things that have made Ava famous enough that her reputation arrived long before her. Her inheritance of the Prophecy, meaning the belief that she's some sort of savior.

And the knowledge that for two years, she hasn't changed. It seems she's the least wolf out of all of us.

"I knew your father, Hunter, I'm glad you're carrying the torch."

I'm glad Noah can't see the wince. I doubt Dad would be proud to see that my legacy involves captive breeding. I decide it's time to lighten the mood. "My mom has set up a room for her," I don't mention it's my room seeing as I barely sleep in there anyway, "and she's looking forward to meeting her. She'll be well looked after."

There's another sigh. I've heard the same sound from my mother. It's the sound of a parent struggling to accept things are moving faster than they'd like and it worries them...but they know there's little they can do.

"Ava is...special, Hunter. We want her away from Furious and away from danger."

I picture a girl walking with bubble wrap strapped around her body. "Well, you've made the right call then. You're sending her to the quietest pack of wolves and neck of the woods you could."

Noah chuckles. "We know."

We say goodbye and I hang up. Leaning back in the office chair, I enjoy the brief moments of solitude here in Resolve. Dawn is deep in the lab somewhere, and she sent KJ to town to buy more of her herbal teas—uncaffeinated lolly water in my opinion. Mom kept Riley at home so they could clean the already three-times-cleaned house before our visitor arrived. The visit from Ava, aka Were royalty according to my mother, has brought a spark to Mom's eye that's nice to see. I'm just glad I could say I needed to man the fort so I could get out of removing non-existent dust particles.

Watching the pups thrive and grow, planning for their release, has put everyone in a positive frame of mind. Hope really flourishes under these conditions. It's been a ripple free year, one where Resolve could probably be left unattended for short periods, but old worries die hard.

Things are going so well I keep expecting golden wolf to disappear. Knowing she has to be a creation of a mind that had considered giving up, the lack of tension in my mind had begun to worry me. But she's been there, any night I'm out as a wolf, and we run together, simply sit together, glorying in our connection.

Relief is a feeling I've been spending some time with, too. It's looser, lighter than what I've been carrying for so long. It means desperate suggestions like KJ made won't ever get air time again. A wolf-Were hybrid. I shake my head, wiping my hand down my face. All hope would have to be dead for me to think that's a good idea. The collective response to this Furious virus shows us what we can achieve. It'll be stamped out before it can do any more damage.

A movement on one of the screens catches my eye and I lean forward. Zephyr is pacing the fence line, the one closest to the car park. This wouldn't normally be an issue, but he was moved into the breeding enclosure a couple of days ago as we wait for Sakari to come in heat again. The next litter of pups is what we all need to feel like our steady progress is gaining traction.

So, the fact that Zephyr is nowhere near his mate is unusual. Add that to the pacing that seems somehow...different, and I walk over to look more closely. Zephyr is panting, and there's an energy to his movements that even the grainy security camera has picked up. Zephyr on edge has me on edge.

I'm about to head out when I see the next screen. Cursing, I rush to the door. The camera on the carpark just showed two people climbing out of a car.

And one of them is Alistair.

I shove open the door, deciding it's time Alistair learns this isn't a place he wants to return to.

"Gloria, honey. I want you to get this."

The woman with Alistair is about twice his spindly width and far more muscled. She lumbers over to him, carrying her phone horizontally. Alistair is indicating towards Zephyr, who's still pacing along the fence.

"Don't worry. I've got you covered," he says as he pats his hip.

They're so focused on getting footage that they don't hear me approach. I decide to let them know I'm here, biting each word off through my clenched jaw. "Get. The. Hell. Out. Of. Here."

Alistair visibly jumps, his fly-away combover flipping up in the breeze. Gloria, on the other hand, looks like she's built from a mountain. She turns to look at me, curious but not alarmed.

Straightening, Alistair crosses his arms. "Ah, Hunter Rendell."

So, Alistair has been doing some research.

"I've come to show some others exactly what these animals are like."

A low growl carries on the breeze, quiet enough that I doubt these two hear it, but loud enough for tension to wind itself around my spine. Now isn't the time for Zephyr to get defensive. "Neither of you are welcome here. I'll be making that formal as soon as you're gone."

Alistair smirks. "Good luck with that. They tried it at Jacksonville and the authorities turned them down. Apparently I don't pose a threat."

Unless he's the one who baited the pups. My hands are fisted so tight they feel like rocks. "You'd need an army to be a threat, Alistair."

The smirk dips and I know I've struck a nerve. Alistair has never been able to gain traction because he's never had any support.

Except today he's brought someone else.

Gloria has been moving, she probably thinks quietly and unobtrusively, closer to the enclosure while we've been speaking. I turn towards her. "Not another step."

She pauses to glance over her shoulder. "No harm in having a closer look."

Zephyr's growls escalate, as does the pacing. I'm not sure

what's got up his muzzle, but I may as well use it to my advantage. "He doesn't think so."

Gloria stops, now a couple of yards away. She takes in the white, alpha wolf and Zephyr stops too. His head drops as his eyes center on her. The next growl is several decibels louder.

"You're fine, honey. This is exactly the sort of stuff we want the rest of the world to see."

I turn back to Alistair, incredulous. He's sending Gloria closer while he stays here? But Alistair is looking at her, nodding encouragingly.

Gloria shrugs, and begins to move again. She hasn't completed a step before Zephyr snaps at the fence, spittle flying from his mouth. Gloria jerks back, her hand coming up to her chest. "You were right, Alistair." She lifts her phone and starts to film again.

This is starting to feel a little out of hand. I've never seen Zephyr like this, even in the wild. He's getting so worked up that foam has started to line his mouth.

And this is just what the world doesn't need to see of these gentle, majestic creatures.

Striding forward, I decide it's time this ends. "You don't have permission to film. You need to leave. Now."

Gloria ignores me, her focus on nowhere but Zephyr. Like he's working himself up into a frenzy, Zephyr starts snapping at the wire over and over. The growls and barks and snarls are full of anger.

"I told you, Gloria! This is exactly what they're like."

Gloria's phone lowers a little as she stares over it. Her eyes are wide as she takes in the rabid animal that's trying to eat its way through the chain-link fence.

Rabid...no, it can't be...

"Get a little closer, this is just what our cause needs." Alistair's voice is full of excitement.

My chest is full of dread. "No, Gloria." I stop myself before I say it's not safe. Words like that would be a jewel in Alistair's crown of victory.

Gloria shrugs her broad shoulders and lifts the phone as she steps forward.

It's like a red flag to angry Zephyr.

He unleashes his violence onto the fence, jumping and throwing himself against it. He does it with such brutality that the fence bows with each collision and spittle flies as he looks like he's trying to break through it.

Gloria has frozen. Her eyes are like two moons in her wide face, her mouth slack. The fence is the only thing that separates her from an animal that seems to want her dead.

My chest feels like a rock has lodged in my sternum.

Something has Zephyr riled, and these are the last two people who need to see this. They'd never believe this isn't like him.

Deciding I'll drag them to their car myself, I take three steps in Gloria's direction. Zephyr will calm once these two idiots get out of his face.

"Just like my father," Alistair mutters behind me. I turn, my heart leaping into my throat when I see what he's steadily raising to point at Zephyr.

Alistair has a gun.

It only takes two steps to be back by Alistair's side. Grabbing the pistol, I yank it from his grasp. "He can't get to her, you fool. He's in an enclosure."

Alistair's face is mottled with red. "This is what he saw. This is what they're all like!"

I jam my face close to his. "This is nothing like what they are like." I hold the gun up between us. "And this would be murder."

Alistair jerks back, smart enough to look scared. "Well…" His voice trails over as he looks over my shoulder, eyes going the widest I've seen them.

Spinning around, Gloria's scream yanks at the boulder in my chest. My blood seems to have congealed in my veins.

Zephyr is leaping, claws digging into the fence as he tries to reach the top. Like a hare on speed, each time he hits the ground, he jumps again. The white around his mouth is now a foam, his growls distorted with fury.

Gloria's scream seems to have loosened her muscles because she starts to move backward. Her eyes never leaving Zephyr, she slowly creates space between them. She seems to realize the fence is designed to be too high.

"Dammit. I told you to leave."

They shouldn't have been in here in the first place.

On the next leap Zephyr takes, he lodges his claws in the wire. Expecting him to drop to the ground, I gasp when he pushes up then slams into the fence again. Almost a foot from the top, he loses traction and falls to the ground.

The hard rock of tension in my chest explodes into fear. It propels adrenaline through my body, spikes my heart-rate. This is too far outside of normal. Wolves aren't supposed to be able to do that.

As Zephyr launches up again, Gloria turns and runs. This time her scream is the sound of a woman who's terrified.

A woman who believes this time he's going to make it.

Just like before, Zephyr's claws latch onto the wire and he uses the foothold to push up again. He hits the wire a foot from the top and I freeze as time draws out what will happen next. I will him to drop to the ground again. Will him to stop whatever he's starting.

For some reason, these two humans have prompted a rage that has Zephyr out of control. And I can't stop it, nor can I shift because of these two humans.

If Zephyr clears that fence, someone's going to die.

The wire bows as Zephyr's claws slam against it. With a violent roar, he pushes up again. Like an evangelical angel, he soars over the fence and lands on the other side.

"No!" My shout is as powered by fear as Gloria's frantic run to her car.

Except the sound doesn't puncture Zephyr's fury. He compresses as he lands, joints folding down, then seems to use it like a springboard as he propels forward again.

Gloria is all Zephyr sees.

Death is all that's stamped in his glowing eyes, his spit stained mouth, his arrow-like trajectory.

"Oh god…" Alistair's voice is barely a whisper, but those two words feel like a slap.

Zephyr powers forward, a white bullet that's found its target.

I raise the gun, holding it with my right hand as I cup it with my left. Training to use the tranquilizer gun was never meant for this. I was supposed to help these wolves. Protect them.

Not kill them because of the very people who hate them.

I track Zephyr's moving body, my arm tracing his trajectory. My breath stops and my heart shatters as I irrevocably, undeniably pull the trigger.

There's the crack of the shot and Zephyr drops as the bullet rips through his chest. He plows into the ground, body crumpling over the gravel. As he comes to a stop he pushes himself up, his body failing, but his mind still intent on killing.

This time I squeeze my eyes shut as I pull the trigger. Except I still hear the sound of the gun firing, still feel the recoil through my arms.

I open my eyes to see Zephyr drop as death claims him.

After I killed him.

My arms drop as my chest feels like someone just took to it

with a sledgehammer. My insides feel like I've been gutted with a pitchfork.

Alistair rushes to Gloria, and as much as I want to go to Zephyr and tell his lifeless body how sorry I am, I know there's one more thing I need to do.

I head to where Gloria was standing, to where she dropped her phone. I stand over it and look up at them as they stand in the center of the parking lot. "Don't come back."

With that, I stomp down on the phone, grinding it beneath my boot. The sound of grass crackling and plastic snapping fills the silence.

Turning away, I head over to Zephyr's dead body. Dropping to my knees I hear them over-rev the car as Alistair and Gloria drive away, leaving behind the damage they've caused.

Zephyr is splattered with blood, his tongue lolling out of his foam-rimmed mouth. Slowly the hollow, gouged out feeling in my gut starts to fill up. Guilt feels frozen and jagged, but I don't try to stop it. Zephyr wouldn't be in captivity if it wasn't for me.

I was responsible for him.

There's no way I can be the one who'll save these magnificent creatures.

30

HUNTER

LEGACY AWAKENED

The pull of my golden wolf is strong today, the strongest it's ever been, particularly considering it's daylight.

But I know I'm not going to shift even though I'm out here.

In all those magical moments out on the tundra, the moments where it was just her and me, there's no way she could have realized who I really am.

What I really am.

And it seems I can't hide it anymore. Losing my father. Starting captive breeding. Losing Miki.

And now Zephyr. All those graves are a testament to what I am.

Stepping back from the mound of soil, I lean on the shovel, but its slender strength isn't enough. I crumble, my legs collapsing under the weight of my failures. I welcome the bite of pain as rocks stab into my knees. I consider staying here the night, letting them worm their way deeper and deeper into my skin. Pain has become my constant companion anyway.

Behind me, my phone vibrates for the millionth time today,

and I ignore it like I have all the others. Riley or Mom were worried about me. Except this time it vibrates right off the quad and drops onto the ground.

Crap. Rising like I have arthritis, I walk over and pick up. Through the cracked screen I see exactly how many missed calls there are. Scrolling through Riley's texts that become progressively angrier, I realize why they've been trying to get hold of me.

Shit. Ava is arriving today.

As I climb on the quad, I almost laugh at the conversation I had with her father yesterday. I promised him I'd keep an eye out on her. That she'd be safe here.

At the time I believed I was someone who could do that.

Accelerating, I welcome the wind in my face and the jarring of my joints. I'm going to encourage her to drop off her cargo, then hightail it back to her cotton-lined home as quickly as she can, despite how much Mom has been looking forward to this. She's a responsibility I shouldn't be shouldering.

Oddly enough, the sense of connection with golden wolf only seems to strengthen the closer I get to Resolve. It doesn't surprise me. The closer I get, the more my body tightens with tension at the prospect of seeing all the people I've let down. And golden wolf has always been the balm to my pain. It makes sense that the more my heart aches, the more I feel the pull towards her.

Entering through the back door, I'm struck by the out of place sounds. There are people here, a lot of them. Sniffing the air, I register the member of my family and pack. Oh yeah. The Phelan princess was going to do some sort of speech.

Heading left, I decide I'm not as ready to face them all as I thought. I'll do all the Alpha formalities this afternoon at home. Maybe I'll go for a run. Pretend one more time that I'm someone worthy of spending time with golden wolf.

Even as I hate myself for being so weak and selfish, my chest feels the first speck of warmth as I reach the decision.

Just for a little while, I can pretend.

Heading to the kitchenette, my plan is to grab a covert coffee, then head back out, but I realize it's not going to be that simple when I hear footsteps down the hall.

The same Were hearing and the same Were smell that tells me it's KJ, means he knows it's me. I glance at the back door, wondering if I can still make it in time.

"You're putting off the inevitable."

Damn Were hearing. Damn Were smell.

Damned cousins who can read your mind.

He comes around the corner, stopping a few feet away. "If you sneak in now, you can pretend you were there all along."

I'm already shaking my head. "I'm going out on patrol."

KJ impales me with his gaze. "We got Zephyr's bloods back. He had Furious."

"The rabies virus?"

KJ sighs. "Yeah, but it's more like rabies on speed."

I take a step forward. "And the others?"

"All clean."

The good news feels so alien it takes me a few breaths to assimilate it. I nod. "That's great."

"Seems the vaccines got here in the nick of time."

Our visitors. More Alpha responsibilities that I don't believe I can live up to anymore.

One last run with golden wolf before painful reality is all I have. That's all I'm asking for. I turn for the door. "I'll be back later."

"You get here late, and now you're leaving early? I get that the patrols are important, Hunter, but you've spent almost every night out over the past two years."

I quell the anger that shoots through my veins. "I don't want to talk about this right now."

"As opposed to all the other times you've wanted to talk about it?"

"KJ. Now really isn't the time. I need...." My golden wolf. "A break. Just for a bit."

"Going out alone again isn't the answer, Hunter. Take advice from an orphan who knows what they're talking about."

I shut my eyes, concentrating on letting my breath out a second at a time. "I'll explain tomorrow."

"You know what? Don't bother. If you want to kill yourself, don't let someone who cares about you get in the way."

KJ spins on his heels and starts to stride away. I open my mouth but then shut it. KJ knows we need to talk about what we're up against. The truth, a trident that spears me right through the chest, hits me.

Sakari no longer has a mate.

Captive breeding may not work.

And now there's a virus we've never heard of.

This time, I find my voice and force myself to say it. "KJ. I think we start it."

KJ stops, then turns back. "What?" He takes long moments to scan my face. "You're serious, aren't you?"

I swallow, wondering if I've just proposed a solution or dug my grave deeper. "We've run out of options."

A squeak, the slightest of sounds, carries down the hallway. We look at each other, alarmed. Someone was listening? I go to walk forward, already reviewing what we just said. No one can know what we're about to start.

For some reason, golden wolf flashes through my mind. The vision, the feeling of connection, is so strong that I stop. It's like she's calling me.

When a girl walks around the corner, I'm glad I'm motionless with some sort of center of gravity—the sense of connection that hits me would have knocked me on my ass.

Her eyes are what grab me first. They're eyes I've connected with countless times before. Wintergreen eyes.

She opens her mouth to say something, and I register there's more than just eyes to this girl. Gossamer blonde hair falls in waves behind her; her fragile, sculpted face is one that belongs in a magazine or an art gallery or heaven. I knew my golden wolf would be beautiful, but I hadn't realized it would be a beauty that would suck the air straight from my lungs.

Oh my god. She's *real*.

And then I register who I'm looking at. Her name slips past my lips. "Ava."

Ava Phelan. The girl in the photo who was holding the wolf.

As the shock wears off, reality feels like too much. "It's true, you're Ava Phelan." A cold, penetrating hardness starts to seep around me. "The girl who never changed."

I'm glad it feels like my chest has turned to stone, I'd probably be doubled over if it weren't.

There's no way this girl can be my golden wolf.

"What?" Her voice is a shocked whisper.

I know I'm being inexplicably rude, but there's no room for manners in my tight body. This girl has just shattered my dreams.

"Hey." KJ steps between us. Damn, I'd forgotten he existed there for a second. I need to get a grip. "What's going on?"

Ava steps back. "It seems I've made a mistake."

KJ is looking from her to me and back again. "Dude, I know you don't get out much. But that was just damned rude."

I have enough guilt as it is. My jaw is so tight it hurts, my body so frozen that I'm scared to move. "Mistakes." I look away, her wintergreen gaze the one thing that could shatter me. "They're not a feeling you want to repeat."

Looking like I've just taken more from her than I've lost, Ava turns on her heel and leaves. I give her marks for the straight back and high chin. I don't know what she's thinking, but I can recognize someone pulling together their armor.

Thing is, I don't know if I can apologize.

KJ turns to me, but I stride straight past him and out the door. I don't have any answers for the questions stamped all over his face.

Outside, I stop. Leaning against the door, I realize I don't know where to go.

Resolve is full of people who believe I'm something I'm not.

The enclosures house the wolves I've failed to protect.

Home is full of family I've let down too many times.

And now the wild is no longer a haven.

I jam my palms into my temples, trying to stop the painful conclusions.

My poor, screwed-up mind created a damn good delusion after seeing Ava in that photo two years ago. Maybe my stupid subconscious wanted for golden wolf to be someone like Ava.

Special. Important.

My hands squeeze tight. *But it seemed so real...*

I crumple over, folding in over the pain. Ava has never been a wolf.

Ava and golden wolf cannot coexist in the same reality.

And the shock and hurt I saw in her eyes were undeniable. Ava is the living breathing child of the prophecy.

I push away from the door, walking forward mindlessly...like a lost soul.

I've just joined the harsh world of reality.

And I'm not sure it's a world I want to be part of.

31

AVA

Waiting for the screens to come alive for the committee meeting, I've never felt more of an imposter. Only the leaders are allowed in the room for this meeting. Dawn is here. Hunter is here, but I haven't looked at him since he walked through the door. The others will be here shortly thanks to KJ's skill with computers.

Fae Elders.
Were Alphas.
And me.
Nothing but a watered-down version of them all.

The first monitor flickers to life, and my eyes sting as my parents fill the rectangle. God, I've missed them. Mom's gentle smile is a balm for the ache in my chest, whilst Dad's quiet confidence is the foundation I wish I still had. We already chatted earlier today as we updated each other on everything that's going on, and I'm glad that the seriousness of everything that's happened masked the strain in my voice. Seeing them though, reminds me that we've decided I'll be coming home soon.

They're the ones I'm letting down the most.

The next one brings up River the Fae Elder, and then my

Uncle Orin. Then there's Uncle Mitch and Aunt Tara, and the Alphas of the key regions—the Lyalls, the Tates, the Bardolfs, even Nian, the sole representative of the Lang pack.

"We're all here, Prime Alpha."

I almost jump at Hunter's voice. He's stepped forward, shoulders square, back straight. Even as I mourn something I never had, I admire the strength he projects. No wonder I was drawn to him, he's my age and can exude the feeling that we have a chance against everything we're facing.

"Thank you, Hunter." Dad pulls in a breath. "We're here to discuss what we're seeing."

John Tate crosses his arms. "We've lost four wolves to poachers in the last week."

There's a rumble of Alpha voices as they all join in. Most have lost wolves to targeted attacks.

Oh god. More poachers? I look to my mother, and find she's watching me. I try not to be weak, but I can already feel the tears catching at the back of my throat.

Dad nods. "It has to be more than a coincidence."

Hunter glances at the faces around him. "You think this is systematic? That someone's coordinating this?"

"We believe that may be the case."

Hunter rubs his chin. "Alistair Davenport?"

Mom sighs. "We don't know yet."

I wish Hunter and I had enough of a connection that he would look my way too. I want to get a sense of what he thinks of this all, particularly when I've been told Alistair has been seen here at Resolve.

Dawn comes to stand beside Hunter. "There's more."

A low rumble collects from each of the screens. My shoulders hunch as I anticipate the blow this is going to be.

"We had a wolf infected with Furious." She sighs. "The therapeutic vaccine didn't work."

There's silence. Full of shock and heavy with implications.

Hunter's shoulders tense, and I know he's thinking of Desna, maybe even Zephyr…both of who he had to kill. How does he manage to stand there, so strong and sure? As much as I don't want to respect someone who's stolen my dreams, I do.

And I'm not sure what that says about me.

Nian narrows her eyes in thought. "And the wolf who we believed was cured?"

Dad's face is somber. "Achak escaped two weeks ago and is still missing."

Hunter straightens. "And he jumped the fence, didn't he?"

Mom and Dad glance at each other before nodding. "We believe so."

He glances at Dawn and she frowns. "Then he may still be infected."

I want to shoot up and deny it, tell them all that Achak had been cured. But I don't. I sit there, mute.

The Lyall Alpha leans forward. "We're going to have to find him."

I close my eyes for the briefest of seconds. They're going to have to kill him.

Before all of this, I would have stood up and fought that decision. Even without proof, with nothing but my conviction, I would have told them they're wrong.

But I've learned too much. I know who I am now.

And that girl doesn't have any belief that her perspective is accurate.

"We are doubling our efforts to find him. We believe he's deep in the reserve. In the meantime, we need to stop these poachers."

There's nods and grunts of assent. The collective strength of Were and Fae is about to be mobilized. Protecting their own is what they do best. It has me straightening a bit, glad it gives me a sense of hope even though I can't be part of it.

"We've already doubled our patrols," one Alpha grunts.

"We're looking at tracking them," says another.

Dad's eyes narrow. "If you come across one of these idiots, you take them to the authorities."

Most of the Alphas nod. One or two slide their gaze away.

"That isn't a request."

I think it's the first order I've ever heard my dad make. It shows you how high emotions are getting. The frustration with humans has the potential to spill into hatred.

There's a muttered round of acknowledgments.

Orin speaks up for the first time. "And Furious?"

"Its spread has been slow," responds Mom, "but for only one reason, and that's the same way we can continue to curb it."

River frowns. "That cannot be your solution."

Mom doesn't falter. "Without a cure, there's no other solution." Dad's arm shifts, and I know he's holding her hand. "Any infected animal must be killed."

Controlling my gasp takes everything I have. I want to shout that this goes against everything we stand for. How can we be the ones who take their lives too? We'll be hastening their extinction.

I take in Hunter's back again, ramrod straight and tight. Is this how he's had to feel? He's given his life to the arctic wolves, and yet he's killed two of them and lost even more.

Mom is watching me, her eyes full of sympathy and pain.

I look away, not sure I have the strength for this. I'm not like Hunter, or Dawn, or any of them. Going home is probably the best thing for everyone.

Everyone signs off, the goodbyes somber and cheerless. One or two glances at me before their screens go black. With everything so bleak—wolves under threat from humans and a virus—

it sure would be nice for them to have some spark of hope. The child born of the Prime Prophecy was what everyone assumed would be the solution in a time like this.

I flick my hair back, although what I really want to do is curve it around me and hide. I couldn't save Kayuh, the dreams I've had for two years have been nothing but romantic fluff, and I have no special ability to help them.

I'm glad I'm going home.

The door opens and Riley strides in like this is any other day and we're about to have a meeting. "So, extra patrols, huh?"

Hunter crosses his arms. "You were listening at the door?"

Riley flips her fringe as she juts out a hip. "I was in the hallway. I can't help it if I was born with great hearing."

KJ and Josh are right behind her. KJ slides into his chair and powers up his computer. "We need to do something about Furious."

Dawn comes to stand beside him. "Like what?"

I lean forward—maybe this is the flicker of hope we've been looking for.

KJ shrugs. "I have no idea. That virus and I are gonna spend some time together in the lab."

I try not to sag. That's not a lot to pin hope on.

"Good thinking, KJ." Dawn heads to her desk. "Let's see what we can come up with."

Riley grabs Josh by the hand and pulls him to the door. "We'll take the next shift."

Josh nods in Hunter's direction. "Try to get some sleep or something."

Riley rolls her eyes. "Or some more coffee."

They're gone, taking all noise and movement with them.

For the first time since I entered the office, Hunter's eyes connect with mine. Today his eyes aren't copper, they're darker, more muted. It's like the fire that powered them has been cooled, almost extinguished. I open my mouth, but then close it again.

I've known Hunter's been hurting from the beginning. He's carried too much, had too many hard choices to make.

But I'm not the one who can fix it. He knows it. I know it.

I stand up. "I'll go check out the fence line."

My bogus job for the useless, non-Were, non-Fae person.

I'm just at the door when a beeping sound cheeps from a computer somewhere. Turning, I see KJ wheel himself to another station.

Hunter strides to join him. "That's one of the boundary sensors."

I stop with my hand on the door. "We have boundary sensors?"

KJ scans the screen and presses some buttons. "Yep, recent upgrade. We set them up along some of the tracks the wolves use most frequently."

"So, it's one of the wolves?"

KJ looks up at me, shaking his head. "Their collars are designed so they won't set them off."

Hunter points to the top right screen. "Bring it up there."

KJ clicks a few times and the screen flickers from the image of Sakari's den to the tundra. I walk forward to look closer. "And you have cameras out there?"

"Just a handful, right around the sensors."

We all look and wait. Dawn and I both jump when a caribou streaks past, a blur of grey zipping across the screen.

KJ leans back, a huff of laughter slipping out. "Always the caribou. Those things are going to make me grey."

Hunter nudges him with his elbow. "You're probably already grey."

KJ yanks down his beanie. "I could be Rapunzel under here for all you know."

I relax again, pulling open the door. These wolves have a dedicated team with some very special skills looking after them.

"Hunter!" It's Dawn's voice, full of alarm.

She's standing in front of the bank of screens, pointing at the one we were all just looking at.

Hunter is like a coiled ball of anger. "Bastard."

"What?" I stride over, wanting to know what they're looking at. I peer at the black and white image, except there's nothing but rocks and ruts.

"I'm on it." Hunter spins and before I can ask, he's out the door.

Dawn frowns at the empty doorway. "Maybe I should go with him."

KJ shakes his head. "We don't want to slow him down. He knows what he's doing."

I look from one to the other. "What's going on? I thought it was just a caribou."

Dawn's lips thin. "It was. And then there was a poacher."

"What?" I spin to look down the hallway, knowing Hunter's long gone. "He can't go out on his own!"

Dawn's green eyes fill with compassion. "This is what Hunter does, Ava. If there are any wolves nearby, he'll make sure they don't get close to the poacher."

Can't they see how he's hurting though? I turn to KJ. "KJ, you should go."

He's already shaking his head. "I don't shift."

"What? Why not?"

KJ opens his mouth, holds it there, but then shuts it again. He looks away.

Dawn rests a hand on his shoulder. "Now isn't the time. KJ is better off staying here and monitoring the situation. We need to keep an eye out for Riley and Joshua."

"But—"

"You're right. Someone should be with him." Dawn heads to the door, giving my shoulder a squeeze on the way through. "I'll go."

She shuts the door behind her. No one suggested that I go out with him. I didn't suggest that I go out with him. I've seen what a helpless liability I am.

Maybe they're right. Everything's going to be fine.

And I haven't actually been right yet.

KJ turns back to his computer. "He's probably long gone anyway. We almost didn't see him. The prick's wearing grey or red or something."

The words stop me, but I'm not sure why. "What?"

KJ shakes his head. "Well, the screens are black and white. He was probably wearing grey considering it's the tundra, but reds look the same—seeing it in four-megapixel resolution is tough."

"He was wearing red?"

He looks at me, a quizzical frown scrunching his brows. "Possibly. Why?"

It's not something I'm ever going to forget. *Not many people wear red out here. He was there for one reason.*

And then when I tried to tell him it was human ignorance that killed his father.

I'm not sure it matters anymore.

The door slams against the wall as I shove myself out.

"Hey!"

I don't answer KJ. My heart is pounding painfully as I sprint out the door and to the shed. My heart clenches as I realize this will be over before I could even try. With Dawn and Hunter both out, there won't be another quad. The relief that floods my system at finding one there is short lived. It means Hunter didn't take it.

It means Hunter went out as a wolf.

My hands shake as I jump on the quad and turn on the ignition. My mind races as I find the thread that's always been different to the others.

If that poacher is the same one who killed his father, Hunter is going to look for retribution for a whole lot of pain he shouldn't be carrying.

And I can't let that happen.

32

AVA

I didn't have time to think of tying back my hair, which means it flies around me like seaweed in a storm. I shove it back, knowing I'm not stopping, knowing I'd cut every last lock off if it'd make a difference.

The thread feels stronger for some reason, and I realize it's because Hunter's in wolf form. He must be using his wolf senses to find the poacher.

Maybe he won't find him.

Maybe he'll come across the wolves first and lead them away.

Maybe I imagined what I heard in his voice that day.

As each of those thoughts come out as a prayer, I accelerate. Too many wishes have failed to come true for me to put much faith in them.

The thread takes me due east, which isn't a direction I've been before. The terrain here slopes up rapidly, becoming rocky and uneven. I quickly find that by half-standing on the quad, I can spare myself the biggest jolts. Slowing down isn't an option.

The tundra fast becomes a series of rises and dips, some full of rocks that've been sheared and sliced by nature, others still holding the last of summer's green and gold. I accelerate up the next one, feeling I'm getting closer, and spear over the top.

Except a fist of rock has punched up through the soil on the other side. I yank the handlebars hard to the right and the quad swerves. It narrowly misses the pile of rock, but the tire hits the edge. The bike tips and I instinctively counterbalance. For seconds I don't know which way gravity will pull me and images of my body tumbling over the rocky ground dominate my mind.

But then the wheels bump back down and I'm powering forward again. I glance over my shoulder, gaping at the near miss. I won't be helping anyone if they have to pick me up piece by piece.

The next rise looks like it's made largely of rock. I have no choice but to slow, having learned I have no idea what's on the other side. The rise plateaus at the top, like Mother Nature has sheared the whole top off a mountain, before disappearing down the other side.

He's close. I can feel it.

I'm about to accelerate as I come to the other side of the plateau, but then I see what's before me. The land falls away into a valley before rising up to another low hill, which isn't much different to the terrain I've been crossing.

It's what's in the valley that has me coming to a complete halt.

To my left, a white-furred body is lying lifeless and I feel the scream echo through my heart. It's one of the pups, it must be Pakak, her life-force already leached into the soil. And kneeling over her is a man in a red jacket. When the sun catches on the silver in his hand, I gasp.

He's going to skin her!

I'm about to power down the hill, knowing I can't let that happen, when my hand goes slack on the accelerator.

Oh god.

A massive white wolf, big and powerful, arrives in the valley on my right. He sniffs the air, sees what I see, and makes the decision in an instant.

No, no, no.

Hunter surges forward, gaze locked on the man kneeling over the dead body of the wolf he raised. With his back turned, his focus on what he's about to do, the guy has no idea Hunter is bearing down on him.

A Were who's looking for justice.

I take in the determination and the speed. A Were looking to avenge the deaths he will forever carry.

Yanking down and accelerating isn't a choice. Careening down the hill doesn't feel fast enough. I can't let Hunter do this.

"Stop!" My scream sounds as full of desperation as I feel.

To my right, I see Hunter's head rise as he registers me coming down the slope. He glances back at the poacher, takes in my trajectory, and drops his head. With the determination of an avenger, he picks up speed.

"No!"

The man looks up, startled. He must follow my line of sight, because he stands and turns. There's a moment where he freezes in time, realizing that another wolf is running straight at him.

Except this one is much, much bigger.

The second he decides to move he starts to run. Wildly and frantically, he sprints forward, even though he'd know a human can't outrun a wolf, and certainly not one as big as Hunter.

As I jostle and jolt down the hill, I do the math. My line will intersect Hunter's before he reaches the man. It's the only hope I have of stopping him before he does something he'll regret.

Pushing up, I shout as hard as I can. "You don't want to do this!"

I know the words register with Hunter because there's the slightest of pauses, but then he lowers his head, and it's like I don't exist. He powers forward, determination a steady thrum as his paws devour the distance between him and his target.

I only have a few seconds, and fear has started to spike through my veins. I can't accelerate any more, but I can keep trying to reach him.

"This isn't you, Hunter!"

I know it's not.

There's no pause this time, it's like my words have hit a sheet of ice and vaporized.

The man is running, stumbling, repeatedly glancing over his shoulder. Terror has his eyes wide and his mouth wider. He knows he won't stand a chance when that wolf reaches him.

I'm close enough to see Hunter's eyes. They're the darkest I've ever seen them. His magnificent face is devoid of anything but determination. There's no hope. No belief.

No acknowledgment of everything he is and can be.

The quad loses speed as my body loses strength. I reach the point he'll pass a second before he does and stop. All he has to do is sidestep me and continue. Just like all the other times, I haven't been able to stop this.

I've run out of time and I've run out of words. All I say is what has had my heart cracking from the moment I learned I wasn't the one he saw on the tundra. As he leaps over me I reach up, letting his fur brush my fingers.

"I'm sorry I couldn't be what you needed."

I don't shout the words, knowing they're my own confession more than anything, and they trail off on a sob.

I couldn't stop the death of Kayuh, just like I can't stop Hunter from altering his life forever.

Altering the trajectory of what's about to become a war between wolf, human, and Were.

I hear Hunter land, imagining his body compressing, absorbing the impact and using it to propel himself forward. I hope I don't have to hear any cries for help or screams of pain. At least Hunter will exact his revenge humanely.

The scrabbling of gravel, a scattering of rocks, has me turning. They aren't sounds that fit into what's about to happen.

What I see has me climbing off the quad. Hunter has skidded to a stop and spun around. His whole wolf body is staring at me in shock.

My words had an impact?

I stand my ground. "I meant what I said. You're the strength and conviction I wish I had. I wish I could be part of."

He doesn't move.

"I'm sorry I wasn't..." I shrug, wishing there was another way to say this. "More."

Hunter steps forward, his copper eyes wide. He stops, shakes his head, then blinks at me.

I don't know why, but I smile. Smiling is everything this moment isn't, but at least my inadequacies have been good for something. The man has seen Hunter stop and is now running with renewed vigor, no longer glancing over his shoulder. I notice the motorbike not far away. Good. I doubt he'll be returning here anytime soon.

Hunter takes another step, his broad body filling my vision. His eyes are studying my face with an intensity that robs me of the ability to breathe. I don't say anything else. I don't have anything else. I've just bared myself to him.

Another step and he's only a few feet away. His copper eyes, the ones that have always been so familiar, are wide with wonder. Our thread pulses and my heart hammers. I'm not sure what's happening, but I step forward too.

Why has Hunter stopped? Why is he looking at me like that?

He's within reach, so I lift my hand. "To be honest, I think I wished I could so hard that I dreamed you up."

Hunter sucks in a sharp breath, his wide chest expanding.

Our thread seems to grow and expand, shimmering and swelling. All of a sudden it isn't a thread anymore, but a golden ball that surrounds us. It feels like if it keeps going, it will swallow us both in its embrace.

We seem to draw in closer, and I'm not sure who it is that moves. It doesn't matter. This is a magic that my whole soul knows is real.

The *crack*, a sharp clap of thunder, makes us both startle. My eyes widen, but then Hunter's flare as he crumples. An anguished moan escapes my lips as I register why.

Red has exploded across Hunter's shoulder. He catches himself, pushing himself up, pain carved into the movement.

Frantic, I see that the poacher has left a cloud of dust in his wake. But Hunter has just been shot…

I look up to the place where I came down. Another man, also in red, is standing on the plateau, a rifle leveled at us.

"No!" I scream. "Stop!"

But the man fires another shot and granite explodes behind Hunter. Hunter leaps, a garbled yelp wrenched past his throat. The glance he graces me is short, sharp, and burdened with emotion, before he spins away. He leaps forward, his right leg already giving out.

I go to follow, but Hunter looks back at me, copper eyes fierce. I shake my head, my denial a whisper. "No."

He moves again, creating more space between us as quickly as his broken body will let him. He's taking the target that he is away from me. Even shot and bleeding, Hunter's working to protect me.

As I look up, I see the poacher tracking Hunter's movements. Another shot is inevitable.

Another shot that will probably kill him.

I want to fight, but there's no way I'll get to the man in time. I want to run towards my wolf, but I know that's not want he'd want.

Instead, I freeze in anguish, watching Hunter move further away from me, not being able to comprehend that this is how it all ends.

The scream that hits my eardrums confuses me. It's not mine, and it's not Hunter's.

But it's undeniably the scream of tortured pain.

It's the poacher's.

Oh god—a wolf is attacking him!

Except it's not the wolves I've been seeing since I arrived on Evelyn Island. This wolf isn't white. It wouldn't blend into a landscape of snow.

This wolf is grey. I gasp. It's grey with an undercoat of red!

"Achak!"

But Achak, the wolf I raised, the wolf that shouldn't be here, has one goal. He either doesn't hear me or ignores me.

The poacher is down on the ground, arms raised to protect himself, pleading for Achak to stop. But the pathetic screams fall on deaf wolf ears—Achak's head spears down over and over, snapping and snarling at the arms that are barely a barrier.

No...

Achak has never attacked anyone, but I know what's going to happen next. The moment the man's arms drop, exhaustion from blood loss and pain sapping his strength, Achak's head bears down for the final blow. Mouth wide, teeth bared, he grasps the man's head. The screams escalate, becoming high-pitched and frantic with fear.

If he knows wolves, he realizes what's coming next.

Achak clamps his jaws shut.

I don't hear the snapping or crushing sound that would be his skull, but I know the moment it happens. The barely-there thread that appeared the moment I saw the poacher severs. The screams stop.

Achak raises his head, the blood lining his mouth apparent from here. Even from here, I can see his eyes are clear. He holds still as I watch and wait.

Oh god. What just happened?

Except there's no time to figure out if I can answer that question. A groan, part wolf, part human, reaches out behind me. Spinning around, my gasp is involuntary.

Hunter has collapsed. As a human he lies on the rocky ground, blood coating his upper chest, his face pale and twisted with pain.

I crumple beside him, seeing his thread grow weak...

Knowing I can't heal him.

33

AVA

"The wolf." Hunter tries to lift his head, eyes searching for the animal that just violently killed the poacher.

I scramble forward, not wanting him to add to the strain. "It's the wolf I raised. Achak. I don't think he's rabid."

Hunter's gaze flies to mine. "He followed you?"

My hands flutter over his chest. There's so much blood and I can't tell where it's coming from. "It seems so. Hunter, we need to do something."

He lowers his head, letting out a breath, then winced as it seems to cause him pain. "The vet pack."

Yes. Why didn't I think of that?

I run to the quad, my hands shaking so hard it takes me three tries to unclip the vet pack. Back by his side, I yank it open and pull out bandages as quickly as I can. Were speed would have been useful right now.

"Pressure." He points to his upper chest. Hunter's face is so pale, every feature tight with pain.

I don't let myself think about what I'm about to do. I grab a wad of cotton and gently but firmly press it down.

Hunter arches, his breath sucking in through tight lips. He

holds himself there for long seconds and I almost pull back. How can I be doing this to him?

But then his body releases and he sinks back to the ground. He keeps his eyes closed, seeming to concentrate on his breathing. I grab some more bandages and ignore the strain in his face as I wrap them around his chest.

"I'm so sorry, Hunter."

I close my eyes, struggling to contain the tears. What have I done? As I look at this strong, amazing protector I don't know how my choices have made any of this better. Hunter wouldn't have been shot if I'd stayed back at Resolve.

"Ava."

I look down and find Hunter's molten gaze on me. Although his face is tight and pale, his eyes blaze bright and sure. "This isn't your fault."

"I can't heal you, Hunter." My voice is choked with helplessness.

He shakes his head. "Why would you think you're not enough, Ava?"

"Because I'm a cross-breed mix that can't do anything."

"You're the most amazing blend of the best parts of us all."

I frown, tears trekking down my cheeks. "What are you talking about?"

Hunter lets out a slow breath, gaze staring up at the sky. When he looks back at me, his face seems to have lost some of its tension. "I didn't think anyone would be able to reach my human heart, Ava. It's been too battered and bruised, chopped and charred."

He swallows, and I wonder if I should say something. Except I can't. Pain and something else have clogged my throat.

"But you did, Ava. With your tenacity and determination. But mostly with your compassion and never-ending belief in good."

I close my eyes as his words wrap around me. Others have told me I'm optimistic and idealistic. They never seemed to be qualities that were of much value. But for some reason, knowing this has touched Hunter gives this moment a bittersweet edge.

"You stopped me from becoming what I was scared I was." His last words are bitten off.

I raise my hand, resting my fingers on his lips. "You were never going to be that person, Hunter. You're so much more than that."

His lips work beneath my fingers, they feel so warm and alive I wish I could keep my hand there forever.

His eyes close again, his breath pulling in past my finger then flowing back out. "You need to go back and get help."

I jerk my hand back. "What?"

He looks at me, gaze unblinking. "You heard me."

"Hunter, you've been shot. I'm not leaving you."

"Well, I'm not riding back like this." He grasps my hand. "It's the only chance we have."

"But…"

Hunter could bleed out. He could be attacked. So much could go wrong as he lies here alone and injured.

"Now isn't the time to argue, Ava."

I try to hold in the sob, I really do, but it bursts past my lips. I squeeze my eyes shut, trying to contain all this emotion. "I can't. I just can't."

How do I leave Hunter like this?

"Ava."

I ignore the call of my name. I know it's childish, but I don't have what it takes to do this. I won't leave Hunter knowing he might die.

"Ava."

The catch in Hunter's voice is what finally has me opening my eyes. It's a catch I've never heard, but I instinctively know it's one I've wanted to hear. Hunter's face is full of wishes and dreams.

"We should have done this differently." He swallows. "I should have done this differently."

His hand comes up to caress my cheek. I have no defenses, nor do I want them. I lean into the palm of his hand, increasing the pressure, amplifying the sensation.

Reaching forward, I touch the face I've wanted to touch for so long. The skin of his cheek is smooth, so much strength underneath. I move down, the subtle graze of stubble a contrast I wish I had more time to explore.

His lips part, and I look up.

Hunter's copper gaze is somehow brighter and deeper at the same time. His eyes glow with promise, and darken with something that has my breath disappearing.

His hand shifts back into my hair, a warm slide of skin on skin. His fingers cup my head and he tugs, his face asking a million questions.

I lean forward, a million yeses pouring from every cell in my body.

It's a slow, delicious trip down. Hunter's face comes closer and closer, his scent, his eyes, his intentions drawing me in. I pause as the last millimeters wait to be claimed. My breath, my heart, my soul all hang in suspended animation.

Is this really what Hunter wants?

His head lifts and our lips meet.

Touch.

Meld.

The sensations—so soft, so hot, so god damned amazing, assault me. The emotions—so true, so eager, so beautifully overwhelming, capture me.

I hold myself there, wanting more, but wanting to be lost in this forever.

Hunter's hand tightens at the back of my head and he increases the pressure. Our lips crush and the heat intensifies.

All of a sudden keeping still is impossible. Passion detonates. Desire explodes. I want to dive into this, see how I can build it higher.

I'm just about to raise my hands, those two points of contact no longer enough, when I remember. I stop and pull back.

Hunter is injured.

But Hunter doesn't let me go. He holds me there, inches between us, our breaths panting and blending. We study each other, the knowledge that something was just born a glorious glow between us.

I open my mouth, wanting to say something, but not knowing what. I may have just been kissing Hunter, but he was stealing my heart. My white wolf or no white wolf, I've fallen for him.

Hunter's eyes flicker over my face before returning to capture my gaze with an intensity that tugs at something deep in my chest. "I want to give whatever this is a chance."

I nod, not wanting to, but no longer fighting the inevitability. If I don't get help, Hunter will die.

I lean down, my lips brushing his gently. Pulling back, I blink several times. "Don't go anywhere, okay?"

His lips tip up in a smile, and the heat in his eyes mellows to something warmer, but just as captivating. "I'll be here."

Without giving myself time to think, I stand and turn away. I'm going to have to drive the fastest I have yet. I'll get help. I'll come back. There's no way this can be how it ends.

Please, please let it be fast enough.

I turn, and a bolt of pain seems to spear up from the ground and through my body. I gasp, but take a step. I don't have time for a twisted ankle or stubbed toe right now.

I'm about to break into a jog, the quad not far away, when

another lightning strike of pain hits me. I arch, teeth gritted. I don't know what's going on, but I can't afford to find out.

Hunter needs my help.

"Ava?"

Hunter's voice is full of worry, but it seems far away. I turn back, confused. There are only a few feet between us. The sight of the bandages and blood snap me out of it. I need to get back to Resolve.

My legs give out and I crumple, a cry wrenched from somewhere deep inside. My body feels like someone just took a flamethrower to it.

"Ava!"

I hold up my hand. "Don't move!"

I try to push myself up, but everything feels broken. My bones feel like they're shattering, my skin feels like molten metal has been poured all over it. I clench my teeth, holding the next cry in. If I let it out, it's going to become a wail of agony.

Another wave hits, bigger and more destructive than the last. I don't know if I want to arch or cave in on myself. I try to bring my hands to my face, only to find I can't.

I look down, the cry finally escaping as I watch my hands shorten. Then thicken.

Then take on a glimmer that's even more impossible.

I haven't taken a breath when I feel the rest of me change. My body contracts then expands. Every part of me is rearranging. Heat explodes from every pore.

I know when it's done, because like electricity whose supply has been cut, it suddenly stops. I push up, adjusting to the unfamiliar, but for some reason not surprised, as four paws are now my foundation. I straighten, feeling like the world has been brought into sharp relief.

There's the increased hearing and sight and smell. All the senses are dialed up. There's the smell of snow, not coming for days, in the air. There's the sound of silence and absence of breath coming from Hunter.

There's all the white surrounding his beautiful eyes as they watch me, wide with shock. "Ava?"

But more than that is the amplified sense of connection. Our thread feels like it's strengthened, no, magnified. It's the same thread it's always been, I'm just seeing it in a level of detail I've never experienced before.

I step forward, coming to stand beside Hunter. The thread is a pulsing, river of golden motes. They flow and whirl, a watercourse of life.

Hunter's hand comes up. "My wolf. My beautiful, golden wolf."

He brushes my face, and it's so much like my dreams. Except this time, I can feel it.

And there's nothing more I'd like to do than glory in what's just happened, but Hunter's hand drops, his face contorting with pain. I'm already crouched beside him as I close my eyes.

I know what I need to do.

The thread, so much more alive and detailed, is there. I tap into it, being swept into the space that Hunter and I have always shared. There, I see him, the essence of this amazing guy. Instinctively, I know what I'm looking for, what I couldn't see before.

I see his lifeforce and go deeper. There, I find that part that makes him Were and breathe life into it. The motes flare and shimmer, throwing out their healing energy. I feel Hunter pull in a deep breath and the particles flame again. The energy expands, discharging through the thread.

There's another breath, even deeper than the last, and I feel his body relax. My own tension abates as I realize Hunter's no longer in pain.

I pull back, leaving the beautiful well of gold, suddenly tired.

As I open my eyes, I'm glad I'm lying beside Hunter, my legs feel like they wouldn't have the strength to hold a feather let alone this great Were body.

This Were body...

I shifted!

But...but that's impossible.

I feel the strength start to leave me, and I know I'm about to transform back to human. I take in the shimmery gold that is my fur. I'm a wolf.

I'm a golden wolf.

I look up at the guy beside me as he sits up.

I'm Hunter's golden wolf.

34

HUNTER

Three days of souped-up Were healing thanks to Ava's unique brand of magic, and my bullet wound is almost gone. Joshua performed his amateur doctoring on me when we got back to Resolve, figuring the bullet must have missed any major organs since I was able to travel back.

I hook my fingers into the wire of the fence, wondering where Sakari is. Ava and I didn't mention the puddle of blood that'd collected where I lay.

No one, not even a Were, could've survived that amount of blood loss.

Which means Ava saved my life. Ava, who was my golden wolf all along.

Sakari leaves her den, all sleek white lines and proud posture. She sees me standing at the fence and pauses. It's been a few days since I've been here. First, I was healing, then there was the fallout from my attack.

I can still remember KJ returning with Joshua from where it all happened. Their job was to locate the body of the second poacher so we could tell authorities.

"It's gone."

I'd almost shot up from the sofa but Mom had quickly put her hand on my shoulder. Ava's hand in mine had anchored me. "What?"

KJ had flopped into the chair across from me as Riley gravitated towards Joshua. "We found where you were shot—that was a lot of blood, dude."

I hear Mom shift behind me, feel her hand flutter around my shoulder, and I frown at KJ. "Luckily I'm fine."

Ava has asked me to keep her shifting and her healing a secret for now. We need to figure out what it all means before we make any announcements. It also means Mom won't find out how close I was to repeating Dad's fate. I suppressed a shudder. I don't think Mom has the capacity to cope with another loss.

"The body of Pakak was there, just as you described, so we've brought her back." KJ shrugged. "But the poacher was gone."

Ava had shifted forward, her thigh brushing mine. "But there's no way he could've survived Achak's attack."

Josh had nodded. "You'd know if he was dead or not, and there was blood there too. But definitely no body."

She'd looked back at me, and we'd stared at each other for long seconds. Was there someone else there? How did they know? But most importantly, who took the body and why?

Riley had frowned. "With no body, we don't have anything to bring to the authorities."

Sakari takes a few steps forward, and I crouch down, wondering if she's going to come any closer. I've killed her mate. I couldn't save her pups. Her species is threatened by a virus we can't control, alongside humans who want their deaths and their skins.

I can understand why she'd choose to hold her distance.

But I think Sakari was born from the same deep well of

compassion and caring as Ava, because she lopes over to me. I stretch my fingers through the wire, brushing the velvet fur of her muzzle. Sakari's eyes close for a moment, enjoying the touch.

"We'll turn this around somehow, Sakari. I won't let you disappear."

I marvel that hope is still alive within me, despite the odds that seem insurmountable, and I know it's due to one thing. One person, to be exact.

I feel her before I see her. Ava's told me about the threads she sees, which explained Josh's comment that Ava would've known the poacher was dead. It also explains why she's always seemed to be able to trace me. We've spent three days talking and touching and kissing and then talking some more. With no barriers, with the knowledge that we spent two years together whenever we could, we've shared so much.

I glance at Sakari, her pregnancy is still in its early stages, and tension knots at the base of my spine.

How do I tell Ava this? How do I tell her what I've done?

KJ had been adamant that we need to keep this a secret, that there's no point even raising it until the pups are born. There's always the possibility the pregnancy won't take. And according to him, if it all goes according to plan we may not need to tell anyone ever. The prospect sits uneasily, jagged and uncomfortable, within my chest.

Ava has accepted me despite everything I've done, and that's a miracle I'll never take for granted. But genetic manipulation of wolf and Were? We've either saved these animals or committed the most immoral crime against everything Were and Fae hold sacred.

If we're wrong...the second option is unforgivable.

Sakari leaps up when she sees Ava, her paws landing high

on the wire. Ava laughs with delight, and the sound lightens my soul. There's no way I'm risking my salvation. Not yet…

Ava reaches through, her fingers tickling Sakari's jaw. Sakari laps lovingly at the hand caressing her, her face alight with a wolfish grin.

Ava's other hand creeps out to the side and wraps around my waist. She doesn't have to pull though, I slide over like a magnet drawn in purely because it's Ava. Is this what I've been missing out on since she arrived?

There's an innocent confidence about Ava's touch, an assumption that it's true and right. It's so natural and sincere that I wonder if she's even aware of it. It's so amazing that it has me wondering how I managed to be a part of all this.

As our sides meld together, she rests her head on my shoulder. We watch as Sakari looks at us both. She seems neither surprised nor concerned. Actually, I think her grin widens. She lets out a bark and drops to all fours. Three more barks are thrown our way as Sakari's tail wags in a way I've only seen when she greets her pack.

Ava sighs. "We just got her blessing."

I blink, not able to process so much emotion at once. How can I ever show this girl what she means to me? Seeing as my capacity for language seems to have left me for the moment, I lean down and press a kiss into her gossamer blonde hair.

Ava looks up, wintergreen eyes shining. "Today?"

My smile is reflexive, a mirror of what's happening in my chest. "Can't wait."

Happiness blazes across her face as she twists in my arms. Face to face, I breathe in her scent. She pushes up on tip toes. "Are you sure you're well enough?"

Her hand flutters over my chest, tracing the place where the bullet punctured my body. I grasp her fingers, squeezing them.

My pulse is jackknifing and it has nothing to do with my recent brush with death. "I was ready two days ago."

Her smile amps up and I realize I'm not telling the truth. My heart wanted this two years ago.

Guilt tugs at my conscience again, adding to the mass already there, and I realize this is one thing I can be honest about. "Ava. I tried so hard not to feel anything for you. I pushed you away every time you got too close." Ava opens her mouth to speak, but my finger on her lips stop her. I need to say this. "I'm sorry. I could have saved us a lot of heartache. I could have saved you a whole lot of hurt."

In a flash of movement I don't see coming, she gently nips at the finger trying to quiet her. My eyes flash open in surprise, and she smiles.

"Hunter, I would never have discovered what I have about myself. I think we both needed to learn some things first."

Why does it not surprise me that she thinks like that?

"Besides." She brushes my lips with her fingers, in the way she's done enough times that it's starting to become familiar. I glory in the sensations it evokes every freaking time. "I fell in love with you in a dream. We never spoke. We never touched." Her smile softens as she studies me. "This way I got to fall in love with you in reality."

My breath goddamned vaporizes. This girl has robbed me of that essential function again. "Ava…"

This kiss is sweet and tender, so full of emotion that I don't care if my lungs never function again. Ava has just become my oxygen. Her arms climb up, brushing my biceps and curling around my shoulders. I pour all the love that was born so long ago and now has life into the place where we connect. The most incredible blessing is that she meets me there.

I pull back. "You've been my light and my hope. Now I give

you my heart and my soul." There, our faces barely apart, I revel as the truth finally sets free. "I love you, Ava."

The next kiss starts with the best of intentions. It's soft and full of love. But in a flash, it deepens…becomes something more. Heat builds at an exponential rate, engulfing us both. We pull in tighter, passion and desire exploding. My hands clamp around her back, a restless energy wanting them to move—

We both startle when my sister's cat whistle blares through the loudspeakers. "I'm putting this up on the big screen, peoples!"

We glance over our shoulder then look back at each other. I raise my brow, knowing what I want to say to my sister, and having an inkling that my playful, cheeky golden wolf may be thinking the same thing. Ava's lips twitch in a mischievous smile.

We reunite, lips and hearts finding each other, giving the passion free reign. Neither of us cares who's watching nor what they're thinking. These feelings have waited too long, they're too big to be contained.

I'm going to grab them and hold them for as long as I can.

"Ew!"

We pull apart, laughing.

Ava's hand slides down my arm to grasp my hand. "Now?"

I hold it tight as I nod, "Now."

Turning, I don't bother to look back. We're going where there are no cameras and no responsibilities and no life or death questions that have no answers.

We're going for a run as a white wolf and a golden wolf—like we have so many times before…knowing we're about to experience it for the first time.

It'll just be two souls who fell in love never knowing whether it was real.

It'll be two hearts knowing reality is so much harsher and harder, but so much better.

THE END

Ready for the next installment of the Prime Prophecy series?
Check out LEGACY ACCEPTED!

THE EPIC LOVE STORY CONTINUES

A love bonded by fate.
A world divided by hate.

Hunter and Ava have everything they want in a mate. Their connection, born in dreams but now so real, is pure passion and power.

Except, their love is blossoming in a world of shifting alliances and increasing tensions. As a deadly virus gains momentum, poachers now have a reason to kill wolves indiscriminately—and it seems they have a leader. Weres and Fae are the last fort of protection, but there's disagreement about how wolves should be protected...and how far their protectors should go to save them.

But it's the greatest secret of all that will threaten the love that seems so right. Because a lone wolf now carries something that's impossible—something that will either unite Hunter and Ava and their ability to lead them all...or tear them apart.

Don't miss the second installment of the breathtaking Prime Prophecy series.
Discover a love destined to leave a legacy.

LEGACY ACCEPTED
Continue the Prime Prophecy Series HERE

Read on to dive into the first chapter...

LEGACY ACCEPTED

Chapter 1
Ava

"This is where we met."

I turn to Hunter, finding his copper gaze glowing as he watches me. "I thought you might recognize it."

"How could I not?"

Turning on the spot, I take in the tundra. The promise of winter is more like a pledge around these parts. Snow already rests in pockets that used to be puddles, waiting to join with the higher peaks that are already white. You know it's only a matter of time before everything's coated in marshmallow.

Hunter rubs the back of his head, gaze a little rueful. "Well, the first time wasn't long ago."

It never stops to amaze me that this strong, powerful Were, the one who's been an Alpha for two years, who's made choices I don't know I could make, is still uncertain, almost shy, with me. I step forward as I smile. "It was the most vivid dream I've ever had."

Hunter's reciprocating smile is slower...warmer...sexier. "Well, I was dreaming with my eyes wide open."

Another step and I'm just where I want to be—in his circle of warmth. "You were pretty surprised."

"Ah, bedazzled would probably be more accurate." He tucks a hair behind my ear. "You, on the other hand, took it all in your stride."

My hand grasps his, bringing it to my lips so I can kiss it. Hunter's eyes flare copper fire in response. "I knew this was where I was meant to be."

With a soft groan, the one that always seems to be connected straight to my heart, Hunter's head leans down. My eyes close and my breath evaporates as his lips touch mine.

Love fills me, starting from somewhere deep within, meeting the matching fountain of feeling that's pouring into me. I push up, wanting, no, needing more. Then, just like I knew it would, it transforms into something hotter.

Something that has me pulling closer, hands rising to find his dark hair. My fingers spear in, holding the strands like they're a lifeline. Hunter's arms wrap around me, crushing us together so all of me is plastered against all of him.

It's my turn to groan, a sound of pure passion that seems to only tighten the arms I hope will hold me forever. Then hands are moving, tongues are roving. Desire and a sense of rightness are all I feel.

Hunter pulls back, breathing like he's just crossed the expanse of tundra. "You are one amazing girl, Ava Phelan."

I lick my lips, loving the taste of our kisses. "I'm your amazing girl, Hunter Rendell."

Hunter blinks, and for the briefest of seconds, his breath hitches. Then he smiles all slow and warm. "You're everything I've ever dreamed of."

I laugh at his words, but I don't miss the blink and the hitch.

I may be the child of the Prophecy, the golden wolf that Hunter saw long before I knew she existed, but I'm not sure Hunter knows his importance in whatever this Legacy is.

Without Hunter I wouldn't have shifted; without Hunter, I wouldn't have discovered who I am.

But more so, without Hunter, the thread that is my lifeline would shrivel up and die.

I'd be nothing but the mixed-blood girl I was afraid I was.

He steps back, grasping my hand. "Come on, let's get this over and done with."

Sighing, I let him pull me forward. It feels like there's never enough time to glory in what we have. It's so startling and new, but so familiar and known. We've spent two weeks literally making our dreams come true. Just like we did in the nights I was asleep, we've run and reveled, sat and reflected.

It's the passion that was the surprise. A pleasant one. Actually, a freaking amazing one. One look from this Were and I'm pretty sure I'll never be cold out here. A fire has been banked and it's waiting for the oxygen that will feed it.

And that essential element is Hunter.

It's only a matter of time before he realizes I'm only something when I'm with him.

As we head back to the quad, I pause, pulling Hunter to a stop. I look at the rock formation to our left. "This is where Sakari set up her den."

Hunter's hand tenses in mine. "Yeah, it was."

I stare as the memories come. "She was all curled up, ready to give birth." I look up at Hunter. "You were so proud."

"That litter was going to mean so much."

Was...I saw those pups the following night. I frown. And I never saw them again. My hand tightens around Hunter's. "They didn't make it, did they?"

Hunter's lips are a tense line. "No, we lost them that night."

"Oh, Hunter."

I wrap myself around him. He's had so much loss in such a short period of time. Each death would be another arrow that stabs straight into the wound of the previous one. I wish they were hurts I could heal.

His hands come up to rub my arms. "Losing them meant we had no choice but try Dawn's captive breeding program." He sighs. "It was probably inevitable anyway."

I look up, knowing I'll find pain in his eyes. "You made the choice that will save these animals."

Something shifts through the copper depths, but with another blink, it's gone. "We're going to find out soon enough."

Stepping back, this time I pull us toward the quad bike. "Yes, you will." I glance over my shoulder. "I already know."

Back at the bike, I finally pause, realizing something that has reality intruding. "The first time we met—I was sleeping at the center at the time. It was cut short because Achak was born."

Which brings me back to why we're here. We've captured the last of the arctic wolves, all three of them. They're now safely held within the walls of Resolve—our own captive breeding center.

But now it's time to bring Achak in.

Hunter's arm slides around me, sending shivers skipping across my skin. "I know this is hard."

I rest my head against him, breathing in the scent that comforts one moment, kindles something completely different in another. "Like you said, as the snow creeps in, he's going to be a sitting duck. His red and grey fur is going to stick out a mile in the white landscape."

His chest rises and falls with a sigh. "Yeah. Doesn't make it any easier though."

It's been two weeks of no poachers and no Furious.

Furious is an unknown entity, but no-one is naive enough to

assume the poachers are no longer an issue. Which is why we're bringing the wolves in—it's the only way we can make sure they stay safe.

I climb on the metal steed that has taken us to all ends of the tundra. Hunter tells me that in a couple of months it will become a Skid-doo. A part of me is excited to see the depth of snow that can accumulate here—I'm sure it's magnificent. The other part has no idea how my newly acquired Were body will cope with it. Will I be just as warm as the others? Or will my watered-down heritage still have an impact?

As I settle behind Hunter on the quad, shuffling forward so I'm wrapped around him as snugly as possible, I mentally flick the concerns away. Hunter's glance over his shoulder means they flutter away without a second thought. The promise in those eyes holds enough heat to melt the polar ice caps.

Hunter accelerates, heading further north, and I tap into the thread that connects me to Achak. Before I shifted I could trace them, but now...now they're like tapping into a live-wire. A glowing, moving river of energy that tells me so much. I discover the layers that make us all—the distinctions and diversity that makes us each an individual. Next are the feelings we all experience in various shades. But then there's the essence of the being that I'm tapping into—an essence that's exactly the same as mine. It's the universal energy that connects us all.

I lean forward, talking into Hunter's ear. "I wish you could see this."

He squeezes my knee. "That's why you're the child of the Prophecy."

He powers forward, following the direction that I point. I sense the thread strengthening already. "He's not far."

"I doubt he ever was."

Hunter knows I have a deep bond with Achak. After raising him because his mother was poisoned, his wild soul called to me. It was his strength that gave him courage and determination, something I always respected.

As Achak appears at the top of a hill, I smile. "He reminds me of you."

Hunter pulls to a stop. "Big and hairy?"

I roll my eyes, the smile growing. "Fierce and protective."

Shaking his head, Hunter climbs off the bike, and I'm not sure which part he's denying. I don't say any more, knowing this isn't the time.

Achak stops where he is, a lone wolf at the tip of the gently rolling hill. My heart lightens at seeing him, just as the breeze gusts his grey coat—the one that means he'll never camouflage when this world is white. I swallow as I wonder how I'm going to communicate to him that we need to bring him in. Achak's spirit isn't designed for captivity.

Standing beside Hunter, I watch Achak watch us. He was the one who saved Hunter's life...by killing the poacher who was about to shoot again. A human body that's never been found. It reminds me that whatever is looming is far more unknown and violent than I'd ever imagined.

That I'm not sure I'm ready for.

Hunter's hand slips around mine, like he knows I need a reminder I'm not alone. I squeeze his fingers, tapping into their strength. "I'll go talk to him."

Hunter's gaze is sharp as he releases my hand, the intensity telling me to keep safe. Despite all the unknowns of how Achak is going to greet me, despite saying that I'd go alone, he nods. "You got this."

With a deep breath, I release Hunter's hand and start walking up the hill. The magnificent wolf who I raised watches me approach, showing no signs of movement. He's not running away, but I also expected him to be a little happier to see me.

Glancing back at Hunter, I noticed he's taken a few steps forward.

The unexpected stillness rams home that Achak has killed a human. He's wilder than I was willing to admit, but at the same time, he's shown the lengths he would go to for those he considers his pack. Is it because Furious was once in his blood?

Could still be?

That frightening thought reminds me why I'm here. A deadly virus we still don't understand. Determined poachers who are more coordinated than we realized.

The undeniable truth is, wolves have never been more at risk of extinction.

I slow as I come closer. Achak is sitting, watching me, and I'm not sure what that means. I tap into the thread, trying to sense how he feels. The happiness that trickles through makes me smile—he knows who I am.

Shaking my head, I take him in. "I can't believe you followed me all the way here, Achak."

Achak looks at me like he doesn't understand why I'm surprised. When I take another step though, the happiness dims. Instead, wariness comes through loud and clear.

I stop, the smile I could feel in my chest disappearing. Is this because I left? Is it because of what happened with the poacher? I hold out my hand. "Thank you, Achak. He," I glance over my shoulder at Hunter, "holds my heart."

If it wasn't for this silent, still wolf that I've known since a cub, Hunter would probably be dead.

I send my gratitude through our connection, knowing he may not understand it, but he'd know it's a peace offering. Considering what I'm about to do, it's the least I can give him. I feel Achak's impulse to step forward and close the distance between us. It's a flash of the Achak I know.

But he doesn't. Like he's made a decision, his body tenses,

becoming even more resolute. His canine eyes gaze straight at me. He's trying to tell me something, but I don't know what it is.

Please let him come with me. Taking in Achak against his will isn't something I want to have to do.

As I take a step forward though, Achak takes a step back.

I gasp, because the movement has him standing---and revealing what he'd been hiding.

Achak's been injured, his hind leg is a mat of dark red, the soil where he was just resting spotted with the thick liquid.

The wind gusts again and I hear Hunter move. He must've smelled the copper tang on the breeze. I don't look away from Achak though, knowing I need to keep our link. "You need to come with us, old friend. It's for your own safety."

And if that wound was caused by a poacher, then the need just became more urgent.

When I take another step, meaning there are only a few feet between us, Achak retreats again, letting out a bark.

He's telling me to stay back.

Except I can't.

"Please...No one will hurt you," I whisper, letting him know through our connection that I'm not a threat. That I want what's best for him.

But it doesn't matter. For some reason, Achak doesn't want what I'm offering. Maybe he remembers that the last time we saw each other, he was in a cage, but for some reason, I don't think so. Is it because he's injured?

"I can help you."

Our thread pulses, and I feel his flash of pain. This wound isn't new, and it's been causing him discomfort. And yet he didn't come looking for me.

My heart aches as I realize something has changed...and I don't know what.

I'm wondering if I should shift when Achak lets out another bark. One I recognize as goodbye.

"No!" I reach out again, like I can hold him here.

Achak can't leave. He has to come with us.

As if he knows exactly what I'm thinking, Achak turns and breaks into a lope, one marked by a pronounced limp. He doesn't look back as he trots over the ridge we're standing on. Turning, he goes to head back down the opposite side of the hill, going back out to the wilds of the tundra.

The crack of the tranquilizer gun makes me jump, even though I was expecting it. Achak yelps and rears as the dart impales his hind leg and I wince. This isn't how it was supposed to be.

Achak breaks into a run and I feel his pain flare. It stings my eyes and I'm glad to find Hunter by my side. I grasp his arm as he pulls me in close. "He didn't want to come."

"I got that impression." We watch as Achak pauses to look back at us, and I know I'm imagining the feeling of betrayal he throws at me, but it hurts nonetheless.

"He's injured, Hunter."

"I know, that's why I got the tranquilizer. We can't afford for him to keep disagreeing." He looks down at me. "Looks like he got a taste for the tundra."

And didn't want to leave. I'd banked on that. Achak coming back into captivity was never going to be something he agreed to readily.

But I'd hoped our connection was still strong enough for him to trust me.

"Do you think...do you think it was a poacher?"

Hunter sighs. "I hope not. Although that would explain why he's so shy and standoffish with you."

Achak's grey body grows smaller and smaller as he desperately creates distance between us. I close my eyes for the briefest moment, willing the moisture to dry up. The wolf I raised and loved is hurting, and more than just physically. Except I don't know why.

Please, let this be the right thing to do.

Hunter drops a kiss on my forehead and I let the comforting brush reach all the way to my heart. "This way you can heal him, and we can keep him safe."

I nod, knowing what Hunter is saying is true. The skills I've discovered since shifting are still our secret. I know they won't be for much longer, but Hunter understood that I want to see if I can understand them a little more before the world of Were knows.

I step back, not really wanting to let him go. "Come on, we'll need to be there once he's unconscious."

We climb on the quad but I don't need the threads to follow Achak. The scent of blood, the sporadic drops of red, lead us both to his unconscious form.

Just like the others, we'll load his body into the cage on the trailer. Just like the others, he'll wake back at Resolve, surrounded by chain-link fence.

Except it will be nothing like the others.

I raised Achak. I know him.

I asked him if he wanted this.

And he said no.

LEGACY ACCEPTED
Continue the Prime Prophecy Series HERE

I'D LOVE TO CONNECT!

Don't miss out on notifications and tasters of my upcoming books (I might be biased, but there's some awesome stories in the pipeline)! Subscribe to be the first to know and to make the most of any deals I have on offer.

SIGN UP HERE

Every couple of weeks you'll get exclusive tasters of upcoming books, awesome offers and bargain reads, and an opportunity to connect (personally, I reckon that's the best bit).

There's also some cool freebies coming your way…

I'd love to see you over there.

Tamar :)

ALSO BY TAMAR SLOAN

KEEPERS OF THE LIGHT

Angels and demons have battled for millennia.

Their inevitable war has begun.

Hidden Angel

Chosen Angel

Marked Angel

Forbidden Angel

Rogue Angel

Cursed Angel

Blood Angel

∽

KEEPERS OF THE CHALICE

A vampire. A huntress.

A cure that will change everything.

Vampire Unleashed

Vampire Unveiled

Vampire Undone

Vampire Undefeated

Vampire United

∽

KEEPERS OF THE GRAIL

Seven Gates of Hell. Seven Deadly Sins.

One impossible choice.

Gates of Demons

Gates of Chaos

Gates of Greed

Gates of Wrath

Gates of Secrets

Gates of Hell

∽

THE SOVEREIGN CODE

Humans saved bees from extinction...and created the deadliest threat we've seen yet.

Harvest Day

Hive Mind

Queen Hunt

Venom Rising

Sting Wars

∽

THE THAW CHRONICLES

Only the chosen shall breed.

Burning

Rising

Breaking

Falling

Extant

Exist

Exile

Expose

Tournaments of Thaw

Conquer the Thaw

The Oasis Trials

The Oasis Deception

The Last Oasis

❦

ZODIAC GUARDIANS

Twelve teens. One task. Save the Universe.

Zodiac Guardians

Libra Ascending

Capricorn Conjured

Leo Rising

Taurus Divided

Virgo Incognito

Aquarius Undone

Sagittarius Charmed

Aries Armed

Pisces Dreaming

Scorpio Sting

Cancer Sight

Gemini United

DESCENDANTS OF THE GODS

Demigods as you've never seen before.

Child of Crossroads

Daughter of Time

Secret of Fate

Son of Poseidon

Blood of Medusa

ABOUT THE AUTHOR

Tamar really struggled writing this bio, in part because it's in third person, but mostly because she hasn't decided whether she's primarily a psychologist who loves writing, or a writer with a life-long fascination with psychology.

She must have been someone pretty awesome in a previous life (past life regression indicated a Care Bear), because she gets to do both. Beginning her career as a youth worker, then a secondary school teacher, before becoming a school psychologist, Tamar helps children and teens to live and thrive despite life's hurdles like loss, relationship difficulties, mental health issues, and trauma.

As lover of reading, inspired by books that sparked beautiful movies in her head, Tamar loves to write young adult romance. To be honest, it was probably inevitable that her knowledge and love of literature would translate into writing emotion driven stories of finding life and love beyond our comfort zones. You can find out more about Tamar's books at www.tamarsloan.com

A lifetime consumer of knowledge, Tamar holds degrees in Applied Science, Education and Psychology. When not reading, writing or working with teens, Tamar can be found with her husband and two children enjoying country life on their small slice of the Australian bush.

The driving force for all of Tamar's writing is sharing and

connecting. In truth, connecting with others is why she writes. She loves to hear from readers and fellow writers. Find her on all the usual social media channels or her website.

Printed in Great Britain
by Amazon